Love
cheryl

BOOK 1

The Heavenly Host

BOOK ONE

The Heavenly Host

The Testings of Devotion

Cheryl Dellasega

VMI PUBLISHERS • SISTERS, OREGON

HEAVENLY HOST SERIES, BOOK 1
The Testings of Devotion

© 2009 Cheryl Dellasega

Published by
VMI Publishers
Sisters, Oregon
www.vmipublishers.com

ISBN: 978-1-933204-70-3
ISBN: 1-933204-70-2

Library of Congress: 2009936131

Printed in the USA

Cover design by Kara Elsberry

Dedicated to the memory of

Paul Joseph Dellasega

1

The angels followed Gabriel, moving closer together as the terrain changed from soft green grass to a stubbly mix of dirt and stone. By the time they reached the stretch of bare shale that tore at their feet like tiny teeth, some were forced to hold hands or lean on each other for support.

"Where are we?" a few whispered as the familiar trees bursting with lush green leaves thinned out and then vanished, replaced by twisted trunks with naked branches that stretched upward like beggars' arms.

Even the smells were different in this new territory. The air of heaven was fragrant with a subtle mix of fresh flowers and young herbs, but as the angels trekked further away, the scent of something rancid and foreboding surrounded them like a heavy cloud.

"This has something to do with Lucifer, doesn't it?" Azazel asked.

He was one of the angels following closely behind Gabriel, his gait determined but his expression grave. Next to him, Sophia winced as a small piece of stone wedged between her toes. Plucking it free without breaking stride, she leaned closer to Azazel.

"I wish we could beg him to change his mind," she said in a low voice.

Azazel's eyebrows lifted. "Lucifer won't be swayed by Gabriel or any of us. No one even knows where he is, much less if he's going to be there once we finish this miserable journey."

"I just can't believe it." She sighed, then, after a moment of reflection added: "Surely he hasn't decided to leave us for good. Lucifer's always been different from the rest of us…but not this different."

"How do you know he's leaving for good, Sophia? You're Gabriel's confidant; has he told you something?"

She *had* asked the archangel about it before they left. Gabriel's answer was so unequivocal that he hadn't bothered to glance up from the scroll of instructions he was reading while they waited for a group of angels to gather at the edge of heaven.

"Sophia, this is the point of no return for Lucifer. He's been wandering between our world and earth since time began, searching for the place where he can live according to his own rules. Now he's defied the Almighty Divine for the last time, and I've been charged with expelling him from heaven. Angels were never meant to cause problems for mortals, but that's exactly what Lucifer has been doing. Had it not been for him, Adam and Eve would still be happily living in the garden, free of wrongdoing."

Sophia shared that answer with Azazel, shivering at the memory of Eden's closing as they continued to trudge side by side toward an uncertain destination. Mortals had been so perfect when they were created that every angel burst into a song of joy at the sight of them. But Gabriel was right, Lucifer had spoiled it.

"I'm with you. Lucifer *is* different, but is 'different' wrong?" Azazel winced as his foot slipped; he grabbed at Sophia to avoid tripping. Steadying himself, he took her arm and spoke close to her ear: "Not long ago he was lecturing a crowd of us about the need to destroy mortals completely so they wouldn't hurt the Almighty Divine with their evil ways. Even when I challenged him, he didn't seem to make the connection that their 'evil ways' were a consequence of his actions. Even when I told him he pushed Cain too far, he insisted he'd done nothing more than encouraged him to protect Adam from ungodly influences."

Sophia shook her head slowly. "It's hard to believe Lucifer could be so…misguided, but if that's the case, why make a ceremony of his choice to leave us? Shouldn't we be trying to help him?"

Azazel shrugged. "Maybe it's a test. That might be why some of us were asked to come along: we can help persuade Lucifer. The Almighty Divine might be hoping he'll turn away at the last moment."

She pulled free of him and picked her way through the sharp rocks to catch up with Gabriel. His gaze was fixed on a point in the distance, and his steps were so measured and steady that, for an instant, he seemed unaware of her.

She pulled on his sleeve.

"Sophia. What is it?" He glanced back, scanned the crowd of angels behind them, and then looked down at her.

"Gabriel, there's still a chance things can be changed. Do you really want to see Lucifer leave the kingdom of heaven? You're closer to him than the rest of us; why not try reasoning with him? You have to admit he's well intentioned, even if he made a terrible mistake."

The features of Gabriel's handsome face turned down in a frown, and his pace picked up.

"A terrible mistake?' Sophia, Lucifer has been challenging the Almighty Divine since he was created! Yes, he is clever and smart and funny, but he knows no limits. Convincing mortals to defy the Almighty Divine was more than a 'terrible mistake.' Now they will never stop experiencing hurt and sorrow, which will make it all the harder for us to take care of them."

"But—"

Gabriel's hand sliced through the air, and although he addressed Sophia, his voice rose so all the angels could hear. "Be warned!"

The crowd behind him stopped instantly, fixing their attention on him, wide-eyed. It was the first time any of them had heard such anger from Gabriel. He turned so he was facing them, his massive hands clenched in fists that rested on his hips.

"Lucifer would like all of you to believe his motives are worthy, but he cares nothing about morals—or any of you, for that matter. If he's told you anything different, it's just one more of his clever lies. Lucifer wants to rule over his own kingdom, pure and simple. His allegiance is to himself, not the kingdom of heaven nor the Almighty Divine who rules over it. "

There was an instant of silence; then, a murmur of concern and disbelief rippled through the crowd. Several angels began to debate the truth of Gabriel's words.

"Defy the Almighty Divine? That's impossible!" a voice shouted from the far edge of the crowd.

"But what if Lucifer is right? What if the Almighty Divine does love mortals more than us?" the angel next to Azazel cried out. She was fair-haired and delicate, but her face was flushed with emotion. "Mortals have already betrayed the one who created them—unlike us!"

Another angel called out in reply: "That's right! We're the ones who have been obedient, and yet we are expected to take care of mortals."

There was an excited buzz sweeping through the crowd. Although she was still at Gabriel's side, Sophia could hear snatches of conversations that seemed to be repetitions of arguments that had been circulating through heaven recently:

"Lucifer's always been favored. Every good thing has been given to him—what more can he want?" asked one angel, his round face twisted with bitterness.

"He's jealous of mortals," another claimed. "That's his motive, pure and simple. He plans to destroy them and then try to come back and take over heaven."

A third voice, further back, was tentative, but insistent. "He sounds so certain when he talks about it, though. How can he challenge the Almighty Divine if he hasn't got some evidence? He even sang us a song about the life we are meant to lead."

"No, no, Lucifer knows mortals will only hurt the Almighty Divine," a fourth insisted, his words measured. "That's what he's trying to prevent. He wants them to stop sinning and inflicting such pain!"

Gabriel held up his arm and waved it back and forth like a banner to silence further debate.

"This matter has been settled. Lucifer will make his choice. He would like all of you to believe he is really doing a good thing for the Almighty Divine, but that's only so he can bring mortals under his control and establish his own kingdom on earth. Make no mistake about that."

He turned and began to walk forward again, his large head bowed even though his massive shoulders were squared back and his posture erect.

Sophia scurried to keep up with him. "If Lucifer chooses to go, the consequences are going to be terrible. He forgets that mortals have free will, just as we do. They will resist him."

"Perhaps." Gabriel's voice broke and he glanced sideways at her. "I'm sorry, Sophia. I don't mean to be harsh with you. It's just…this is so very hard. I love Lucifer as much as I love every other angel."

She put one small hand on his forearm. "We all love him. I'm glad I'm not in your place. It would be horrible to have to turn against another angel…and yet I guess that's what we are all about to do. How I wish mortals had tried harder to resist Lucifer's temptation! It was such a small thing!"

Azazel joined the two of them in time to hear the last part of what she said. He gave a quick snort of laughter. "Are you serious? They didn't try to resist at all—in Eden or since."

Gabriel frowned at him. "It's not our place to judge mortals. As for Lucifer—his will is strong, but it may be his undoing. If he refuses to submit to the Almighty Divine, he's choosing to live in the world of chaos."

Sophia took a sharp breath in. She felt pity for Lucifer but also horror at the thought of any angel choosing to dwell in a world dominated by unpredictable events and disorder. In the beginning, the Almighty Divine had brought it all under His control, but when mortals refused to live by the few rules He had given them, thanks to Lucifer, the peace had been shattered. Absorbed in a multitude of conflicting thoughts, she continued walking next to Gabriel and Azazel in silence.

Please, she prayed, *do not let this happen.*

They reached a point where the ground was flat and slimy, oozing a rank gray vapor that seemed to pierce Sophia's spirit. It was the first time she had experienced any kind of discomfort, which gave her new empathy for mortals. This must be just a taste of what it was like to live on earth, removed from the Almighty Divine and confined to a body that was no longer perfect.

Gabriel halted, gestured for Sophia and Azazel to join the rest of the angels, and waited while everyone found a place to stand. Judging from the puzzled sounds around her, Sophia guessed she wasn't the only one repulsed by the sensations of the moment.

Gabriel spoke. "Just beyond us, you can see the outer borders of the kingdom of earth, a place where few of us have been permitted or even wanted to go. Our brother Lucifer, however, has often wandered there and even taken it upon himself to test the allegiance of mortals to the Almighty Divine. We are here now to give Lucifer the same choice he offered mortals: obey the Almighty Divine or not. If he refuses, he will be exiled from the kingdom of heaven."

Sophia couldn't contain herself from protesting. "But what if Lucifer repents? He could realize he's wrong, and if he does, the Almighty Divine loves all of us enough to forgive. Lucifer loves music! Perhaps we can sing a special song of love for him so he will see that we still want him to stay with us."

Azazel snorted. "Always the optimist, aren't you, Sophia? I'm telling you, Lucifer will never change his mind, no matter how many pretty songs you sing."

Gabriel looked at her and for an instant his face mirrored the same hope Sophia had just voiced, but then the blue of his eyes went blank. When he spoke, there was a dull finality to his words.

"The Almighty Divine has appointed me to offer Lucifer the choice to obey or not. He alone can decide whether he will be cast out from the kingdom of heaven or welcomed back as a brother."

Sophia saw the careful neutrality of his expression, but sensed he was nonetheless struggling with the same emotions as she. After all, he was the one who had roamed the heavens with Lucifer, monitoring the universe for the Almighty Divine and carrying out appointed missions in tandem. There were many archangels, but it was well known that Gabriel and Lucifer shared a special bond—or had until Lucifer went off on his own.

Gabriel took a deep breath and narrowed his eyes until they were dark slits. He shifted his gaze across the crowd of angels, looking out beyond those who stood close to him. "Each and every one of you must stand firm if I exile Lucifer," he instructed. "Not one of you can react to anything he says or does."

Peering in the distance, Sophia saw a river roiling with orange and yellow flames erupting up from the dark. Beyond its farther bank, geysers of red liquid randomly spewed up with such force that the ground shook, and intermittent bolts of lightning illuminated terrifying scenes: wild beasts ripping apart a carcass, one mortal torturing another, the churning water of the river surging up to smash against its banks.

This was what the world of chaos was like. Earth had become the battleground where she and the rest of the heavenly host fought for the souls of mortals. She shuddered at the sight of a brutish mortal man dripping blood from his mouth as he devoured a raw animal carcass.

Luckily, she and the others carried out their part of the warfare from the safety of the kingdom of heaven. Judging from what she saw before her, she knew Lucifer's thinking must be horribly misguided. Why would any angel want to live in such a place?

2

An agonized scream sounded from beyond the river, an eerie counterpoint to the joyful choruses angels often sang when gathering for important events.

"Almighty Divine, please have mercy!" Azazel gasped, shifting his position and then flailing a bit before regaining his balance.

Gabriel stood unflinching, but out of the corner of her eye, Sophia saw one angel reach out and clutch another's hand, teetering to stay upright or seeking comfort. With a shiver, she curled her toes against the slick rock and tried to mimic Gabriel's stance so she wouldn't slip.

Another volley of long, tortured screams sounded. There was no discernable source of the sounds, but they began and ended with such intensity that Sophia's head throbbed. The distance between the angels and the riverbank was shrinking, while the ground beneath them seemed to shift and slide.

"Lucifer, show yourself!" Gabriel lifted his chin slightly, resting his hands on his hips again. Through the fine material of his robe, his well-muscled arms were tensed, as if ready to strike out.

There was no answer.

The archangel took several long strides toward the river. As he moved, he grew taller and larger, glowing with a white light brighter than the flames of fire before him. Sophia knew that this was Gabriel in all his glory.

Screams tore through the air and heavy black clouds massed overhead, firing long spears of fire down on Gabriel, who merely brushed the flames away. The ground in front of him quaked with such violence that it cracked open, releasing clouds of steam that drifted backward so Sophia could smell the stench.

"Gaaaabrielll…" The musical lilt of Lucifer's voice floated above the echoes of the rumbling thunder. "My brother of brothers, friend of friends."

Sophia trembled, both from fear and because the ground was actually quaking beneath her. If Lucifer was determined to leave, why couldn't he just go without such a terrifying scene? None of the angels were prepared for this. Until now their existence had been spent in the serene confines of heaven, where the only difficulties were earthly ones they watched from afar.

She couldn't believe it when Gabriel threw his head back and chuckled, as he did when he was genuinely amused. "What's wrong? Singing a ditty because you're afraid to face me, Lucifer?"

The current of the river snapped and writhed, as if trying to leap free of its boundaries. A swell of oily liquid flew into the air and floated toward Gabriel, slowly taking shape.

It was Lucifer, wearing a black fur robe that flowed gracefully down from his shoulders into a train hemmed with precious stones. His slender figure was clothed in an elegant silk tunic with a belt of ivory at his waist; as he walked, the fine leather boots on his pointed feet moved easily over the slippery ground.

When he came to stand in front of Gabriel, Sophia saw that Lucifer's eyes, once a delightful mixture of all the shades of sky and light, were now hooded, glittering, and dark. A heavy crown crusted with jewels covered the top of his head; underneath, his lush ebony hair fell free to his shoulders, curling slightly at the ends. His ringed fingers clutched a heavy gold scepter set with jewels that matched the crown.

Licking his lips and smiling, he nodded toward the crowd of angels and paused, as if expecting an exuberant welcome. When there was only silence, he took a small step closer to Gabriel.

"Behold, our brother," Gabriel announced, extending one arm to touch Lucifer's shoulder and tilting his head back with a half smile on his lips. Did he really find something about the situation funny or was it a clever act, designed to reassure the angels who had been summoned to watch?

Sophia decided if the latter was true, it worked. Something within her relaxed slightly at the sight of the two archangels side by side, and Gabriel's apparent ease assured her he was in control of the outcome, whatever that might be.

No one spoke, but all eyes were riveted on Gabriel and Lucifer. Gabriel was glowing, his posture relaxed, and his hand loosely cupped on Lucifer's shoulder. The short blond hair he normally wore tied back fell free like rays of bright sunlight, and every feature of his face seemed composed, as if chiseled from the smoothest, purest marble. While the linen shift draped over the curves of his body was simple, the material hung more luxuriously than Lucifer's elaborate garments and shone with a soft light. The broad belt around Gabriel's waist, no more than a band of hammered gold with a large medallion clasp in the front, pulsed out rays of power. He directed his gaze to the crowd of angels before him, deliberately avoiding even a glance in Lucifer's direction.

"Brothers and sisters of the heavenly host, we are gathered here to witness who the archangel Lucifer will choose as his master. On behalf of the Almighty Divine, I now ask: Whom shall you serve? Yourself, or the One who created us?"

Lucifer's eyes blazed as brightly as the flames in the river behind him. He knocked Gabriel's hand away with the scepter and stepped in front of him to address the angels.

"Look at me! Am I the only one who sees the truth? The Almighty Divine loves mortals more than us, and what do they offer him again and again? Pain. Sorrow. Suffering. Has one of us ever caused such sadness?"

When no one responded to Lucifer's taunt, Gabriel spoke.

"You have," he said. "Of all the heavenly host, you alone have caused the Almighty Divine infinite pain and sorrow and suffering, Lucifer."

"No. No, I have not," Lucifer screamed, throwing the scepter down and stomping on it with one foot. "Listen to me: the Almighty Divine offers mortals unconditional love when they're worthless…beyond worthless. All the effort we've put into helping them will amount to nothing. You'll see. His love for them will be His undoing."

Gabriel put one hand on Lucifer's arm, as gently as he might if trying to soothe a child. "It's not too late to ask the Almighty Divine to forgive you. He's still the Almighty Divine, and He will take you back, even now," Gabriel said with a combination of determination and kindness only he possessed. "What is Adam to Him, when you are one of the created angels, eternal and everlasting?"

Lucifer lifted his chin slightly. "I will not. I will be my own master and you will see! The Almighty Divine will see! I will break His beloved mortals and then He will realize we—the angels who have existed since the beginning of time—are the ones He should love the most. He should never have created man."

Lucifer's restless eyes, clouded with emotion, moved to take stock of Sophia and the other angels around her. Leaving Gabriel, he moved toward her with the ease of a panther, coming so close she could see the sheen of moisture on his cheeks and forehead. Pressing his narrow lips together thoughtfully, he addressed her. "Sweet Sophia, come with me. We can stop these wicked mortals from ruining eternity for the rest of us. In fact, we'll be doing them a favor by speeding up their destruction."

Sophia sensed the angels on either side of her freezing in place, but the intensity of Lucifer's gaze was enough to make her take a tiny step backward, despite Gabriel's admonition to stand firm. Her feet twisted on the slick surface, which gave Lucifer the opportunity to leap forward, grab her hand, and draw her nearer to him.

"I need a woman. None of the others who have agreed to come along with me have your sensibility."

Over Lucifer's shoulder, Sophia saw a shocked look transform Gabriel's expression briefly, but then he composed himself and stayed where he was, watching impassively. Lucifer's voice continued to beguile her with one of his famous songs, a long poetic description of a world where they would reign together. As he spoke, he turned to gesture back at the scenery she had glimpsed in the distance. Before, it had looked so dismal; now it had changed.

"See, Sophia, this is the way the world will be," Lucifer sang in her ear. "A beautiful place. A place of our making, full of pleasure and good things."

She shut her eyes, trying to ignore him, but when she opened them she still saw a coursing river of clear water, and beyond it, a landscape much like the comforting glory of the kingdom of heaven. Everything about the scene was orderly and inviting: beautiful birds called cheerfully to each other and dipped through the air in a playful dance, while a soft breeze stirred the glossy green leaves of trees and bushes. A group of joyful mortal men, women, and children danced together in a field of flowers, their voices raised in song.

"If we control mortals, they won't be able to hurt the Almighty Divine, and earth will be a better place for it," Lucifer continued. "It will be like the beginning."

Sophia stared at the mortals beyond them, as fair as any angel, and remembered the early days in the garden when even Lucifer had delighted in these new creatures. Was it possible to undo all that had happened and go back to that time?

Lucifer clutched Sophia's fingers in his, but lifted his head and raised his voice so the others would hear his song, which was full and throbbing with emotion. "Stay in heaven and you will serve mortals for the rest of your existence. You'll spend eternity correcting their mistakes and trying to prevent them from acting on the evil in their hearts. Come with me and you will be free, free to live as you want. Mortals will, in fact, serve you and do as you bid." He took a deep breath and sang with his full capacity: "Come with me; come my angels. Many of you feel that I speak the truth, so come and rule with me. Be free."

He stepped away from Sophia and extended one hand to Azazel, smiling. The angel hung his head for a moment, but then stepped forward to stand next to Lucifer.

"Come with me and be free. Speak the truth and rule over earth. Teach mortals the right way to live." Lucifer repeated the invitation over and over, his voice hypnotic as he reached out to the crowd, his long fingers arrayed with rows of rings made from different metals and every color of jewel.

At first there was no response, but then a few angels from the middle of the group pushed their way forward to join Azazel, defiant looks on their face. Clapping Lucifer on the shoulders with their hands or hugging him briefly to their chest, they called back to the others, "He's right! Lucifer is right!"

"Come with me, then! Stand by my side!" Lucifer spread his arms out wide in invitation and began to back toward the river.

Suddenly, angels surged forward.

"Don't listen to him," Gabriel shouted, but only Sophia obeyed. The rest shoved past her toward Lucifer, crying out jubilantly, "Lucifer! We believe in Lucifer!" Several fell and were trampled by the others, but when Sophia helped them up, they pushed her away and continued limping forward. Pulled along by the crowd, Sophia turned toward Gabriel and held out her arms in a desperate plea. He reached in her direction and she found herself drawn steadily to his side.

"Can't you do something?" she asked, clutching his robe once she was safely removed from the tangle of angels trying to make their way toward Lucifer. He shook his head, eyes moist as he watched the mob.

Before long, Sophia was the only angel who stood with Gabriel. As soon as the others chose Lucifer, their white robes vanished and the soft caps of light that distinguished those created at the beginning of time disappeared. They seemed unaware of these changes, smiling and nudging each other as they spoke excitedly about their new home on earth and the blessings that awaited them there.

"Begone!" Gabriel's command echoed to the skies and caused the ground to shake again with one mighty heave. "Woe to you, Lucifer, and woe to all of you who have chosen to follow him. You, like him, will now wander earth throughout eternity, and may not come back to heaven with your true brothers and sisters. You will be judged at the end times and cast into the abyss for eternity."

"I think not." Azazel said with a sneer. "We're going to have our own kingdom, and it will be far better than heaven! Death and destruction to the mortals!" A triumphant cheer from the others punctuated his defiance.

"Before long, earth will be ours. Look how easy it was to break the first mortal, one woman tempted by food." Lucifer tossed his hair back, raised his fists high into the air, and shook them. In the midst of his victory cheer, he caught sight of Sophia, who was cowering behind Gabriel in horror. Anger seized his face.

"Get Sophia! We must not leave one angel behind!" he cried, leading a charge forward.

"Get Gabriel too! Get the messenger!" Azazel snarled, leaping toward her. Along with him, hundreds of Lucifer's followers flew at Gabriel, dragging him to the ground and wrestling to keep him pinned down. Although the archangel was stronger than any one of them, the large group was quickly able to immobilize him and pummel him with kicks and punches.

Lucifer leapt on Sophia with animal-like ferocity, grabbing her from behind and wrapping his arms around her waist in a vise that seemed impossible to escape. He lifted her up so her feet could only strike out at the air, but still she refused to stop trying to wrestle free of him.

"You aren't thinking clearly, Lucifer. Stop this nonsense and come back to your home in heaven," she panted.

"You are my special prize!" he roared, ignoring her pleas. With one hand, he gathered the tumbled curls of her hair, yanked her head back, and began dragging her away. His wild laughter sounded almost like the screams she heard earlier.

"To the river!" Azazel ordered, taking command of those who held Gabriel prisoner.

Before they could make another move, the air began to stir, circling Azazel with a violent wind that tore into his naked flesh like a blade. He cried out in pain and fell to his knees as the whirlwind drove away the other defectors. Lucifer looked up, so stunned by what was happening that his grip on Sophia loosened. Swiftly, she jerked free and ran to Gabriel's.

"Are you okay?" she cried, kneeling down at his side. There seemed to be no wounds on his arms or legs, and no damage to his clothing.

"Sophia, I'm an archangel." He stood and brushed himself off. "They could hold me down, but that's about the extent of it."

Beyond the river that was again made of fire, a great cracking sound distracted them, splitting apart the happy scene Lucifer had projected. The illusion of an idyllic kingdom on earth melted away, and the ugly chaos Sophia glimpsed before returned. Without warning, a violent storm of ice and fire exploded from the water, shooting high in the air and then pelting down on Lucifer's new followers. They were still crouched on the ground, their arms wrapped around their bowed heads, crying out in agony and begging Lucifer to protect them. It was useless. Their formerly perfect figures were burnt and frozen into misshapen lumps by the torrent of the angry storm, despite their attempts to bat away the furious tongues of fire and ice.

Seeing this, Lucifer dropped to all fours and began to lope off in the opposite direction. Before he could get very far, a brilliant beam of light burst out of the skies, and a figure on a large white horse came charging forth, hurling a white orb at Lucifer with one easy thrust.

The orb trapped Lucifer in place and, as Sophia watched, the features of his face dissolved, as if wiped away. Two hollow slits formed in place of his eyes, and his mouth was replaced by a red slash that opened and closed reflexively to reveal a set of rotted, broken teeth. The smooth skin of Lucifer's naked body was covered with flaking gray scales that he instantly began to scratch away with the long nails curving out from the ends of his clawlike fingers. Each time he did, a thick green liquid poured out and crusted over the opened spot.

The maelstrom died down, and Sophia could hear the moans and whimpers of the fallen angels who hadn't moved from their places on the ground a short distance away. Still grabbing at his exposed skin, Lucifer trotted over to his followers and prodded one or two of them with the sharp ends of his toes.

"Get up! You're fine! We have a battle to fight!" he shrieked.

Sophia looked up at the archangel Michael, who was as tall and strong as Gabriel, with silver hair cut straight to his shoulders and gray eyes flecked with white. His robe was simple, but the fabric was of such an elegant weave it seemed to magically move around his being. On his feet were slippers woven from metallic thread, and the sword he carried had a blade so bright, she knew only an archangel could look directly at it. He slid from his steed, radiance streaming from his being.

"Must I always rescue you?" he asked Gabriel with a playful twitch at the corner of his mouth.

Gabriel shrugged, straightening out his garment. "There were hundreds of them and one of me. It's only fair you should join the fight."

How like the two of them to make light of something so traumatic. Sophia wondered if heaven or earth would ever recover from it.

"This has been a terrible thing," she said quietly.

"Yes." Michael sobered and sheathed his sword. "The fall of Lucifer is one of the most terrible things that will ever befall heaven and earth, but surely you know that Gabriel and I often hide that which we feel deepest, while you speak it openly. Both ways help us do what we must to serve the Almighty Divine."

"You alone know His will. Finish this, I beg of you," she said, lifting one hand to shield her eyes. "I can't stand to watch any longer"

Michael nodded and took out his sword again.

"Lucifer and those of you who have chosen to follow him, you are now banned from heaven. Begone, and never again curse us with your evil trickery," he ordered, lifting the sword high. "From this point on, the Almighty Divine has decreed that we shall be archenemies. Your every action shall be recorded in the Judgment Book, so that you will be held accountable for any mortal who stumbles or falls because of your influence. Both you and the mortals you caused to sin will be brought before the Almighty Divine and judged accordingly at the appointed time."

Lucifer held one hand in front of his face and pretended to bow down in submission, but then he sprang up and grabbed at the sword, crying out in pain when he was scalded on contact, but refusing to let go. Using all his strength, Michael ripped the weapon from Lucifer's grasp and threw it to Gabriel, who easily caught it by the handle.

"Why doesn't Michael just strike him down with the sword and be done with it?" Sophia asked miserably. "I can't stand to watch this."

"You're the one who reminds us that he's still our brother. No matter what, we cannot harm him without the Almighty Divine's permission or express wish," Gabriel answered, his azure eyes riveted on the scene before them. "Michael will only fight to free himself."

Michael and Lucifer flew up into the air, locked in combat. They wrestled furiously, shoving free of each other and then grappling back together in battle. Charion, the perfect horse who had carried Michael there, trotted over to stand protectively in front of Gabriel and Sophia.

"You, of all the angels, should understand," Lucifer shouted. "You have enough power to help me teach mortals a lesson, once and forever."

"Never," Michael answered, pushing free of Lucifer. "We were created to serve, not choose our own way, Lucifer."

It seemed as if the confrontation would never end, because neither figure overpowered the other. Lucifer's gang slowly recovered and got to their feet, calling out encouragement to their leader and sneering at Gabriel and Sophia, but Michael was unmoved by their ridicule. Behind the fallen angels, the river crackled and snapped, sending up sprays of fire that fell around the warring archangels. Charion maintained his stance in front of Gabriel and Sophia, a massive barrier between them and Lucifer's followers.

Just when it seemed there would be no victory, Charion reared up and another bolt of lightning flashed down from the sky, curling Lucifer's foot with a rope of fire and severing him from Michael's grasp. With agonizing slowness, the rope snaked around him until he was covered with flames and howling in agony.

Sophia looked away, unable to watch what was happening to the other fallen angels, whose jeers quickly turned to cries of pain as they were similarly bound up. She clung to Gabriel's arm as the ground shook, and a long roar thundered through the air. Then, Lucifer and his minions were gone, and there was silence.

She peeked up to see Michael striding toward them.

"Well. That's that." He pressed his lips together and looked back at the river.

"Michael, what will we tell the rest of the heavenly host? I mean, there's no chance Lucifer is right, is there?" Sophia bowed her head so the archangel wouldn't think her question was meant disrespectfully. "He is—was—an archangel too, just as pleased as the rest of us when the Almighty Divine created mortals. It's hard to believe our ranks could be split apart because of them. So many of our brothers and sisters chose to join him—could they all be wrong?"

Michael was still studying the river. His reply was barely audible above the roar of the raging current, which mingled with the grunts and screams of the former angels who had been sucked beneath its surface.

"Lucifer may have pretended to be pleased by mortals, but he never really was. From the beginning of their creation he sought out other angels who agreed with him that mortals must be destroyed. Now we've been purged of them, and Sophia, you were brought to witness it all."

Her hand clutched at the front of her robe. "Is that why I was chosen to come too? Surely you didn't think I doubted the Almighty Divine?"

"No," Michael answered without pause. "In time, you will understand, but for now let me say that you must inspire the remaining angels to accept the will of the Almighty Divine without question."

"But this isn't the end, is it?" Gabriel said, his eyes fixed on the spot where Lucifer had last stood. "The real hardships are about to begin, thanks to Lucifer's defiance."

"Yes," Michael answered, his eyes fixed on the same spot as Gabriel's. "The battle between good and evil will never end until earth time is completed, thanks to our departed brother."

3

Michael lifted Sophia onto Charion and swung up in front of her, with Gabriel mounting easily behind them. The mammoth steed effortlessly glided into the air and carried his passengers back to a place where the rocky terrain began to be interspersed with patches of soft green grass, and a few slender trees festooned with a lacework of pine needles poked up from the bleak landscape. Recognizing the outer border of the kingdom of heaven, Sophia relaxed her grip on Charion's mane slightly.

How amazing to think that her existence prior to this point had been so free of suffering and pain. Yes, she felt tremendous sorrow for mortals and the difficulties they faced almost every day of their lives, but it wasn't a personal grief. The defection of Lucifer and the others made her feel as if part of her spirit had been ripped away. It was shocking to think that an angel greater than her would make the choice he had, and equally disturbing to remember the fleeting moments when she thought Lucifer might possibly be right.

There was much she still didn't understand, but she knew that since the moment of her creation, Lucifer and the other angels had been there, sharing her existence. Now nearly a third of them were simply gone, and neither Michael nor Gabriel seemed particularly concerned about bringing them back.

"Let us refresh," Michael said, guiding Charion to a lovely area where bushes tipped with golden leaves surrounded a plush carpet of velvety moss. A small stream twisted through a field of brilliant orange flowers nearby. The three of them sat and joined hands, closing their eyes and releasing their spirits into a deep state of relaxation that filled them with peace and comfort.

This was the way angels nurtured themselves, and too often, Sophia realized, she neglected to do it, opting instead for extra time in prayer. As a contented stillness renewed her soul, the terror of what she just experienced began to dissolve, replaced by an overwhelming love for the Almighty Divine. Gradually, she lost awareness of the feel of Michael and Gabriel's strong hands holding her small ones, and the music of the water trickling on its course nearby seemed to sing, "You are loved. You are loved completely."

Eventually, Michael broke their silence with a deep sigh, and when Sophia opened her eyes, he was smiling. "All will be well, no matter what happens with Lucifer. You know that, don't you, Sophia?"

She nodded and smiled back. Gabriel was the last to break his reverie, releasing their hands and clasping his own together with the fingertips pointing upward. He rested his chin on them for a moment and then spoke.

"Many things must change now," he said. "There will be greater struggles for mortals than before, if possible, but we are blessed with the power of the Almighty Divine and can help them."

"What has He revealed to you?" Michael leaned forward, his gray eyes thoughtful.

Gabriel stood and began to pace as he described what the future would hold. Those angels in the heavenly host who remained faithful will be given tasks to perform on behalf of mortals. "For example, you will be a dedicated prayer angel," he said, nodding at Sophia. "The Almighty Divine is much pleased with your love of interceding for mortals in this way."

Sophia clapped her hands together in delight. To dedicate herself more fully to prayer and become even more accomplished at connecting with the Almighty Divine was the best assignment she could hope for. As Gabriel continued to describe the role of the other remaining angels, she recognized the magnitude of the difference that was about to occur among the heavenly host.

Previously, the angels had been free to act on behalf of mortals in whatever way they felt would please the Almighty Divine, unlike the archangels who received specific orders directly from their Creator. Now they would all be charged with more specific tasks, and as Gabriel emphasized, it was important that they do exactly what they were assigned—no more or no less. It would require absolute subservience and belief that the Almighty Divine, in His wisdom and goodness, knew what was best for both the kingdoms of heaven and earth.

"What if an angel doesn't care for the task he or she is assigned to?" Sophia asked, thinking ahead. At one time, it would seem unlikely that might happen, but Lucifer had set new precedents for everything.

"Just as Gabriel and I and the other archangels obey without hesitation, so too must all of you," Michael said, as if the answer was obvious.

Sophia bit back her reply, knowing that part of what he said was true. She and the others had been taught that angels were made to carry out the wishes of the Almighty Divine—in fact, they had no independent existence without him. But Lucifer and the others had shown that wasn't completely true. They might not have a blissful existence on earth, but they would be allowed to stay there and do as they pleased, or so it seemed to her.

A slight breeze tickled the back of Sophia's neck and she shivered, realizing that Lucifer and his followers might also choose to try to come back; he had seemed so determined to take her with him that for a brief time she had thought she might not escape his grip on her hair.

"There will be a different organizational structure too," Gabriel was saying to Michael. "You and I and selected others will be dwelling on what will now be known as the Second Level of heaven. The Almighty Divine will be on the Third and highest Level." He turned to Sophia. "You and the rest of the heavenly host, along with the souls of deceased mortals, will be on the First Level. They will be kept in a separate resting place and looked after by selected angels and one of us."

He waited, as if knowing she would protest.

"But…that means we won't gather in the presence of the Almighty Divine as before." Her last words were choked as she considered the implications. Being in the presence of the Almighty Divine and receiving His blessings while they sang praises to Him was something all angels loved beyond any other activities. It was what made their existence meaningful. It was also, she noted, the level closest to Lucifer.

Gabriel nodded sadly. "Yes."

Michael looked at Sophia, then focused on Gabriel again. "He will never abandon the heavenly host or mortals. The two of us will bring His blessings regularly, and when you refresh, you will feel His love as strongly as if you were standing before Him."

There was a silence as Sophia rubbed the still tender spot on her head where Lucifer had seized her hair. As if reading her thoughts, Michael added, "We will also protect you from harm."

"Yes," Gabriel repeated, seating himself so he was on eye level with the other two. "And that is why all angels must refresh as often as possible. In that way, it will be even better than before." He took Sophia's hand in his and gave it a gentle squeeze. "Surely you know the One who brought us into being would never abandon us. These changes are not what any of us would desire, but because of Lucifer, we must form our own strategy to fight for mortals, just as surely as he is conspiring this very moment to destroy them."

"He destroyed everything," Sophia said bitterly. "How can Lucifer have such power? I can't help thinking he will quickly come to see the error of his ways."

Michael took her other hand. "Just like mortals, we always have a choice, Sophia. He and his followers have made a bad choice, which makes our job more important than ever. I suspect Lucifer will target both mortals and angels now. Believing that the Almighty Divine is just that—all powerful and supremely good—will help us win this battle."

"It's a lot to work through," she said. "I'm glad I'm not an archangel with such heavy responsibilities." Another thought occurred to her and she gripped Gabriel's hand harder, tilting her face up to his. "I will still see you, though, won't I?"

"Of course!" He hugged her to him. "You will be my inside connection to the first level."

Michael gave an exaggerated sigh. "I suppose you're not much bothered by having less contact with me?" Nearby, Charion heard the tone of his master's voice and snorted, throwing his head back so that his long mane rippled.

Sophia nudged Michael's foot with her own. "Of course I'm bothered by seeing less of you, but I'm well aware your special confidant is Isaac. The two of you have much in common."

"That's another change," Gabriel said, nodding in agreement. "The Almighty Divine recognizes that a more formal system for maintaining order and coordination on the First Level is needed. He has decided there will be a Senior Servant who will lead the efforts of the heavenly host. That person will work with two Selected Servants to make sure the efforts of all angels are coordinated, but just as prayer is your mission, service is the mission of these three. They are not in any way to be seen as superior to the rest of the heavenly host. Isaac is to be appointed as the Senior Servant, but he will receive direction from Michael, who will be relaying the Almighty Divine's wishes."

Sophia rubbed her forehead, trying to imagine all the changes that were about to occur, and the new threat of Lucifer actively working to undermine all their good works. Isaac was certainly a good choice to be the Senior Servant: he had tremendous energy to rally the angels in praise songs or celebrations of a mortal's decision to worship the Almighty Divine and no other. Being given permission to help mortals by immersing herself in prayer was a tremendous blessing, but it would doubtless take tremendous effort for every angel to make all the adjustments Gabriel and Michael were describing.

"There's one last thing," Michael said. "We must protect the borders of heaven from Lucifer and his followers. They cannot be allowed back in or they will bring the chaos we just saw into the First Level and attempt to lure away more of the heavenly host, as they just did."

You mean like me? Sophia wanted to ask, but she bit her lip and stayed silent. Clearly, a plan was in place that she had no part in creating, but Michael charged her to obey without question, and that's exactly what she would try to do.

Summoning Charion, he unhooked a brass instrument from his saddle, lifted it to his lips, and blew once. A blast echoed around them, and instantly, a legion of new angels appeared, some still in the midst of what they were doing when summoned. A tall woman with hair that cascaded down her back like a rippling waterfall of blonde waves was singing a song of praise; another man with his eyes closed and hands clasped together continued to recite his prayers. Quickly, they realized where they were, and huddled together with looks of dismay on their faces.

"Brothers and sisters, don't be afraid," Michael assured them. "You have been summoned because you were chosen by the Almighty Divine for a special mission, and as such are under His special protection."

Not many members of the heavenly host had personal conversations with archangels; Sophia could see a few of them trembling or clutching their neighbors for reassurance. If only there was a way to calm their fears—but Lucifer had changed that. Now the angels would know pain and suffering, just as mortals did.

"Many things about heaven are about to change. These changes will all enable us to better serve the Almighty Divine, and have come by His direction," Michael told them, stroking Charion's mane in an absent-minded way that contradicted the seriousness of his statement. Sophia looked up, concerned about his ability to downplay the horror of what had just happened, but Gabriel spoke next.

"As many of you know, Lucifer has long believed the creation of mortals was a serious mistake. He has his reasons for thinking this, but more importantly, he has chosen to follow his own way, instead of living in obedience and submission to the Almighty Divine, as we do. Unfortunately, many of our brothers and sisters have chosen to leave heaven and follow him. For that reason, they have been banned from our world, and destined to stay on earth."

There was a collective gasp from the angels who had been summoned, and a few furtive glances were exchanged. For some time, Michael and Gabriel wandered among them, soothing those who were weeping over the loss of their loved ones.

Sophia looked down and noticed a circle of red around her wrist where Lucifer had held her and said another silent prayer of gratitude for her escape, trying to banish the queasiness that returned to her spirit when she thought of him and his new band of devotees.

Eventually, there was silence again, and the summoned angels looked to Michael and Gabriel for more information.

"Know that the Almighty Divine is just as grieved by this turn of events as each of you," Gabriel said.

"But what does that mean for us?" the woman with the beautiful blonde hair called out, her voice quavering. "How will we go on when we've lost so many of those we care about?"

Gabriel nodded. "Good question. As you know, the boundary between the kingdom of earth and the kingdom of heaven has always been hidden, and only those of us who had permission from the Almighty Divine were allowed to travel between the two. Unfortunately, we now need to know where that boundary is at all times, and guard it zealously, since we have reason to believe it might be broached by Lucifer and his followers, with ill intent."

More expressions of distress sounded from the group, which made Charion whinny and paw at the ground. Michael steadied him and turned back to the angels, his voice still soothing.

"Again, I tell you that you must not be afraid. We are protected at all times by the Almighty Divine, who is far more powerful than Lucifer. Establishing a guard here is a caution."

"So what are we supposed to do?" the angel who had appeared in the midst of his prayers asked.

Michael took out his sword and swept it through the air in a wide arc. Instantly, an immense barrier of solid silver appeared, stretching in either direction and upward as far as they could see. In front of them was a gate made of filigreed posts set with pearls and diamonds, which swung slowly open. Just inside, they could see the beginning of the Great Way, a path paved with pure white marble that wove throughout the kingdom of heaven. As one of the new arrivals took a step to pass through the gate, Gabriel barred his way.

"You must remain on the outside, my friends. There is an invisible barrier surrounding this one that will keep you secure, filled with clouds you may rest on or stand behind. As long as you remain within the area of the clouds, you will be safe and well able to protect whoever enters this gate." He lifted his arms. "We bless you, Watchers, our new guardians of the entrance to heaven."

Michael said, "There will be others appointed too, so you may regularly rejoin the heavenly host for prolonged refreshing. I'm also asking Sophia to dedicate part of her prayers to your efforts."

Sophia studied the beautiful gate, which sparkled with points of light so brilliant, she knew they were signs of the Almighty Divine's myriad blessings. Seeing it, and the comfortable border of clouds that surrounded the outside of the wall, the new Watchers seemed delighted by their new assignment, running from one spot to the other and exclaiming over the smoothness of the pearls in the gate and the brilliant flecks of light. Overcome with laughter, the woman with the long blonde hair settled in to sit on one of the floating clouds that had drifted in to surround the entryway.

"I can't see anything unpleasant about this assignment," one of them said, twisting to look in all directions. "How can I guard something I can't see?"

"You will find that many come this way," Michael said. "Some are meant to enter the kingdom of heaven, but others are not. The only question you need ask is whether the being who seeks to enter serves the Almighty Divine. Those who cannot bow down and worship His holy name cannot enter, but those who respond with complete conviction can."

He gestured for the Watchers to come together and join hands. Together, he and Michael went around the circle and blessed them by saying: "You are gifted with guarding our kingdom. May you be ever strong and vigilant."

Sophia sank to her knees and prayed for the Watchers to manifest these very qualities, and to be confident of the love of the Almighty Divine even though they would be operating in relative isolation for long periods of time. When Michael finished, one of the angels lifted his hand timidly.

"What about Lucifer?" he asked. "He has often boasted to me about his ability to go back and forth between both worlds."

"That will be no more. Lucifer has declared himself our enemy." Michael slid his sword back into its sheath and crossed his arms over his chest. "Under no circumstances must you let him past this gate."

Michael waited for further questions or challenges about the importance of their efforts to guard the dividing point between heaven and earth. When none were offered, he prepared to depart, but before climbing back on Charion, he told the Watchers he intended to check on them frequently.

"You can count on us to keep heaven secure," said an angel who was slightly taller and more muscular than the rest. "I will never fail you, Brother Michael and Brother Gabriel."

Gabriel rested one hand on the man's shoulder. "Thomas, I will count on that. In fact, although we have no hierarchy here, I would suggest that you might be the one to develop a system for maintaining vigilance and a process for reporting any issues to Michael. Thereafter, you can rotate this responsibility among yourselves."

The rest of the angels raised their voices in a cheer for Thomas, then sang a farewell song to Sophia, Gabriel, and Michael. The three of them climbed on Charion, who easily galloped upward into the sky and then playfully dipped back to the ground.

"He's feeling frisky today," Michael noted, reaching around Sophia to ruffle the creature's mane. "I wish I shared his emotions."

4

S ophia saw the familiar sights of what would now be called the First Level of heaven and sighed with relief. The Great Way, a road of polished white marble, curved through the lush landscape like a satin ribbon. Ultimately, it led to clusters of buildings, each a different fluid color that regularly faded into another slightly different shade that blended perfectly with the flowers and trees surrounding it. The roofs and doors were tipped with crystal that created a kaleidoscope effect. Inside, each angel had a special place to refresh, either alone or in groups.

The Cleansing River ran next to the Great Way, its surface glinting like the facets of a diamond. When it reached the heart of the First Level, it split to create a moat around a magnificent building that gleamed like pearl, situated high on a mountain covered with a blanket of thick dark green grass. Beyond the building, the Cleansing River plummeted downward in a spectacular waterfall that filled a pool of still water surrounded by a border of sandy beach.

"What is that?" Sophia asked, leaning back so Michael could hear her.

"That is the new Operations Central," he said. "Isaac and the Selected Servants will spend most of their time there."

A few angels were pointing at the new building, and one or two others were actually flying down into the waterfall and soaring effortlessly back up into the air, shrieking with delight. For the most part, though, things seemed much as they had been before Sophia left. She could see the Prayer Chamber from the air, a yellow dome surrounded by a soft glow.

If they only knew, Sophia thought, watching her colleagues walk hand in hand or with their arms around each others' shoulders, deep in conversation or smiling with delight at their conversation. Deep inside that building that was the color of pale gold, she knew there were angels voluntarily immersed in prayer. How would they respond when all the changes Gabriel had described took place and some of them were assigned to completely different duties?

Charion landed on an empty stretch of the Great Way, and Gabriel dismounted, holding up one hand to help Sophia down. Michael looked at the two of them and nodded grimly.

"I guess we must get started with this new way of existence. As you can imagine, my role is changing too. I will be patrolling the kingdom of earth more closely, along with an additional force of archangels assigned to help me. If what we have seen so far is a battle of wills between Lucifer and the Almighty Divine, this is all-out war. Gabriel, can you orient Isaac and introduce him to the two Selected Servants? I will meet with him later. And Sophia, it will be your job to keep the prayer angels consistent in their work."

"No problem," Gabriel said, giving Charion's flank a final pat.

Sophia nodded in agreement, but as the two of them walked away, she frowned. "The Almighty Divine is all-powerful. How can Lucifer have any notion of prevailing against his own creator?"

"Mortals," Gabriel said. "The weak link."

Sophia frowned again, not sure she understood his answer.

"All Lucifer has to do is to come between mortals and the Almighty Divine and he destroys them, in one way or another," Gabriel continued, his eyes deepening to a hard blue and a pained expression shadowing his face. "Because mortals have free will, like us, they can choose to live their lives in service of the Almighty Divine or not."

"No one would choose to serve Lucifer," she retorted, hugging her arms around her waist and shaking her head.

"No?" Gabriel said softly. "I think we've just seen that angels will believe his lies, Sophia, and we're much stronger than mortals! Look at what has already happened to them—Adam and Eve introduced sin to the human race, courtesy of Lucifer. Their son Cain believed he was right to kill his brother Abel—who do you think suggested that idea? Without our protection and intervention, Lucifer will continue to destroy mankind by planting these kinds of ideas. Once mortals are under his control, earth is his."

They walked side by side on the Great Way without speaking, the rippling of the Cleansing River a soothing song in the background. As they made their way to the Praise Plaza, a gathering place for the entire heavenly host, another thought, more troubling than Michael's predictions, occurred to Sophia.

"Lucifer singled me out back there, Gabriel." She held out her hand and showed him the smudge of red that remained around her wrist. "Does that mean something I should know about?"

"You're not an archangel, Sophia, but the Almighty Divine does have special plans for you," he answered. "Although what we just witnessed was not planned, in many ways, your ability to resist Lucifer was a test of devotion. You were the only angel there who listened to what I said and believed me, despite all the things you saw to the contrary."

"Does that mean I won't be on the First Level with the rest of the heavenly host from now on? Tell me that's not the case—I'm dedicated to praying for mortals. It brings me great joy. What I've just seen motivates me to work even harder."

She was only being partly honest with Gabriel. It was true that she found complete bliss when her soul was caught up in prayer, but there was a part of her that wouldn't mind being assigned to the Second Level of heaven, which was what the words "special plan" sounded like to her. Until Lucifer got over this willful behavior and stubbornness and returned to them, the farther away from him she was able to keep herself, the better. She shivered, remembering how compelling his words had been, and suddenly, she wasn't sure she could resist his wiles a second time, if it came to that.

They saw some other angels in the distance, calling out in recognition and beckoning them closer. Waving back, Gabriel put one hand on Sophia's shoulder and spoke in a low voice.

"If you're asked about the missing angels, say only that they chose to go with Lucifer to earth. It's best if they don't know all the details or feel as if they might be attacked."

"You mean, like I do?" she asked, clenching her fists. "I think Lucifer might target me specifically, Gabriel. He hates to lose at anything, and I'm the one who didn't go with him."

"You will be protected, and I promise we will meet often. Just keep praying."

"Gabriel! Sophia!" The angel who ran toward them was Isaac, his face full of joy. He hugged Gabriel, his long hair clustered in waves of a rich chestnut color that spread out against the archangel's chest. When he turned to embrace Sophia, his brown eyes were tender, with the rich sheen of polished wood. She felt nearly smothered when his strong arms surrounded her and pressed him to her chest, but for a moment, she let herself rest against him, appreciating the support.

"Is everything okay?" he asked, when she finally broke free. He looked from Sophia to Gabriel, concerned. "I was hoping to see Michael—is he coming to join you?"

"We must talk," Gabriel said, and as he described all that was about to happen, Sophia trailed behind the two men, feeling like mortal children must when they were relegated to following their parents from place to place. She was smaller than most angels, and something about her perpetually tousled blonde hair, full cheeks, and big green eyes added to her perception that she somehow looked younger than most of the others in the heavenly host, especially with Gabriel and Isaac in the lead.

It was curious, though, that since the beginning of time, she had been the angel Gabriel sought out when he wanted an opinion on how things were going among the heavenly host. She had been the first to encourage him to talk to Lucifer, believing he was just misguided and could be helped to reconsider his behavior. Their relationship wasn't automatically as close as those among the archangels, but she, of all the heavenly host, seemed to be his special confidant.

Now, as they arrived at the Praise Plaza, and Isaac summoned all the heavenly host to hear what Gabriel had to say, she remained at the back of the crowd, distracted by her own thoughts. She must work hard at her assignment to pray, and maybe the favor she had somehow found with Gabriel would increase. She might even somehow be allowed to advance to the Second Level of heaven, the dwelling place of the archangels and a level closer to the Almighty Divine as well as a level further away from Lucifer.

"Sophia, what do you make of all this?"

The angel standing nearest to her nudged her slightly and moved closer. She recognized Hector, one of the angels who had been trusted to go to earth and comfort mortals directly. He had also been the one who alerted her to Lucifer's strange comings and goings between the two king-doms and the discord he sensed the archangel was causing.

"Does this have something to do with Lucifer?" Hector quizzed, pulling her away so the other angels couldn't hear their whispered con-versation. "Different levels of heaven? That sounds like a serious change."

She looked at him, wondering how to limit her answer without being openly dishonest. Hector knew she was close to Gabriel and had seen her leave with the hundreds of angels chosen to witness Lucifer's choice—the same angels who elected to follow him out of the kingdom of heaven.

"I can't speak of all that happened." She smiled apologetically. "But Lucifer and all of the angels who went with me as witnesses chose to live on earth now. You're right about all these changes. They've come about because Lucifer and his followers have rejected the authority of the Almighty Divine."

"I can't believe it." He looked around, his round blue eyes searching the back of the crowd. Like her, he was too short to see very far, which led him to sigh in exasperation and run one hand through the curly gray hair that covered the top of his head like a small cap. "On the way here I was looking for Azazel, but no one has seen him. Now I know he won't be coming back."

"I have to trust that we're all better off not knowing the particulars of what's happened to them," she said carefully, "but what I saw was horri-ble. The rest of us must have enough faith to believe in the Almighty Divine's wisdom and trust that the changes taking place are for the best."

Hector's face relaxed, and he laid one hand on her arm. "Of course you're right. 'Doubt is the beginning of unbelief'—how many times have we been told that? Come, I can hear the details of Gabriel's plan later. I'm sensing you need to refresh, and I certainly can too."

She realized he was right—she longed to sink down into the com-fortable recliners they used when they refreshed and clear her spirit of all anxiety again, even though the time with Michael and Gabriel had seemed to offer total relief. Following Hector to one of the nearby houses that was a nearly transparent shade of emerald, she gratefully collapsed onto the lounge chair conformed to her proportions. Hector pulled out a similar chair reserved for guests next to her and settled himself in.

"Praise to you, Almighty Divine," he murmured, his voice trailing off.

Sophia crossed her hands over her chest and let her eyes flutter shut, wishing she could slip into a state of refreshment as easily as Hector. Instead, she saw ugly images before her like a series of photographs, each chronicling the scene of Lucifer's ejection. It was surprising that, once alone, the horror of what had happened still felt raw inside her.

Eventually, she slipped to the side of her chair and knelt on the floor, bowing her head and clasping her hands together. Quickly, she lost herself in a prayer of thanksgiving for the safety she had been given and an appeal for similar guidance to mortals. Gradually, her thoughts stilled, and she felt herself drifting into a state of refreshing, but not before one last petition.

"Thy will be done," she whispered, "but if possible, please bring Lucifer back to us and stop this terrible thing from happening."

5

Sophia had struggled to put the situation with Lucifer behind her, but eventually her dedication to praying for mortals and their well-being became all-consuming. Among the Prayer Angels she became a leader of sorts, always ready to stay and continue praying when the others left to refresh. Sometimes she couldn't help laughing with joy because she was blessed with a responsibility she thoroughly enjoyed.

"Something funny?" Gabriel asked on one such occasion.

She had just finished a passionate prayer on behalf of Sarah, a woman who had cried out to the Almighty Divine in distress many times after being unable to conceive a child. Now, her request had been granted, and Sophia rejoiced along with Sarah as she shared the news with her husband.

"The Almighty Divine is so good," Sophia told Gabriel. "Just when I think I have seen the limits of His love, He surprises me by doing something even greater."

"Be prepared to be further amazed. Sarah shall bear not one but many children," he said, as Sophia leaned back against the cushioned satin wall and clapped her hands together in delight. All around them, the voices of angels praying for different mortal needs filled the air with a soothing chant.

"But that's not why I'm here," he continued, so stern she feared she had somehow offended him without realizing it.

"Wh-what is it, Gabriel?" she finally asked.

He took both of her hands in his, and they were instantly transported to a place that she had never visited before. The walls were an almost translucent turquoise, like the cloudless sky over an earth desert. The floor was the same color but as soft as fleece, and in a semicircle, there were arranged three cushioned chairs with curved backs, each a slightly different shade of blue. One wall had a large window set into it, covered with white silk and rippling in a slight breeze. A pleasant blue vapor wafted in from the other walls and down from the tapestried ceiling, caressing her face and soothing her spirit as she breathed it in.

"Where are we?" she asked, eyes shut to better enjoy the sweetness of the moment.

"This is my Refreshing Room," Gabriel said. "It's removed from the First Level for protection and privacy, but not part of the Second Level, for the same reasons."

His voice was so grave her previous concern returned. "Gabriel, why have you brought me here?"

He paced back and forth, clearly distressed. "How are things on the First Level?"

She reviewed her recent interactions with other angels and anything else that might have been unusual. "Although it took some effort to adjust to the new order in heaven, things are now organized and peaceful. The angels I have contact with are happy. We feel Isaac is a good Senior Servant and enjoy dedicating ourselves to jobs the Almighty Divine has commissioned us to do." She hung her head briefly. "I think some of us—myself included—may feel a bit guilty about not being this dedicated before."

She waited while he studied the opening in the wall shielded by the shiny covering, and sighed. "Well, at least that's good news, as opposed to what I must show you. We've been betrayed by the Watchers. You heard Michael tell them they weren't supposed to speak to Lucifer, but they disobeyed. Somehow, Lucifer and Azazel began to engage them in conversation. At first it was nothing worrisome, but eventually it became a debate over why the Watchers had to spend so much time outside of heaven. From that point, it was easy enough for Lucifer to convince them to join him on earth, where he assured them they would be treated like royalty. Of course, Azazel was there to confirm the absolute truth of Lucifer's lies."

Sophia made a sound of dismay. "Does that mean Lucifer and his followers can enter the Portal now?"

Before Gabriel could explain further, Michael descended from above, his white hair and garments standing out against the blue of the room. Michael's silver eyes narrowed for a second, as if still trying to figure out how the news could possibly be true. His eyes met Gabriel's first, in a hooded look that suggested secrets. Then he turned to Sophia and inclined his head in greeting.

"Blessings to you, Sophia," he said, then rested one hand on Gabriel's shoulder. "It's true. Hector just gave me a report."

Sophia looked from one archangel to the other. "What's happened? Is Hector okay? I didn't know you put him in charge of the Watchers."

"Secretly, I did." Michael nodded. "I felt that Thomas needed extra supervision, since this was a new job. Unfortunately, Hector's the only one who followed my instructions. The rest of them spoke to Lucifer, who wouldn't relent until he convinced them they should descend and live on earth. Made it sound like a regular paradise. Hector said he overheard Lucifer tell Thomas that Azazel is busy teaching mortals how to make music and tools, read the stars, measure time…things they were never meant to know. It will change everything again."

"Incredible," Gabriel said, disgusted. "Lucifer just can't stop. He knows the Almighty Divine has rules for what mortals were to know and not know. Surely He's angry over this latest development?"

Michael looked away from Gabriel and Sophia, then took a deep breath and met their eyes. "He hasn't been the same since Adam and Eve disobeyed. You know Lucifer kept telling him that was just the first sign of the rebellious nature of mortals, but the Almighty Divine wouldn't destroy them then, and He won't now. He believes their love for Him will be stronger than any other motivation."

Sophia spoke up. "He's right. There are good mortals. Look at Seth— Lucifer may have gotten to Cain, but he couldn't sway his brother. He's done everything the Almighty Divine hoped mortals would do—and he isn't the only one. There are many good mortals."

The satin curtains parted, revealing a telescopic view of earth. Sophia and Gabriel took turns pointing out different mortals who were faithful to the Almighty Divine, but Michael countered each instance with a situation of complete discord and chaos. Their debate was interrupted by Hector, who had been charged with going between the heaven and earth to monitor the defection of the Watchers.

At the sight of him raising his arms toward the Refreshing Room,

Michael leapt to his feet and drew Hector upward to join them. "What has happened?"

Hector struggled to speak, clasping his hands together and lowering his eyes so only his frosted curls were visible. They waited until he composed himself and looked back up, his expression distressed.

"It's Azazel...he's taken a mate from the mortal women. They've had a child...a monster."

All four of them looked down on earth, shocked into silence. They saw dozens of Watchers roaming the civilized parts of earth, selecting mortal women who appealed to them and, willing or not, impregnating them. It was hard to judge all that happened, since heavenly time was without boundaries, but as Sophia watched the generations flow, children from those unholy unions mutated further, so large in size that birthing them was often the death of their mortal mothers. The children grew into horrible giants, driven by evil and determined to populate the earth with their own kind, an idea encouraged by Azazel and Lucifer.

Hector elaborated. "The Nephilim, as mortals call them, are truly evil, and while they aren't immortal like angels, they can cause tremendous damage while they are alive."

"And they can have children who carry on the destruction," Gabriel added.

"We must find a way to help mortals," Michael said, sweeping one arm in front of the screen so it went blank. "Above all other duties, we are charged to intervene on behalf of mortals whenever we can. Gabriel, we must bring this to the Almighty Divine immediately."

Without a word of farewell, the two of them vanished.

Hector looked at Sophia and sighed. "Just for once, I wish they would take me along. I know I'm not an archangel, but I long to gather in the presence of the Almighty Divine like we used to do before all this 'First Level' stuff. Can you remember what that was like?"

Sophia shared his feelings, but instead of commiserating, she dropped to her knees and began a prayer for protection over the mortals who had, so far, resisted the temptations of Azazel and the others. She also prayed for those who lived in fear of the Nephilim, and finally, she stood over Hector, who had collapsed on one of the chairs, and prayed for his perseverance.

By the end of her prayer, Michael returned, joining her in the closing with a special prayer song of blessing. His voice was deep and resonant, filling her spirit with hope. The song of an archangel was like no other, but it took special occasions like this for them to occur.

"The Almighty Divine can't help reminding us of Lucifer's intentions," Michael said quietly. "By trying to wipe out mortals and populate earth with some form of angel—even a fallen one—he thinks he's preventing a future tragedy. You know I disagree with that."

Hector rubbed his eyes and sat up. "How can the Almighty Divine even care about Lucifer's motives at this point?"

The archangel frowned. "You know there is no end to His compassion."

They went back to the screen and turned it on to watch. The situation on earth was already worse, with mortals living in fear, surrendering to whatever request the Nephilim or Azazel made of them, without hesitation.

"I must go down and try to help Gabriel," Michael said grimly. "Clearly a message from him isn't changing anything."

Soon, Sophia and Hector saw both archangels on earth, flying from one city to another in an attempt to convince mortals to abandon their misguided ways. None of their efforts worked, as mortals and Nephilim alike continued to multiply, inflicting misery on each other.

Hector was rubbing his chin. "I have an idea," he said, leaving for earth just as the two archangels returned to the Refreshing Room.

"Where is he going?" Michael snapped.

Sophia gave a small shrug of her shoulders. "To earth, it appears."

"What makes him think he can change the course of history when we couldn't?" he said, slamming his massive hand against the screen so the images on it disappeared. From behind Michael, Gabriel rolled his eyes at Sophia and put one finger to his lips.

When Hector reappeared, a mortal who appeared to be several hundred years old was with him. The man was dressed in rags, had a curly gray beard that reached his chest, a walking staff that was taller than he was, and shrewd brown eyes that peered out from a wrinkled face at them.

Michael looked the figure over from head to toe. "And who might this be?"

"One of those 'good mortals' you saw when we looked down on earth," Hector explained with a smile, then glanced sideways at the man. "He might not look the part, but this is Enoch, who truly lives for the Almighty Divine. Enoch, meet the archangels Michael and Gabriel. Sophia is a regular angel, like me."

Sophia tried not to gape at Enoch, whose wispy beard reached his chest. The mortal's brown eyes moved constantly from one of them to the other, taking in every detail, and there was a bemused expression on his face. Although half as tall as Gabriel, he stood with his shoulders back and head up, as if honored to be in their presence.

"Greetings, dear ones. I can say that, can't I? I feel I know you well, although this is our first meeting." Enoch smiled wistfully. "How can I be of help?"

"Welcome," Michael said, bowing ever so slightly. "I doubt there's much you can do, Enoch. By earth time, it's been centuries since we've tried to conquer Lucifer and his followers, but even when I appear directly to a mortal, it seems not to matter. Although our existence is not governed by time, it seems that, for mortals, the voice of Lucifer has become what controls their lives. For every Nephilim I slay, two new ones seem to arise."

Michael waved Hector and Enoch aside, going back to the screen and leaning against it, resting his forehead on what appeared to be empty air. After a few minutes, Enoch crossed over and seized hold of Michael's wrist.

"This cannot be!" he said. "Perhaps they will believe me—a mortal who has witnessed the glory of heaven in person. Let me go back and tell the others what I've seen. I promise I'll try with all my being to change them."

Michael and Gabriel eyed each other, considering. Finally, they shrugged and told Hector to take the old man back in one last effort to convince mortals of their wrongdoing.

"This will be it, though," Michael warned, as Enoch prepared to leave. "Let them know they won't have any more chances."

"Pessimism is a very unbecoming trait," Sophia told him as they watched Hector escort Enoch back to earth.

Again, generations of earth time passed as children grew to adulthood and bore sons and daughters of their own. Enoch did as he promised and traveled from town to town, exhorting those who gathered to change their evil ways before it was too late. He toiled to write about his experiences and spread the documents to others so they might be convinced of their wrongdoing. To a person, they responded to his speeches with scorn and ripped the pages of his writing to shreds. Sometimes they even hurled a stone or two at him to chase him away or threatened to summon a Nephilim to beat him.

"I must confer with the Almighty Divine," Michael finally said, shaking his head regretfully. "These efforts aren't going anywhere."

He flew upward and out of the room as Sophia returned to her prayers. Hector descended to take one more survey of the damage on earth and offer help to Enoch wherever he could.

Gabriel paced back and forth, whispering encouragement to mortals to repent before it was too late. Finally, out of frustration, he told Sophia he was going to join Michael and see if the Almighty Divine had need of him.

"I think Hector must bring Enoch's time on earth to an end," he added as the ceiling parted to allow him passage. "For all his efforts, he will be rewarded with immediate entry into heaven."

When Michael and Gabriel returned, their expressions conveying relief. They summoned Hector back to the Refreshing Room, assuring Sophia that Lucifer's plans were about to be turned against him. When Hector arrived, he had Enoch at his side.

Michael looked at the mortal, then withdrew his sword and placed the point on the elderly man's head. "With this sword, the Lord I serve has directed me to both give life and take it away," he said. "For your sincere efforts to help us, you will not die a mortal death, but will stay here with us in the kingdom of heaven. Thank you, servant Enoch."

Enoch's eyes filled with tears and he collapsed to the floor, covering his head with his hands. "Blessed be the Almighty Divine. If only others could understand His goodness."

Sophia dropped down and comforted him, rubbing the frail man's shoulders gently until he stopped sobbing and was able to stand up. She kept one arm around him and turned her attention to Michael, who told them what had been decreed.

"In a short time, rain will begin and water will cover the face of the earth, destroying mortals and Nephilim. It grieves the Almighty Divine to do it, but at least it will be a chance to start over. However, at Gabriel's direction, a mortal named Noah was told to build an ark. His obedience means that he and his family will live through the flood and repopulate Earth."

"I can't believe it. Noah is my grandson, many generations removed!" Enoch said. "Only a man like him could build such a boat when everyone will ridicule him. I knew he was meant for great things when he was born."

Hector asked Michael, "What about Lucifer?"

"Unfortunately, the flood won't affect Lucifer, just as it wouldn't hurt one of us. The Almighty Divine will never put an end to him, but it will be interesting to see what happens when he loses his followers."

"You mean the Nephilim?" Enoch asked, looking at both of the archangels, who nodded in unison. "What if they're not destroyed? I wouldn't be surprised if Lucifer found a way to shelter them. They're..." He choked up, his voice dropping to a whisper. "They're evil in a way you can't imagine. The only power we mortals have against them is our faith."

Michael and Gabriel exchanged a look, not daring to question what might happen if somehow Lucifer did find a way to keep the Nephilim alive. Enoch tottered over to the screen that had transformed into a window offering them all a view of earth. Enoch leaned out and rent the strips of his robe in grief.

"Fools! Can't you listen to the wise ones? And Noah, be steady, despite the scorn of others. You can do this." He turned back to the angels and, rubbing the small of his back with one hand, winced. "I guess I haven't left my mortal body behind yet."

"It will take some time for that to happen, but when the process is complete, you'll have no complaints, I assure you," Gabriel said, then inclined his head as if hearing something. "Sophia, Hector, if you'll excuse us, Michael and I are being called to meet with the Almighty Divine. Enoch, you're to come with us."

"I guess it's back to earth for me," Hector said, "even though we all know what's about to happen. Maybe if I take Isaac with me, it will make a small difference."

After he vanished, Sophia lingered in the Refreshing Room, touching the cushions and breathing in the wisps of soothing vapor, but her mood was more unsettled than calm. She was worried about the mortals, but it also bothered her that Enoch was granted a blessing she longed for. Being in the immediate presence of the Almighty Divine was supreme happiness, but since Lucifer left, everything about heaven had changed. Until now, only archangels were granted that privilege. Could she even remember what it felt like to bask in the glory of her Creator?

"Sophia, how can you tolerate this?" She heard Lucifer's singsong voice surrounding her. "Mortals being gathered up from earth and allowed to mingle with angels in heaven, yet somehow here on earth that's a bad thing? The Almighty Divine is going too far now."

She fell to her knees and clasped her hands together, wishing Gabriel or Michael or even Hector were there to help her. She remembered the mistake the Watchers had made: being enticed into a seemingly innocent conversation with Lucifer. That would not happen to her.

"Have no doubt, even if some are lost in this flood about to come, others will survive," Lucifer said, laughing softly. "And you will never find me, or my followers—but you can be *my* messenger, Sophia. Tell Michael and Gabriel to check out a place called Sodom in a few hundred earth years. I've already decided it will be my next project."

Sophia squeezed her eyes shut and threw herself face down on the floor, but the voice continued: "Tell Gabriel what you know, Sophia, and I have a special message for that fool Enoch who somehow thinks the world will be different after the flood! It's already over, and one of Noah's daughters is happily pregnant with the child of a man who doesn't even know he carries the Nephilim gene."

She couldn't stop listening, biting back the retorts she felt Lucifer deserved. The memory of him being dragged into the river of fire on the day of his departure made her grimace. Only Lucifer could project a demeanor of pathos and evil.

"Go away, in the name of the Almighty Divine, go away," she said, crossing her arms over the top of her head and bowing deeper into the floor as if it would offer her an escape. "You know what you're doing is wrong. You belong here with us, doing good, not on earth spreading evil."

There was a strange stillness, and then the sound of weeping. At first it was distant and muted, but before long it exploded into wails that vibrated through her spirit.

"Why?" Lucifer asked. "Why doesn't He see that they will break His heart over and over unless I stop them?"

When she found herself suddenly transported back to her prayer chamber, Sophia discovered that she too had tears in her eyes. Would mortals really undo all that the Almighty Divine worked so heard to create?

It was her own voice she heard asking the most reasonable debate of the day: *That all depends on who you trust the most, Sophia: Lucifer or the Almighty Divine.*

6

In the centuries that followed, Sophia never stopped believing the Almighty Divine would triumph, regardless of how grim things looked on earth. Michael and Gabriel remained steadfast too, and when Lucifer's prediction about Sodom had proven true, they fought valiantly to destroy what could have been the first of many evil kingdoms on earth.

"But it's mortals too," Sophia confided to Hector one time when they had found the opportunity to refresh together. "They don't seem very eager to be rescued."

"Lucifer has a ready audience, I'll admit, but earth is different, Sophia. When you're there, you desire the pleasures that can be found in material goods. The Almighty Divine is far away, but a bottle of alcohol or a night of debauchery with your best friend's wife is right at hand. I'm not sure I can explain it well, but I do understand, even if I don't approve."

Hector's explanation hadn't stopped her from praying as diligently as ever, but when Gabriel summoned her to his Refreshing Room, she sensed that something significant was about to happen. He did not disappoint her.

His request made her drop to her knees, but instead of pressing her hands together as she usually did when she prayed, the tips of her tiny fingers rubbed her forehead in worry. The lashes of her eyes were dark with moisture, and loose strands of short sandy hair had fallen over her face, but she continued to contemplate Gabriel's request without moving.

"What you've just asked of me…well, I'm not myself," she said by way of apology, brushing her hair back and patting her flushed cheeks.

"It's understandable," Gabriel said, and gestured for her to come and stand next to him. She steeled herself with a deep breath and leaned forward on the frame of the window.

It would be different if the millennia since Lucifer fell had gone as they thought it would. Unfortunately, restructuring heaven and assigning angels to specific tasks had only inspired Lucifer to copy their strategy, grooming the fallen angels to become demons of the worst vices: murder, greed, idolatry, adultery, and so on. Soon after the flood, humankind was no better than before—worshiping the foreign gods of the demons placed before them, and turning their back on the covenant they had made with the Almighty Divine.

One servant prophet after another had been sent to try to persuade them to return to the Almighty Divine and live a life of submission, and while a few had been successful, it was almost as if her observation to Hector was true. Mortals seemed more attracted to evil than good.

Sophia looked down and took a sharp breath in. Many of the countries of earth had disappeared completely, and those that remained looked like pieces of shredded fabric.

Following her gaze, Gabriel said: "Yes, Lucifer inspired it all. He caused earthquakes, volcanoes, and fires to make one land after another slide in the ocean or be consumed in bottomless canyons of earth." He pointed to the eastern border of the country. "He also created such conflict between mortals, it led to nuclear attacks in the north and chemical warfare in the south. The land is unlivable."

"So where did everyone go?" she asked, then realized most must have died.

"Those who survived gathered in the center," he said, pointing at an area in what was formerly the Midwest United States. It was the size of a small country, heavily fortified by a wall that was wide and tall, topped with laser lights whose beams met in a point high above the colony.

"The Bible Belt," Sophia mused.

"That's not by accident, but it doesn't mean everyone within this colony is immune to Lucifer's wiles. There are other colonies scattered around the world close to holy places too, but they are tempted as fiercely as mortals have been since the beginning of time."

He touched the window, and it turned into scenes of other countries she recognized from ancient history. Some had been rendered inhabitable due to landslides, floods, and pollution. Others looked like scorched black holes—the unmistakable insignia of a nuclear attack. Still, where mortals had managed to survive, there were colonies with barricades of protection that extended into the sky.

"I thought the Almighty Divine controlled the forces of nature; am I wrong?"

Gabriel shook his head slowly. "After the flood, the Almighty Divine promised He would never again turn the forces of nature against His people. What you see down there are the consequences of mortal actions: weapons of destruction used against each other to destroy life, squandering of natural resources, pouring pollution into the environment, and so on. All inspired by greed for a quick fortune that didn't account for long-term consequences. Here's just one example." He focused the window on an enclosed territory where hundreds of mortals in shabby clothes were sifting through mountains of discarded medical equipment for radioactive materials that had been discarded. Their hands and faces were rotting away from the effects of the toxic but valuable substance they were mining. "These people will die, but the merchants they sell their products to will be rich. Eventually the whole colony will die, even the children."

He turned away, his expression tortured. She waited until he waved her into one of the blue chairs she found so comfortable, then sat with her hands held together loosely as if ready to pray. He sat across from her.

"It's a great honor to be considered for the position of Senior Servant of the First Level, Sophia. You'll be helping the heavenly host carry out our mission, and you'll have two devoted Selected Servants to help you," he said softly.

"But what happened to Isaac? Everyone was so pleased when he was appointed as Senior Servant, and the reports on his performance were all positive, at least as far as I could tell from my little place as a prayer angel."

"We're not to speak of Isaac," Gabriel said, and although he looked away from her, she could see his expression harden.

"Why can't I know? If Lucifer enticed him to earth because he was the Senior Servant, that means I would be targeted too. If Isaac wasn't strong enough to resist—"

"Sophia, take it up with the Almighty Divine when you come before Him."

"That's not likely to happen anytime soon, I guess," she said in a small voice. "I'll never be admitted to the Second Level of heaven or be given an audience with Him if I refuse to do this."

Gabriel leaned over and patted her foot, his eyes crinkling with amusement. "You and the Second Level! You're obsessed with it, and I'm not sure I understand why."

"It's safe there. You and Michael are there. I'd be closer to the Almighty Divine. What other reasons should there be?"

"Sophia, fear is never a good motivation. As long as Lucifer thinks he can tempt you, you're vulnerable. We all are. Think about it: what better way for him to reach the Almighty Divine than by causing Michael or me to fall in some way? He hasn't been able to accomplish that, so he destroys mortals, pretending his motivation is love."

"But what if he really is acting out of love? What is he is trying to protect the Almighty Divine from the hurt mortals will inflict on Him? Look at the Servant Son and all the ones like him—"

Gabriel seized her wrist in the very same spot Lucifer had grabbed her so long ago, but his grasp was gentle. "Sophia, that is dangerous talk, and from you, of all angels. You've been the one to believe in the good of mortals since the beginning, and now you think that they come up with evil ideas on their own? I assure you they do not. The mortal who is not connected to the Almighty Divine in some way is an unhappy mortal."

She jumped to her feet and paced over to the window, glancing down and then shuddering. "I did believe in mortals…I mean I still do, but never would I have believed so many could turn away from the Almighty Divine."

"If it can happen to angels, why not mortals?"

She looked at Gabriel in surprise. "You mean there are still angels who are forsaking heaven to live on earth?"

He nodded, clasping and unclasping his big hands. "Yes, unfortunately."

Stunned, she sat back down and buried her head in her hands, trying to make sense of it all. The Almighty Divine was pure goodness. He should be triumphing over evil, and yet Gabriel was suggesting the opposite was happening.

After a moment of silence, Gabriel spoke again. "You're a good angel, Sophia. Your petitions have blessed many mortals, and throughout the ages you've caused many horrible situations to be used for good." He turned to smile at her. "Mortals think of them as miracles, but it's you and all the other angels, intervening on their behalf, that make the difference in any given situation. It's a great honor for you to be considered as Senior Servant!"

His words made joy surge through her. "You're absolutely right. Who would ever think I could earn such favor? I've been blessed by the Almighty Divine, and that pleases me, and I will do everything I can to carry out His wishes. Lucifer won't win this battle, if I can help it." She straightened out her robe, which tended to twist the wrong way from so much kneeling, and pressed her hands together. "I'm ready to do everything asked of me, just tell me what it is."

Gabriel patted her shoulder. "I know you will do well, Sophia, and we desperately need that. Earth is very corrupt right now. We've seen these cycles before, and hopefully this one will pass soon, but I admit that when I go down there, I am greatly grieved by what I see. But there is a remnant of those who believe in the Almighty Divine, and that is what we must focus on."

She leaned forward in her chair, eager for her lessons on servanthood to begin. As Gabriel spoke, Sophia's sense of awe grew. How little she had realized of the Almighty Divine's vigilance in assigning angels on the First Level of the kingdom of heaven to help all mortals in any way possible.

Gabriel spoke at length, describing the role of the Senior Servant and how she would be working as closely with him as he did with the Almighty Divine. Next, he gave her a brief history of the two Selected Servants she would be working closely with: Miriam and Faras. They had been in their positions for a long time and knew the workings of Operations Central, the heart of the First Level of heaven, very well.

The amount of information presented could have been overwhelming, but they were in the Resting Room where the soothing blue mist and peaceful atmosphere allowed her spirit to open and understand everything. Relaxing into the curves of the soft chair and listening to Gabriel's rich voice was actually a pleasure Sophia never imagined possible. Before long she found herself looking forward to her new assignment and believing that somehow she might make a difference.

Finally, Gabriel laid one hand on her knee.

"You will always have questions, but now you must go, and find everything on the First Level of heaven just as I said it would be. Your two Selected Servants are at work as usual and will help you learn further."

As if in farewell, she found herself lifted up and then down, deposited at the beginning of the Great Way, which would lead her to Operations Central, her new home. On either side of the pathway, there were the rainbow clusters of crystal mansions, reflecting soft rays of ever-changing color. They stretched as far back as she could see; each was bordered by a carpet of lush green grass. Some housed prayer angels, others off-duty guardian angels, and, in those closest to her new home in Operations Central, intervention angels were always on call.

As Sophia headed on her way, thousands of angels separated to allow her passage. Those closest to the Great Way smiled or gave her a fond glance as she passed by, clearly aware of the change in her position.

"Good going, Sophia," one said cheerfully, lifting his arm in a salute as he walked by.

"Blessings on you, sister," said another woman, squeezing both of Sophia's hands in her own.

Quickening her steps, Sophia continued to return their greetings with genuine emotion, surprised by how happy their responses made her. If her very presence was enough to cheer the heavenly host, her new position might be an even better opportunity to serve the Almighty Divine than she initially thought.

Lifting her chin, she decided she would not only carry out every instruction given, she would be an inspiration to the heavenly host and make her allegiances clear. If Lucifer was offending the Almighty Divine, no matter what his motive, he was offending her. From now on, he was her sworn enemy.

But what if Lucifer was just misunderstood? What if, as he claimed, he really meant to save the Almighty Divine from being hurt and betrayed by mortals?

No. She cast those questions aside, knowing the time to ask them had ended. Lucifer's actions were the very things that led mortals to disobey. Her job was to help change that.

Smiling, she looked to her left and right with tenderness, extending her spirit to those who would now consider her a role model in serving the Almighty Divine. Each of the angels she saw were like snowflakes, possessed of a unique and delicate beauty that gladdened her. Even as she came within sight of Operations Central, she couldn't resist stopping to quickly touch or hug those who reached out, drawing energy and excitement from their support.

She caught sight of Miriam and Faras in the distance, waiting on the porch of a tall white building that seemed to give off light as soft and bright as moonlight on a clear earth night. When they saw her, they hurried down the stairs and across the bridge spanning the moat as if Sophia had been the Senior Servant forever and they were entirely used to seeing her come up the Great Way toward Operations Central.

Miriam, tall and slender, reached her first, seizing Sophia's arm. "It's terrible."

Faras, shorter and more rotund, caught up to them. "There's no time to waste, Sophia," he said.

Sophia quickened her pace. "Tell me what's happened."

Faras's forehead wrinkled as he fell in beside them. "It's horrible. Let's hope we can intervene in some way that will help."

They ran together toward the building, crossing the bridge and mounting the stairs effortlessly. Miriam led the way, turning back to update Sophia. "There's been a bombing at a school in the U.S. Many are dead."

"Where did it happen?" Sophia asked, wondering if there would now be one more dead spot on the aerial view of the United States that Gabriel had shown her. With Miriam still in the lead, they crossed the porch and went through the massive front doors, which opened automatically in anticipation of their entry. Faras stepped aside to allow Sophia to enter, then continued with specifics.

"There was a missile that made it through the laser shield. It hit a building where hundreds of students and teachers were in the middle of their usual lessons," he said. "It's complete chaos because no one had any warning the shield could be breeched in certain spots...and this is the first time young people have been targeted."

They continued down a long hallway punctuated by wide doorways, each bordered by a light so intense it seemed to pulse with power. At the end of the corridor, they paused in front of a final larger doorway that was brighter than the rest. Miriam pointed to a white rectangle set into the floor and indicated that Sophia should step forward.

When she did, a cone of blinding light surrounded her and a disembodied voice said, "Senior Servant Sophia, enter."

She stumbled forward, blinking, as Miriam and Faras went through the same process.

"This is the heart of all we do and the most important room in Operations Central: the Guidance Room," Faras said, without pausing to explain further. "You'll get used to the light."

Although Sophia had heard whispers about Operations Central and had some idea what the Guidance Room would look like, in other circumstances its actual experience would have made her pause in wonder. Each of the thin crystal walls magnified the light entering to such intensity that she had to briefly shield her eyes. When her vision finally adjusted, she saw an enormous, transparent globe before them. Its surface was covered with an elaborate network of wiring, and the entire structure revolved slowly, as tiny lights flashed on the surface.

Faras went to a flat podium and tapped parts of the panel on top of it so the model of earth spun faster, then tipped toward them and stopped. Miriam touched a light that was bigger and brighter than the rest, blinking red with such fury that it seemed like a distress beacon. This led one of the walls behind the globe to change into a giant screen, where the angels saw frightened students running away from a building surrounded by police. A few adults seemed to be trying to take control and direct the younger people to a safe place, but their faces were panicked too. Many bodies lay on the ground, immobile, and a few others were being carried away by emergency workers.

"What could have gone wrong?" Faras's voice choked. Feverishly, he wrung his hands and bit his lower lip.

Miriam gave Faras a sharp look. "Does it matter what caused this? Right now we need to send help."

Without knowing what she was meant to do, Sophia closed her eyes and lifted her spirit to receive direction. In response, she heard Gabriel whispering in her ear. There was a tense silence in the room as the others waited for her to share the message.

"Faras," she said, finally, "block all the mortals who would create more pain in this situation, and put a protection around the families of those who lost a child. Miriam, you've already sent angels and helped some mortals act with great courage, but have Hector send everyone available for the time being. We also need mortals who are good people to be led there so they can begin helping everyone heal."

Sophia opened her eyes, but couldn't turn away from the screen as police officers and firefighters charged into the building where most of the carnage had occurred. She couldn't help murmuring, "Somehow, in some way, good will come from this tragedy. We have seen it throughout history, and so will you. The Almighty Divine—"

"—turns trials into triumphs," the other two seasoned angels said in unison. It was a cliché, but one of many the heavenly host loved to repeat. The three of them exchanged a glance of understanding.

The Selected Servants worked feverishly as Sophia watched from behind them, calming herself to receive any further instructions, should they be given. She couldn't help noticing how smoothly the two of them worked together, almost as if they didn't need her there at all.

Finally, Miriam turned away from the screen and said, "We've done everything you told us to do. Now it's time to turn things over to Hector."

Faras looked at Sophia, and in an unguarded moment, she guessed he was thinking that, until recently, Hector had been giving her directions too. Her initiation into her new role had been haphazard, but at least it spared any conjectures over why she and not one of them had been appointed Senior Servant.

On the screen, they watched a new multitude of angels descend to the scene of the bombing. Of course, they were invisible to mortals, but their presence was felt through whispered words of support to the victims, beams of steel that were shifted slightly out of the way to uncover trapped students, and the incredible strength of one student who somehow carried a wheelchair-bound classmate on his back and out of the debris. Quickly, leaders from nearby communities also arrived to offer assistance, and dozens of nurses and physicians volunteered to work with the staff of the already beleaguered local hospital.

Miriam made a sound of satisfaction and turned away from the screen. "It looks like things are under control now, and I, for one, am ready to refresh."

"I'll say," Faras agreed, patting the curly cap of his hair. "What do you think, Sophia? Maybe we can continue your orientation later."

They headed for three plush recliners arranged in one corner bathed by the bright light Sophia found so overwhelming when she first entered the room. The two Selected Servants settled into chairs they seemed accustomed to, leaving the third for Sophia. Had it been Isaac's?

Miriam's eyes were already closed, but her eyebrows raised. "I'd say Sophia has already had some intensive on-the-job training."

"True," Faras agreed in a faraway voice, his hands folded across his stomach.

Sophia eased herself into the chair, expecting to feel uncomfortable, but it was as welcoming as the chairs in Gabriel's Refreshing Room. As her eyes fluttered shut, she felt herself lulled into a reverie all the deeper for the intensity of the white light that seemed to flow inside her and renew her spirit, cleansing all anxieties and insecurities.

When she stirred, Faras was walking toward her, his hands pressed together and a small smile on his full face. "Only five students were killed in the bombing, and they are already here with us in the Community of Resting Mortals."

Miriam leaned up on her elbows. "There were thousands of students in that building! What a miracle only five were killed."

Faras's deep brown eyes were troubled nonetheless. "I can't imagine how someone found a weak point in the laser shield. I thought those things were impenetrable."

"Every mortal creation is fallible. Be glad the damage was minimal," Miriam said. She swung her feet to the floor, straightened out her robe, and extended one hand to Sophia. "Shall I give you a tour of the building?"

Sophia's forehead wrinkled. "Where's the Community of Resting Mortals? Gabriel told me they were on the First Level with us, but no one has ever seen them."

"You can see them if you want to," Miriam offered. "After mortals die, the Almighty Divine goes through a life review with them, and they're either admitted through the portal and taken to the Community of Resting Mortals or sent elsewhere."

"Elsewhere?" Sophia echoed.

"Sometimes they go back to earth to try again," Faras explained. "The rest are sent to Lucifer. What he does with them is anyone's guess."

"The Community of Resting Mortals is very pleasant. Much like the First Level of heaven, except the mortals aren't assigned jobs."

"Their work—for better or worse—was done on earth," Faras said. "I thought you knew all this."

He and Miriam chuckled, which made Sophia uncomfortable. She shrugged her shoulders. "I was a prayer angel. Why would I know the secrets of heaven?"

"We heard you were Gabriel's confidant and that you've been at his side since the beginning of creation," Faras said, frowning.

"That's true, but…well, I guess the subject of what happens to mortals after they die never came up. I *do* know what happens to the ones who choose to serve Lucifer."

Miriam linked her arm through Sophia's. "Come on, I'll show you your room." As they went back through the splash of light at the entrance to the room, she said: "What you might not know is Lucifer also claims all those who don't make a choice one way or the other."

Sophia stopped short. "You mean if mortals live a good life but never declare they serve the Almighty Divine, Lucifer still gets to call them his own?" When Miriam nodded, Sophia wrinkled her forehead. "But why? That doesn't seem right. They aren't doing anything wrong."

"Perhaps not, but what I've been taught is that Lucifer's greatest advantage in this spiritual war between him and us is that most mortals are completely unaware of it," Faras said, and then his eyes grew distant for a few moments. "Whether that's true or not, I can't say, but among angels, would you take the risk? Carry out your responsibilities, but not out of submission to the Almighty Divine?"

Miriam patted his arm and tilted her head toward Sophia. "Faras tends to be a bit more philosophical about it than I. I see it as good and evil, black and white. Ah, here we are." She turned and led the way into a room that was lit with pale yellow lights, casting a golden glow over the contents.

On the floor, Sophia's prayer cushion rested. "Although we almost always refresh together, if you wish to be by yourself, this is your private chamber."

A recliner dominated the room, its surface reflecting the muted tone of the lights. Miriam sat on one edge of it and crossed her long legs. She gave the surroundings an appraising look and then looked to Sophia questioningly. Faras, however, was still stuck on his earlier debate.

"It's not that clear-cut, Miriam. Sophia, we are all here because we've made an active choice. Every moment of our existence we choose to be here, serving the Almighty Divine. Why should mortals be any different? Are they really the Almighty Divine's beloved children if they don't acknowledge and serve Him during their time on earth?"

Sophia thought back on the awful moment when Lucifer and the others chose to leave heaven, and realized both of them were right. Those who stayed in heaven were here by choice and were supposedly doing everything they could to serve the Almighty Divine. Why *should* mortals be any different?

7

Sophia heard Gabriel call her name as Miriam continued to examine the spare contents of the room that would be hers. As the Selected Servant played with the control panel of the smaller Earth Viewer, she described the way she and Faras worked together to handle a crisis.

"We both have our roles—"

"Sorry to interrupt Miriam, but Gabriel is summoning me. I must go," Sophia said, but before she could explain further, she found herself in the Refreshing Room.

"So, what do you think?" Gabriel asked. "It appears you handled your first situation well, and Miriam and Faras don't seem averse to working with you."

"I guess not," she said slowly. "But they are a bit...jaded, I think."

"They've been doing this for a long time," Gabriel said. "Perhaps they need a break, or maybe you are just the angel to bring a new enthusiasm to their work."

"I'll try." Sophia wondered exactly how she would accomplish that, but Gabriel moved on to another subject before she could reflect further.

"You know about the Community of Resting Mortals."

"We were just talking about it."

"The Almighty Divine decided angels and mortals should be kept in separate parts of the First Level because our purposes are so different. We exist to serve Him; they are waiting for the end of time when mortality as they know it will cease to be." He gestured to the wall that was part window and she looked out.

Miriam was right; the place was much like the First Level of heaven, and the mortals there all seemed to be having a wonderful time, playing games or singing, eating splendid foods, or relaxing contentedly by themselves or in groups. Although they were different shapes and sizes and colors, just like mortals on earth, there was no sign of conflict between them, and their bodies were free of disease or disability.

"They stay there until the end times?" she asked.

"Traditionally."

"Uh-oh. When I hear 'traditionally' from an archangel, I start to listen closer."

Gabriel smiled and waved her toward a recliner, taking one last look at the Community of Resting Mortals.

"Of course you would, Sophia. That's why you were chosen as the Senior Servant." He leaned against the wall next to the window and crossed his massive arms over his chest. "Mortals are allowed to look down on earth, just as you and I do. They see what is happening to the loved ones they left behind, and how corrupt and challenging life has become for all of humankind. Many of them are here because of disasters in their countries—a nuclear bomb or a deadly virus cultivated for the purpose of killing millions. Some died slow and painful deaths, either from starvation or sickness, and they fear for their descendants."

Sophia nodded. "Of course they would, but hasn't that always been the case? Maybe mortals want to warn those left behind, but every time the Almighty Divine sends prophets, they are usually ignored. Somehow, though, a remnant of believers has always managed to survive."

"Mortals can never have the view of history that you and I do, Sophia, but recently we've had an unusual request from the Community of Resting Mortals. They want to help."

"Help? Isn't it a little late for that?"

"No, I mean help as in help from up here, and to be truthful..." He bowed his head and paused for so long she feared his next words. "To be truthful, we've lost many more angels than most of the heavenly host realizes. Hector may suspect, but it's not something we're eager to broadcast."

"How bad is it?" She sat forward in her chair to get a better look at his face, which was partly hidden by strands of hair that had come loose from the binding he usually wore. Eventually, he lifted his head and smoothed back the locks of hair, his eyes holding hers.

"Bad. Just as Lucifer has gained influence over mortals, he's been able to persuade angels away when they see what is happening on earth. They either give up on serving the Almighty Divine, who seems powerless to stop the immorality, or they join in. So, it does seem as if Lucifer is winning, so to speak."

"Is that what happened to Isaac?" She pressed, needing to know what her predecessor had faced.

Gabriel sighed. "We're still not sure what happened to Isaac. One moment he was standing next to the Portal and the next, he was gone. He's not anywhere on earth, that Michael's been able to track, but that's not your worry." He came to sit next to her. "We've decided to allow a mortal to come to this part of heaven to work with you and Miriam and Faras. A special mortal."

"I take it this 'special mortal' is one of the ones who has asked to help?" At his nod, she continued. "I wonder how Miriam and Faras and all the others will feel about that. How will I explain it?"

"No explanation is needed. This comes directly from the Almighty Divine, so just as we don't question His other decisions, true faith will prevent them from questioning this one."

She made a deliberately wry face. "I might have to remind them of that a few times. But of course I will obey absolutely—in fact, it seems a reasonable plan. Tell me more."

"You will greet her at the Portal and then orient her to the First Level of heaven."

"What?" Sophia drew herself up with a start. "Me? Didn't you just tell me Isaac may have been sucked out through the Portal? Anyway, I thought the Selected Servants had oversight of the Community of Resting Mortals."

Gabriel's fingers flexed restlessly. "That's true, but in this case, it's His will for you to do it."

A direction from the Almighty Divine trumped all others, so Sophia held back further objections, reminding herself that she of all angels needed to be role models of absolute obedience. "My tenure as Senior Servant might be very short if you or Michael don't come along to protect me."

"Remember, we change the location of the Portal constantly. Sophia, belief is trust. You'll be safe."

She prayed that it would be so, but the pleasure she had persuaded herself to feel over being named Senior Servant had already diminished. If Gabriel noticed, he gave no sign, as he helped her to her feet.

"I am here to help you, just as you are on the First Level to help mortals. We'll meet regularly so you can always understand and act in accordance with the Almighty Divine's will," he promised, then disappeared.

She was lost in contemplation. Allowing a mortal to comingle with angels on the First Level was a daunting way to begin her new role, especially since she only had secondhand information on what really happened to mortals after they died. There were still so many unknowns associated with her position as Senior Servant that she paused to say a quick prayer to the Almighty Divine for extra wisdom and fortitude.

"Oh, and thank you for your belief in me," she added as an afterthought, feeling herself beginning to slip out of the Refreshing Room. That was what she should concentrate on, wasn't it? Of all the angels who could have been chosen, the Almighty Divine had picked her.

She found herself deposited on the Great Way, next to Lara, a prayer angel known for her beautiful language and ability to sing in the most blessed way possible. Sophia kissed her cheek happily.

"Lara, your words are always so uplifting," she said, smiling at the tiny angel whose copper hair circled her face in a fiery tangle of curls. "Can you walk with me and sing something soothing? I'm on my way to the Portal, and I have to tell you, I'm a little nervous."

Lara's laugh was like the tinkling of silver bells. "Sweet Sophia, why do you think I'm here? Hector sent me to join you. Don't be troubled. I've helped Miriam and Faras many times, and it's actually very simple. After passing through the Portal, the mortal is greeted by the heavenly host. We sing songs of welcome and praise, then one of the Selected Servants escorts him or her to the Community of Resting Mortals. It's a joyful ceremony."

"But you know this mortal is coming from the Community of Resting Mortals, not from earth? And he—or she—is going to stay here on the First Level."

Lara stopped and looked at Sophia, her green eyes amused. "You're teasing me, surely?"

"No, it's true. Gabriel just told me she would come through the Portal very soon."

Lara sobered and continued walking. "If it comes from the Almighty Divine, who am I to question? But why is she coming through the Portal, and why must we go through all this ritual?"

"I'm not sure. Maybe so it doesn't seem secret?" Sophia guessed, wishing she had asked Gabriel.

"Anyway, I suppose you would like to read her Life Review—or at least the parts of what I've been given." Lara held up a scroll. "Each mortal has one."

"Did Gabriel tell you when she would come in through the Portal?" Lara asked as Sophia unrolled the scroll.

"He just said I was to meet her there soon. You know, maybe there's some kind of barrier between the Community of Resting Mortals and us that makes it necessary to come in through the Portal?"

Lara just shook her head in reply, a troubled look on her face. When they reached the area leading up a slight incline to the Portal, a crowd of angels fell into place. Lara picked up a large flag woven with gold and silver threads from a stand within reach of the Portal, hoisting it easily.

"Angels aren't allowed too close to the Portal without specific permission or invitation," Lara said, waving the flag slowly back and forth. "This is the signal for them to gather, but only you and I are allowed in front."

Sophia couldn't help studying the Portal from top to bottom and then side to side. A shimmering curtain of transparent material covered it, large enough to allow a human to pass safely through but thick enough to hide what was on the other side—not that she wanted to know.

Was she too close, or too far away? She stood up straighter, determined to be a worthy role model for the angels stirring in anticipation behind her. A quick scan over either shoulder confirmed there were legions of them, all exquisite and facing forward, occasionally touching shoulders as they shifted positions or leaned close to exchange a few words with their neighbors.

She heard snatches of whispers:

"—Sophia here?"

"What do you think of her as our new Senior Servant!"

"Why would the Senior Servant be here?"

Suddenly, the Portal began to ripple so that filaments in the fabric flickered and then changed color, taking on an intense pink hue that vibrated with power. Lara's face was serene as waves of energy radiated out to fill Sophia with warmth, and the angels burst into song. She joined them, eyes closed so she could concentrate on understanding what she was supposed to do next.

When the song finished and Sophia opened her eyes, the Portal was bigger. It could easily admit an army—or Lucifer and his followers, if they discovered where it was. She automatically took a step back and those behind her did the same.

As the rustle of movement died down, she heard the angels laugh with relief. Maybe they thought she was being playful, which was far better than having them realize how afraid she was that Lucifer might have figured out where the Portal was. If he had, she would most likely to be the first one targeted to be sucked out and down to Earth.

Sophia shuddered, knowing how dangerous Lucifer could be, even though he was only part angel. Who knew what fate would await her if he ever lured away from heaven?

8

L ife Review for the Beloved Mortal, Ruth March:
This Beloved Mortal came from a poor family and began her time on earth as the middle of five children born to abusive alcoholic parents. Her father abandoned them when Ruth was eight, which improved her life somewhat, since her mother returned home to live with her parents. Still, social workers visited the home frequently because Ruth's teachers reported suspicious bruises or marks on her and her siblings.

The picture of Ruth receiving her sixth grade graduation certificate made Sophia smile.

"She's adorable," she commented to Lara, noting the delight on Ruth's face.

At age sixteen, Ruth met and married Ray March, a sergeant in the Army she met at the diner where she worked after school. (Again, there was a picture of Ruth clutching Ray's arm, beaming with happiness.) While her husband worked, Ruth was content at home, spending time with other Army wives, doing volunteer work, and sending money home to her siblings when she could. When Ray discovered she was supporting her family with his salary, he became enraged. Until that time, Ruth had never known him to be physically violent, but his assaults became more frequent and intense. After miscarrying the only child she would conceive due to a beating from her husband, Ruth moved to a homeless shelter and rebuilt her life.

Sophia quickly looked past a picture of Ruth in the emergency room, clutching her abdomen while a nurse gently patted her swollen face with an ice pack. She must have made a sound of disgust because Lara moved closer.

"Is something wrong?" she asked, peering at the scroll.

"Sometimes everything seems wrong for mortals," Sophia replied, pointing to the picture. Lara sighed and rolled the scroll so it was no longer visible.

"It's best to move through these quickly," she advised, staying next to

Sophia so she could read over her shoulder. "See, things improve."

The scroll continued with a description of Ruth's life post-recovery: she took classes to become a nurse while working as a nurse's aide during the day. As an RN, she found a job in pediatrics caring for terminal children, and joined the First Church of God. There she befriended Pastor Ephraim, his wife Anita, and their ten children, most of whom were adopted. Ruth volunteered to be part of many church activities and regularly brought new nurses to services with her.

At the request of Pastor Ephraim, she took in her first foster child, Tamika, age three.

"How cute!" Sophia said, tracing the photograph of the little girl with one finger. "She must have made Ruth very happy."

Ruth began to work part-time nights so she could accept more foster children. Eventually her church bought and renovated a house so there would be more room, and one of Ruth's younger sisters (Dorcas) came to help with the blossoming brood of cast off children..

This picture stood out on the scroll like a mug shot.

"Hard to believe she's related to Ruth," Sophia murmured at the sight of the scowling woman, moving on to read what was written next.

After two months of living with Ruth, Dorcas stole everything in the house of any value, emptied the bank account, and disappeared. Ruth refused to press charges against her sister.

Lara said what Sophia was thinking. "That's the work of Lucifer for sure. What a terrible thing to do to those children, let alone her own sister."

Sophia closed her eyes for a second and imagined a dejected Ruth at the bank teller's window, discovering she had again been betrayed by someone she trusted.

The Life Review continued.

With the help of the church and her friend Anita, Ruth gradually recovered from the loss of her money and trust. (With a jolt, Sophia realized that in the past she had made a special prayer effort for Ruth, who was described as a Beloved Mortal who lost nearly all her belongings, as well as her trust in her sister. There had been dozens of angels sent to earth too, directly intervening by prompting extra donations of cash and goods, arranging for

Ruth to receive a promotion and raise at work, and comforting the foster children over their losses, which were sometimes as trivial as a worn-out stuffed animal.)

When Ruth was fifty-five years old, Pastor Ephraim asked her to come to the hospital and help care for a crack baby who had been left at his house in the middle of a cold winter night. Ruth nursed the baby through several crises and became so attached to him that she named him JoJo and adopted him. Raising JoJo led her to create the first facility in her city for the care of crack babies, which she called The Sanctuary. Many infants were helped there, but unfortunately, several of Ruth's own children strayed from their mother's teachings and succumbed to the temptations of Lucifer. Most difficult to accept was JoJo, who dropped out of high school and became addicted to crack cocaine by the age of eighteen.

Ruth died traumatically at home when she was seventy-two.

Sophia took one look at the final picture and met Lara's eyes, too shocked to speak. Slowly, she rolled up the scroll and tucked it in her sleeve, wishing she could be rid of it completely.

Lara pulled Sophia closer to the Portal so the other angels couldn't hear what she had to say. "We witness the death of each Beloved Mortal who passes through this Portal, and then they are taken away from us to be with their own kind in the Community of Resting Mortals. Those of us here have already seen Ruth's final days, but you have not. I'm not sure what to do."

Sophia drew back from her. "I don't know what to tell you, Lara. Gabriel only said that I was to meet her here, but—"

Before them, the Portal began to shimmer and move as the angels broke into a low chorus of chants that sent swells of sorrow through Sophia's spirit. Slowly, images began to form on the space that was previously empty.

"I think you must watch," Lara said, nodding at the Portal.

The first figure Sophia saw was a young man, a bit scrawny, but nonetheless well-dressed and obviously cared for. He came through the front door of a house, whistling happily.

"JoJo," Lara mouthed.

The boy went upstairs, taking the steps two at a time and returning a short time later with a gym bag stuffed so full he couldn't zip it. Dropping it in the hallway, he disappeared into the kitchen, then returned with a bag of cookies and began wolfing them down.

In front of him, Ruth had been dozing on the sofa while a television show played at low volume, but the noise of JoJo moving through the house woke her. She picked up the remote, turned the television off, and heaved herself to a sitting position.

"Hey there, handsome," she said, twisting around to look at her son. Then she noticed the bag. "Going somewhere?"

"I'm moving in with T-Jay and getting a job," he told her cheerfully, pausing just long enough to kiss her cheek on his way to the front door. "School just isn't for me right now. Be cool, memaw."

His cavalier farewell in combination with the use of his nickname for her made Ruth struggle to her feet and look him over from head to toe.

"There's something wrong about this," she said. "I don't like it."

Sophia bit her lip as she watched. She didn't like what was happening either.

"You worry too much," JoJo teased, giving Ruth another kiss. "I'll be fine."

"I expect to see you in church on Sunday," she called after him, but the door had already closed.

Sophia thought perhaps her inclinations were wrong. Initially, JoJo was loyal and loving. He went to church and visited his mother on birthdays and holidays, always bringing a gift. Once it was a large print Bible, identical to the tattered old one she treasured but could no longer read without a magnifying glass. Another time, he donated ten dollars in her name to The Sanctuary. The most special present was a newborn kitten he named "Trouble."

"You and me, memaw, we don't need to call trouble—it comes anyway," he told her, laughing as he handed over the tiny creature.

Just when Ruth (and Sophia's) dismay over his choice to move out seemed misguided, JoJo's behavior changed. His calls and visits tapered off and he stopped attending church. When he did show up at the house, he never stayed long, as if wary of her love. Once, he kicked Trouble on his way out the front door.

Not long after these observations, Pastor Ephraim heard street talk that confirmed what Ruth dreaded. Some residue of the crack in JoJo's blood at birth was now a cancer that had drawn him back into the world of drugs.

"He entered this world in recovery and he can do it again," Ruth insisted, urging Pastor Ephraim to say special prayers for her prodigal son.

JoJo's sporadic visits declined into angry confrontations, and the lifetime of bitter tears Ruth refused to cry finally flowed forth, but only in her bedroom at night when she was by herself. Sophia gripped at Lara's arm, wanting to look away but unable to. She was clearly far better at praying for mortals who were suffering than witnessing the events first hand.

On the night of her death, Ruth was deep in sleep when JoJo kicked the door of his former home open and tore up the stairs to his mother's bedroom.

"Memaw, give me cash, now," he said, flinging back her thick comforter and throwing it on the floor. "I know you hide money here somewhere."

He began pulling open drawers and rifling through their contents as Ruth huddled on the bed. Without her dentures or glasses, and in a nightgown thinned at the elbows and jagged at the hem, she looked like a fragile old woman. When she realized what was happening, her appearance changed and she hobbled out of bed and grabbed her son by the shoulder.

"Boy, you go back out there and knock like a normal human being before you come in and wake me up," she croaked.

It didn't matter. The boy before her wasn't JoJo, but a creature possessed. His eyes were wild and his body restless as he danced around the room on a mission. After searching the clothes in her closet and the contents of her purse, his only find was a slightly torn ten-dollar bill.

"Give me some money, bitch!" JoJo screamed, shaking her until she was nearly unconscious.

The commotion roused Ruben, Tamika's son, who was "temporarily" living with his grandmother. He was an anxious child and a notoriously light sleeper.

"Gramma, is everything okay?" he asked, rattling the locked doorknob.

JoJo shoved Ruth's ATM money card in her face and hissed, "Tell me the number or I'll kill you, and him too."

"Then I'll be dead and you still won't know it, because your mother will never give you money for drugs," she said, her voice raspy.

"Gramma!" the voice from the hallway called, on the verge of panic.

JoJo made a snarling sound and shoved Ruth so violently that she stumbled and hit her head on the corner of a heavy wooden dresser.

He hoisted open the single window in her room and climbed onto the fire escape, pausing to give Ruth one last look of fury. The final image of the Life Review was Ruth, sprawled on the floor, staring blankly back at her son.

"I love you, and I forgive you."

By the time the words were out, she was dead.

Lara picked up her flag and began to wave it. In response, the angels gathered nearby lost their looks of bewilderment and burst into song.

"Louder, my sisters and brothers, louder!" Lara called to them. "If anyone deserves our welcome, it's this woman, even if we are greeting her for the second time. Sing, Sophia."

And so she did, lifting her voice in a tribute to the first mortal woman she was about to meet.

9

The Portal turned transparent and Sophia took a breath in, not sure what to expect. Out of nowhere, Ruth appeared and came forward, passing through the opening with her hands clasped and lifted up. She was not the victim from the final scenes of the Life Review, but rather a woman with her mouth caught open in wonder and tears trickling from the corner of her dark brown eyes.

"Glory be!" she said, looking from side to side as the heavenly host burst into a chorus of welcome.

Sophia joined the others, but inside she was miserable. Here she was: the new Senior Servant, a former prayer angel who had never witnessed anything like Ruth's Life Review, *and* the angel in charge of orienting the first mortal to be admitted to the First Level of heaven.

What else will I be asked to do that I'm totally unprepared for? she wondered. Her second look at Ruth suggested the woman harbored no bitterness or resentment over the end of her mortal life. She had grabbed Lara's hands and was dancing as she sang along with the rest of the heavenly host.

When the prayer song ended, Sophia stepped forward.

"I'm Sophia, the Senior Servant here," she said, drawing Ruth into a long hug. "I'm so glad to meet you, and so sorry for what happened."

"Are you the one in charge, then?" Ruth asked, studying her up and down.

"Yes. Well, no. Not really. No one here is 'in charge.' We all exist to serve, but I guess you could say I act as a guide, of sorts," Sophia said nervously, then laid one hand on Ruth's, sobering. "It made me very sad to watch what happened to you on Earth."

"But that's all over, sweetheart. I put it behind me the first time I came through that Portal, and now I'm in the real heaven, not just waiting with other mortals for the end of time," Ruth exclaimed, shrugging the apology away and lifting up her arms. "No pearly gates like I expected, but it'll do just fine."

A titter of amusement ran through the angels who had gathered behind Lara to observe closer. At Sophia's nod of dismissal, they hurried back to their jobs, some pausing to give Ruth a final pat or hug before they left.

"We're all glad to have you here, Ruth March," Lara said, putting one hand on Ruth's cheek. "Good-bye for now, but blessings on you until we see each other again."

"You can't beat that for friendliness, even among mortals," Ruth said, as the angel drifted away. "And what a voice! I thought my friend Anita sang like an angel, but compared to that one, it was nothing. So what happens next? I guess everyone here but me is a real angel?"

Sophia searched for the right words. "Yes. We were created at the beginning of time and have existed to serve the Almighty Divine—the one you call God—since then. All of us make up the heavenly host."

"So, will I be some kind of substitute angel?"

It was an excellent question, and one Sophia immediately wished she had clarified with Gabriel.

"In a way," she said, but luckily, Ruth was quickly distracted by her surroundings.

"Well, glory be," she repeated, turning in a full circle. "It's more beautiful than I could have ever imagined, and we're pretty spoiled over there in that other place—what do you call it, 'The Community of Resting Mortals'?" She went over to the closest tree, touched the velvety bark on its trunk, and breathed in the fragrance, tipping her head back. "It even smells amazing."

Sophia couldn't help laughing, both at Ruth's personality and her clear enthusiasm over surroundings every angel probably took for granted.

"You're right: everything is very calm and peaceful here on the First Level. We're blessed with beautiful surroundings, bodies that have never suffered pain or discomfort, and the freedom to worship the Almighty Divine continually. You'll see for yourself, but right now, we need to get back to Operations Central." Sophia led Ruth toward the Great Way, checking over one shoulder to see if the Portal was secured.

There was nothing to indicate it had ever been there at all.

"Yes, I'm eager to get started helping you all. In fact, I have a couple of ideas about what you could do with all those drug dealers that seem to have taken over half the world," Ruth said, stopping every few steps to touch the polished white stone of the path, or feel the smooth trees that bore white flowers instead of leaves.

A constant stream of angels passed them, caught up in conversation, praying as they walked, or sharing a laugh. Each time they saw Ruth, who wore the white robe of an angel but lacked the halo of light that hovered over everyone else's head, they stared for a second, but then quickly wished her welcome.

Ruth pointed at the sparkling white cloud cover stretched as far overhead as they could see and asked, "Is God up there?"

Sophia tipped her head back too. "No. That's what we call the Separation Zone between the First and Second Level of the kingdom of heaven. It's a bit like the boundary on the other side of the Portal that separates earth and us."

"But that's not in the Bible," Ruth said. "Heaven is heaven."

Sophia's face settled into a smile. "There are many mysteries about the Almighty Divine I don't understand, and I imagine it's even more mysterious for mortals. That's why we rejoice when one of you joins us. It means you have believed despite all the unknowns."

"But that's part of the deal, isn't it? I help out, and I get to see God," Ruth asked. "I mean that bright light stuff and those wonderful angels who came after I died were incredible, but we mortals have this saying: 'ain't nothin' like the real thing.' So when do I meet Him?'"

Another question Sophia couldn't respond to. Of course, the angels had all been in the Almighty Divine's presence when they were first created, but that was before everything changed. Who knew if she would even see Him again, let alone a mortal who was an unheard-of precedent on the First Level?

She stopped and faced Ruth. "The Almighty Divine exists on the Third Level of heaven, where none of us have ever been. That and the Second Level are the province of the archangels and other holies."

The glow vanished from Ruth's face, prompting Sophia to give her another hug.

"Believe me, you will feel greater contentment here than ever before. We are safe from chaos and calamity, and exist to serve the Almighty Divine. That gives us incredible joy. Ruth, when we get to Operations Central, the Selected Servants can probably help you with these questions," she said, hoping that was the truth. "They have oversight of the Community of Resting Mortals."

Without waiting to see if her explanation satisfied Ruth, Sophia picked up the pace toward their destination, relieved when the familiar white building came into view. Ruth's eyes were wide as she tried to take it all in, her head continuing to swivel from side to side as they passed the houses of gently changing colors and hundreds of serene angels caught up in their work: praying, tending to the gardens, singing praise songs, or just resting with others.

"Here we are!" Sophia said, holding out one hand toward the bridge that led over the moat and to the stairway leading up to Operations Central. She'd been hoping Miriam or Faras would be there to greet them, but neither was in sight.

"Oh my." Ruth clasped her hands over her chest, frozen in place. "I think that place is way too fancy for me. Maybe I made a mistake leaving the Community of Resting Mortals."

"You didn't." Sophia took her arm and led her to the bridge. The river beneath was a deep emerald, its surface sparkling and the flow of the water moving in a happy chorus of splashes and gurgles. Ruth held on to the polished wooden banister of the bridge, as if afraid it might dissolve underneath her if she let go.

"I've never walked on marble before," she mused when they started up the steps. "Feels pretty nice."

The instant they reached the top, a dozen angels burst from the front doors of Operations Central, their arms wide open and delighted smiles on their faces. For several minutes they serenaded Ruth, forming a circle around her and Sophia so that the sound of beautiful voices surrounded them. When they finished, Miriam appeared in the doorway and gave the group a fond look.

"Thank you, angels, that was lovely as always," she said. "You may go."

She swept forward to Ruth, who still looked overwhelmed, and folded both her hands in her own.

"This is Miriam, one of the Select Servants," Sophia said. "She and I work together."

"Welcome, Ruth. Come inside and meet Faras, the other Select Servant, and let me show you around Operations Central."

They went down the same long hallway Sophia had traveled before, but Ruth's comments led her to see it with new eyes. The walls were truly like pearl, polished and glowing with a soft white light, and the marble floor beneath them was swirled with silver. When they reached the end of the corridor, Miriam winked at Sophia and touched a button on one wall. It slid quietly up to reveal a window that looked out on the back of Operations Central and the waterfall that plunged down from the moat into a oval pool where a few angels were using their wings to flit back and forth above the surface.

"Wow. That looks like fun." Ruth turned to examine Miriam and Sophia. "You two don't have wings."

Miriam shrugged. "We choose not to use them, but we can anytime we want. Sometime I'll take you flying, Ruth, I promise, but now, let's show you the room where Sophia, Faras, and I spend most of our time."

She stepped on the plate before the doorway, and the same voice as before granted her entrance. The other two followed the same procedure.

Ruth repeated her astonished examination of the contents of the Guidance Room, which Faras was only too happy to display for her and describe at length. Watching the two of them, Sophia looked up at Miriam, who had a guarded look on her eyes.

"Is the Community of the Resting Mortals so different from here?" she asked.

Miriam's eyebrows arched. "You should make a point of informing yourself about things like that, Sophia," she chided. Sophia couldn't help looking crestfallen, and the expression on Miriam's face softened a bit. . "It's a place, that's all. Pleasant enough for mortals, but I wouldn't want to spend most of eternity there."

Another challenge, Sophia thought. *Miriam and I seem to be very different spirits.*

When they stood side by side, the physical contrasts were obvious: she was petite and fair, with a short crop of pale blonde hair and eyes the color of sky on a balmy day. Miriam was imposing, tall and dark, with deep violet eyes that seemed to flash with the same purple highlights in her long glossy black hair.

Their appearances in many ways mirrored their personalities. She could already tell Miriam was forthright and outspoken, while she often held back before speaking for fear she would say the wrong thing. Gabriel had told her Miriam sometimes became concerned over whether others were being given favors she deserved, in contrast to Sophia, who worried about her worthiness to be anything more than a prayer angel.

"Miriam," she said softly, "Don't be displeased. I know the Community of Resting Mortals is your and Faras's province, and I didn't ask to be the one to usher Ruth into the First Level. If anything, I feel totally incompetent. You two could answer her questions far better than I."

Miriam considered Sophia's words for a second and then seemed satisfied. "The Almighty Divine makes a judgment about the life of the mortal at the moment of death. Those who are chosen to go there have a comfortable existence. Nothing is expected of them, and many have led such hard lives on earth that they need a long time of rest just to recover. Their surroundings are closely guarded from Lucifer, so he can't lure them back to earth—but it still happens from time to time, despite our efforts. Some can't let go of the life they led before death, or their attachments to other mortals."

"So after they come through the Portal, you or Faras takes them directly to the Community of Resting Mortals?"

Miriam nodded. "Along the way we answer any questions they have about the kingdom of heaven—at least the ones we can. They're not very deep thinkers, these mortals."

"And Ruth is the first one to ask to do more than exist in luxury until the end times?"

Miriam bit her lip, concentrating, then said: "No. That's the strange thing. Many of them ask to help out, but she's the first one who's been allowed to." She turned on Sophia. "There must be something special about her. Do you know what?"

Since Sophia didn't know specifics, she shook her head innocently. "Gabriel just told me to go get her and bring her here. I assume we'll find out more soon enough."

What would Miriam say if she knew angels were in danger of being outnumbered, and Ruth was an experiment to see if especially good mortals might be able to help out in the spiritual warfare they waged with Lucifer? It might be totally demoralizing for any of the angels to hear such news, but she knew Gabriel had information from the Almighty Divine that would, in time, make sense of everything.

Sophia went to a semicircle of plush wide recliners on the other side of the room and sat down, patting the one next to her for Ruth. "So, this seems like a good time to orient Ruth to how things operate here. Miriam? Faras? Would you join us?"

"You were the one sent to the Portal," Miriam said, coming over but remaining on her feet with her arms crossed over her chest, a doubtful expression on her face. "Are you sure we're supposed to be part of things now?"

"Absolutely. You and Faras are part of this."

The firm answer seemed to satisfy Miriam; she sighed softly and flopped down into a chair while Faras lingered at the podium, seemingly lost in thought. Sophia knew, courtesy of Gabriel, that he was less impulsive and often slower to act than Miriam, and often put more effort into decision making and intervention than most angels.

And how has Gabriel judged me? Sophia wondered, realizing that Ruth and Miriam were watching her, expecting further direction.

"Faras, can you join us, please?" Sophia said, waiting until he reluctantly joined them before going on. "I just started to tell Ruth about the First Level when we got called back here, so she has lots of unanswered questions that I know you two can answer far more capably than me." She looked at each of them expectantly. "So, who wants to get us started?"

10

There was a short silence, then Ruth leaned forward in her chair, first looking to her right at Sophia and then left at the Selected Servants. "I know God, I mean, the Almighty Divine, created all the angels before He even set to work on earth," Ruth said. "And I know from the Bible some angels and human folk got together and made babies, so does my coming here mean I'll get to be an angel?"

Sophia looked at Miriam and Faras, waiting for one of them to answer, since they knew what to tell mortals about their destiny far better than she did. They looked back with questioning expressions.

Finally, Faras stroked his chin and said, "Mortals have never become angels. Some have become holies and saints, and get to exist on the Second Level of heaven with the archangels. Some may even make it to the Third Level, now that I think about it. There have been some incredible mortals, brave soldiers against Lucifer." He looked at Ruth, his face still wrinkled in concentration. "But mortals turning into angels is one of those beliefs used to comfort during times of bereavement."

"You know how someone will say a person who died is an angel in heaven," Miriam elaborated. "It's comforting, but not really true."

"For now, that doesn't really matter," Sophia added quickly, "because you'll be treated the same as any angel here. Everyone on the First Level is equal, and all of us exist to serve the Almighty Divine—in whatever way He deems appropriate."

She didn't point out the obvious differences between them: mortals had known suffering and sin, and their vulnerability to Lucifer's temptations would always be greater than any angel's. Perhaps that was why Ruth, who so often turned her earthly sufferings into service rather than sin, had been chosen to come here.

"But think of it." Faras touched Ruth's knee. "We've existed since earth began, so we've had a lot longer to learn how to serve. We help mortals here and on earth. That pleases us, because we love you and know it's the

Almighty Divine's will for us to guide and support you."

"It might be hard to imagine right now, but you've already seen that each angel you've met is perfect in appearance, and yet none is exactly like the other. In the same way, no one angel is thought of as higher in status than another," Sophia offered, thinking that her explanation probably sounded completely improbable to Ruth.

It was Miriam who changed the awkwardness of the moment. "It's like your faith on earth, Ruth. There are clearly times when it makes no sense at all and yet it is the only thing that makes sense."

"Amen to that," Ruth said after a brief reflection, nodding at Miriam. "But what about God—do I get to see Him now? Pastor Ephraim said I would, and it was pretty disappointing when you whisked me off with the other resting mortals instead of right to the Glory Throne."

"That's a common question," Faras said, fingers drumming on his bearded chin. "Come to think of it, I can't remember a mortal that hasn't asked. Can you?" He turned to Miriam, who shook her head. "So far that hasn't happened other than at the moment of death. Do you recall a bright light, so bright you almost couldn't look on it?"

Ruth squinted her eyes and then her mouth fell partway open. "I do! Now that you mention it, I do."

Faras held up one hand, as if presenting an exhibit in court. "There you have it. For mortals, at the moment of death, they face the Almighty Divine. But as to whether you'll come into His presence again…that's another one I'd refer on to Gabriel." He looked at Sophia meaningfully. "Sophia's the only one who has private communications with the archangel, and he in turn meets with the Almighty Divine to see what the heavenly host is to do next to serve Him."

"I don't mean to sound pushy, but can you check it out next time you talk to him?" Ruth asked, turning to Sophia. "It'd be kind of nice to know where I'll be spending eternity, and what I'll be doing."

Miriam and Faras exchanged a look that might as well have said, "Ah, mortals, how can we teach them to be more like us?" but Sophia's laugh was like the whisper of wind through delicate glass chimes. "It sounds like a letdown, I know, but that's only because you're still so mortal. Everyone loves being on the First Level."

"Each with their own mysteries," Faras said. "Even we have questions that challenge us to trust in the Almighty Divine and not worry," Miriam said, directing a genuine smile at Ruth. "I have many unknowns about the Second Level and the future, but they don't concern me to the degree yours do about all this. That will change as you learn to trust and submit."

Faras added, "Miriam's right. Any opportunity we have to submit to the Almighty Divine we welcome. We don't worry and hopefully, eventually, you won't either."

But was that really true, Sophia wondered? She worried plenty. Could Faras and Miriam have discovered some secret to angelhood she didn't know? She filed that away with the other questions she had to ask Gabriel when they met again.

"What do you mean about being happy to submit?" Ruth's forehead creased as she turned toward Faras.

"Our beloved Almighty Divine always gives us the opportunity to choose to believe or not, otherwise our love for Him wouldn't mean much. Like mortals, angels still have free will," he answered. "I find it hard to understand, but even some of our own choose to go live on earth as mortals."

Sophia felt herself relax. Ruth was now in experienced hands, and the Selected Servants were setting aside whatever concerns they had and doing their best to help with this divinely directed project.

Ruth was one step ahead of Faras's patient explanation. "So, maybe I'll be like a replacement angel for one of those created ones who leave?"

Faras raised his eyebrows at Miriam, a small smile twitching at the corner of his mouth. "Ruth, you have an interesting sense of humor," he said, then grew serious again. "To answer your question, no one can replace the angels who leave. It grieves us all. You're here because you wanted to help, and the Almighty Divine decided to give you that opportunity. You know how chaotic earth is at this point."

"I sure do. Pastor Ephraim kept saying it was close to the end times, but I have some unfinished business left down there that I wouldn't mind taking care of. There're a lot of people who don't realize what's ahead."

Miriam's eyes were thoughtful. "One of our biggest challenges is the mortals who never make a deliberate choice to serve the Almighty Divine.

It's perplexing since the way seems clear to us, but increasingly there are those who live good lives, but not because they feel the Almighty Divine is leading them to do so. The problem is, Lucifer can claim them as his. He says anyone who doesn't actively reject him is for him."

"I've known some of those types," Ruth said, then paused and thought. "I think it's because we don't see enough of you all. I know my Bible pretty well and there used to be angels all over the place. Now the only ones we hear about are the ones that people think are some kind of magical servants who will do their bidding. Maybe you all need to make more appearances on earth?"

Sophia considered what Ruth had just said and realized she was right. There were incredible earth angels, but it had become such a difficult job to survive outside of heaven that few wanted to do it. Another topic to discuss with Gabriel.

Ruth went on. "So what do you all do about eating and sleeping? We had the most amazing banquets back there with the other Resting Mortals, and I never put on a pound." She patted her midsection and sighed. "And the sleep—I never had such rest or such beautiful dreams."

"Now, that's a good question," Faras answered, trailing one hand across the surface of his chair. "There's no night or day here, and instead of eating or sleeping, we Refresh, which is one of my favorite blessings. We go into a state of complete peace where we receive all that we need from the Almighty Divine—the most incredible nourishment we could ever need. I wonder how that will work for you."

"Hmm…I don't think a mortal will be able to get the same benefits from it as we do," Miriam said.

"Maybe we should try it out and see what happens," Faras suggested, his fingers again stroking the plush surface of his recliner. Before they could pursue his idea, a light began to flash frantically on the Earth Viewer. He jumped up and rushed over to the control panel.

"What is that?" Ruth asked, pointing at the giant computerized replica of earth. "I'm not sure I understood his explanation."

"That is the Earth Viewer. It's how we monitor situations on earth so we can help mortals," Miriam said, rising to follow him.

Sophia gestured that Ruth should join them at the podium. "You can guess that the red lights on the surface mean danger; orange, a warning; green, stable; and blue, one of those rare places of total peace. There's an automatic surveillance system in place, but we can also touch one of the lights to see more of what is happening in a particular location. Something bad is happening right now."

The situation that had attracted Faras's attention was a light that pulsed a persistent dull red. He zoomed in on it and instantly the image of crowds of starving children and their mothers appeared on the supersized screen.

"That's one of the refugee camps we've been tracking," Miriam said.

Dozens of angels hovered over each child on the screen, invisible to the mortals, but nonetheless offering encouragement and support. Others were assisting health care workers, making packages filled with food bars and first aid supplies dropped by a remote-controlled plane lighter to carry.

"We really are working actively in the world to help," Faras said over his shoulder. "Mortals just don't realize it."

No sooner had he spoke than a streak of smoke trailed across the screen, colliding with the plane and destroying it completely. The refugees ran for cover as pieces of flaming debris dropped to the ground.

"I guess you can see *my* point," Ruth said. "It's hard to see the goodness of angels in that situation when your buddy Lucifer turned it around so easily."

"Not necessarily," Miriam said. "All the food was delivered, and that was a remote-controlled plane. You can see the angels got everyone to a safe place, so there weren't any injuries. Still, I think I can understand what you're saying. On earth, so many bad things are happening that mortals rarely see the good anymore."

Faras watched until the situation at the refugee camp calmed down, and then moved back to the podium. It was a sturdy silver structure that branched off into three different sections, each inset with a screen. "This is how we control the Earth Viewer. If we want to go backward in time, or direct a divine intervention we've been given, we use these smaller Earth Monitors on either side. Sometimes that's helpful."

"Can you see the future?" Ruth asked. She was standing next to him, and although they were the same height, Faras's body was trimmer, and the tight waves of hair that capped his head trickled down into a soft fuzz of beard covering his chin, while hers was so short, the sheen of her scalp showed through. They both had intense brown eyes, which met as he answered her question.

"No, only the Almighty Divine can, but He often gives us an indication of what is likely to happen. Why do you ask?"

"Like I said, there're some things I'd like to take care of down there," Ruth said, nodding at the screen in front of them.

"I hope that's not why you volunteered to help us," Miriam said quietly. "None of us acts out of our own will here. We only do what the Almighty Divine assigns us to do. It would please me greatly to pray or praise Him all day, but that is not my job, so I do as I am directed. But please, dear sister, come and sit again. Faras loves to show off the toys we have, but since only the Senior Servant and her Selecteds can use them, we need to focus on you, not us. "

Hesitantly, Ruth moved to join her, still studying her new surroundings. She perched on the edge of one of the recliners and it instantly sprang into an upright position. Carefully, she turned around and leaned back.

"I definitely could have used this for my aching human bones back on earth," she said, crossing her hands in her lap. "So, what will my job be?"

Faras and Miriam's interest in the answer to that question was obvious; the look they exchanged warned Sophia to tread carefully. "Ruth, your role will be revealed in time, but I assure you, we all are given responsibilities that make best use of our unique talents," she said.

Miriam's eyes narrowed and she jumped to her feet, stepping closer to Sophia. "What's going on here? First Isaac vanishes and no one tells us where he's gone, then we get a brand new Senior Servant we don't even know. Now for the first time ever we have a mortal on the First Level. Gabriel is being a bit too secretive on this one, if you ask me."

Sophia, trying to stay casual, gestured Miriam back to her seat, more curious than shocked by the outburst. "I don't know why Ruth is here, Miriam, but it might help if I shared some of the things I learned about her during her Life Review."

Avoiding Ruth's eyes, she summarized what she knew about all of Ruth's trials and triumphs during her time on earth. With each new detail, Miriam seemed to repent, turning away from the large screen and covering her eyes with one hand when Sophia asked Faras to project the awful images from Ruth's last day on earth.

"I'm sorry," Miriam whispered, slipping to the floor and kneeling in front of Ruth. "I've never met a mortal with a Life Review as challenging as yours. It was wrong of me to question the wisdom of the Almighty Divine for bringing you here with Sophia, or to make you feel unwanted. Please, will you forgive me?"

11

There was a short silence, then Ruth straightened up in her seat and sniffed.

"Don't start getting boo-hooey on me, or I'll think this really isn't such a great place to be after all," she chided. "I didn't want to admit it, but I knew in my heart all along that JoJo was drawn to that bad way of life, even if it wasn't where he belonged."

Sophia rested one hand on Miriam's shoulder. "There does seem to be something special about Ruth, but we must wait for the details. In the meantime, how should we continue with her orientation to the First Level?"

Miriam stood up and paused before returning to her seat. "I guess we should answer any other questions she has. This is new territory, Sophia, so until you hear more from Gabriel, it seems best to help both her and you adjust to the way we work in Operations Central."

Was her answer a subtle reminder of Sophia's inexperience? Before Sophia could make too much of the comment, Ruth frowned and looked over at the Earth Viewer.

"Can you show me what's happened to my kids? Especially JoJo since…well, you know?"

Faras took her hand. "Mortals who come through the Portal almost always want to know if they can see what is happening to those they left behind. In His wisdom, the Almighty Divine requires that earthly attachments be surrendered once you die. If that wasn't the case, mortals would be too distracted and distressed by the loved ones they left behind to enjoy their time in the Community of Resting Mortals. In special cases, the Almighty Divine might permit that kind of awareness, and it's not unheard of for a mortal to be allowed to give a loved one on earth some kind of brief message or assurance."

"But it seems only fair that I should get to help the ones I love now that I can." Ruth stared at Sophia, her lower lip trembling.

"Dear one, we all care about your children, including JoJo, but it's important to share that love and concern. Carrying it alone would be too much of a burden."

Miriam said, "Surely you remember how powerful it was when you united forces with other mortals to achieve a common goal on earth? It's even more so here because we all have the same mission, which is helping mortals."

Sophia closed her eyes, lulled into a state of relief as Miriam went on to explain the reason for the way of existence on the First Level. What a blessing it was to have a Selected Servant who could explain all this new information so clearly.

An alarm shrieked from the Earth Viewer, and this time a group of red lights flashed in unison, interrupting the brief calm. Miriam leapt up, ran over, and touched the screen.

Faras drew in a sharp breath when he saw what was happening, and uttered the one word every angel dreaded: "Nephilim."

The brute on the screen was indeed a giant, just as his ancestors had been. The four of them watched in horror as he advanced on a little girl whose eyes were dazed with fear. She was crouched beneath a small table, which the man picked up and threw across the room, then grabbed her with one hand and jerked her to her feet.

"Mister, don't hurt me," she pleaded, but his face hardened into a mask of hatred.

She tried again. "Please, Mister, I don't know why you grabbed me, but I never did anything to you."

Roaring, he threw her on the floor and fell on top of her. She kicked, screamed, and clawed at him with all the power her tiny body could muster. With a vicious punch, he knocked her unconscious and began to tear off her clothes.

"Do something!" Ruth said, grabbing the sleeve of Sophia's robe.

A few miles away in a small town, the kidnapper's accomplice was in a car, on his way back from a trip to buy beer and food. Following a series of quick instructions that spilled from Sophia's lips, Faras caused the man to run a stop sign, resulting in an accident that totaled his car. The local sheriff happened to be cruising nearby, and when he arrived to help, the first thing he saw was a girl's pink backpack on the passenger seat.

"I just got a bulletin about a young girl with one just like that who was abducted on her way home from school the next town over," he told the driver. "Know anything about that?"

It didn't take much to get the accomplice to moan out the location of the abandoned cabin where his partner was in the process of attacking the little girl. Within seconds, the sheriff raced off to rescue her. When he arrived, she was lying in a crumpled heap, alive but unconscious. Close by, her tormentor had collapsed in a drunken stupor.

Ruth was furious. "You should have done something! That poor child—"

She broke down weeping, but when Sophia put out a hand to comfort her, she pushed it away. "Doesn't God get it? That's just the kind of thing that make people wonder how He could exist and allow such terrible suffering."

Sophia turned away from the screen, understanding why the scene would provoke such a violent reaction. Still, it was surprising that Ruth would ask such a question now, when her own life was evidence that Lucifer, not the Almighty Divine, was at the heart of every evil deed.

"Let me handle this," Faras whispered to Sophia. "I think it's not surprising. While she was on earth this kind of thing was commonplace, but now that she's here and sees the alternative, it's harder to witness suffering."

Sophia stared at him for an instant, not sure he understood that she shared Ruth's dismay. Then she decided revealing any more of her weaknesses to the Selected Servants might not be a good idea and so nodded as he and Miriam led Ruth back to the recliners and sat on either side of her, leaning in protectively.

"We hate to see things like that too," Miriam said. "We wish we could stop evil completely, especially for such innocents, but that man was a Nephilim, one of Lucifer's own. They're free to roam the earth until the end of time."

"Nephilim?" Ruth took her hands away from her tear-streaked face. "What kind of crazy story are you going to tell me now?"

Faras inclined his head toward her. "You said you read the Bible. You know the story of Lucifer, and how he and many other created angels were cast out of heaven because they wouldn't submit to the Almighty Divine. They were able to lure other angels away too."

Miriam went on, "And as you mentioned, those fallen angels took mortal women as partners, creating a race of superhuman monsters. Over the generations, some have become less hideous, but no less hateful. They're the Nephilim, just part of Lucifer's legion of destructive forces on earth."

Ruth's expression stayed skeptical. "God destroyed all of the bad people in the flood—remember? If you knew the Bible like I do, you'd remember that was the whole reason for Noah."

"There are many mysteries that remain about the universe. Even those of us who have existed throughout eternity don't know everything," Faras said. "It could be that a Nephilim survived by crouching on the roof of the ark. Another ancient myth suggests that Lucifer built a tower high enough for some of his chosen to survive. It's even possible that one or more of Noah's own children or grandchildren secretly carried the trait and was clever enough to conceal it. Explaining how they survived isn't important. The Nephilim exist, and they're the cause of the worst and most unexplainable suffering on earth—as you just saw. Anytime there's a senseless tragedy and mortals wonder how one of their own can be so completely evil, it's likely the Nephilim are involved. Even the fallen angels don't go to the extremes of those monsters."

Sophia wasn't about to confirm what Lucifer had told her about the survival of the Nephilim or reveal their "conversations." She wasn't sure what Isaac had experienced as Senior Servant, but it might undermine Faras's and Miriam's fledgling trust in her if they knew she had been approached by their greatest enemy.

"Ruth," Miriam said, "Think about your life. Would you have been the same giving person if you grew up in privilege, with a different mother and father than the ones you had?"

It was a desperate attempt because Sophia knew Ruth probably was one of the rare mortals who turned out the same no matter what circumstance life put them in. Still, there was a flicker of emotion on Ruth's face as Miriam pressed on.

"It really is true that the Almighty Divine turns trials into triumphs, again and again. But that doesn't mean Lucifer stops being evil, which is why we must be especially vigilant during the tragedies he inflicts on earth. If mortals don't believe in the Almighty Divine, they often break down completely when that kind of thing happens."

"Sometimes, even when they are believers they lose their faith," Faras added.

Miriam pivoted around to face the Earth Viewer screen, which lit up again, showing the little girl who had been kidnapped. She was now in a hospital with her mother sitting on the side of her bed, holding her tightly and stroking her hair. Unseen to all but those who were watching from the First Level, dozens of angels hovered over the child, singing songs of comfort.

"Mommy, I wanted you so much," the girl said between sobs. "But then I remembered what they taught us in Sunday School and I started praying for angels to come and rescue me."

"I think they did, sweetheart," her mother answered. "That man was a very bad person." She didn't tell her daughter that the remains of three other little girls who were not rescued had just been located in a shallow grave behind the cabin.

Only Sophia heard the laughter of the Voice, quickly steadying herself so the others wouldn't suspect anything was amiss. If angel music created the ultimate sacred sound, what she heard now was pure profanity.

"Sweet Sister Sophia, how very convincing these lies are. But how can you really believe them when, every day, you see angels and mortals choose to follow me and my helpers, just as happened in that little home movie? Only I can control the evil of earth, no matter what you've decided to believe."

Lucifer would love to draw her into a lengthy debate, she knew. Forcing herself to focus all her attention on the situation before her, she realized the other three were watching her warily.

"You look really pale. Are you okay?" Miriam asked.

"Yes, sorry. Please, go on."

Miriam gave a little shrug, and continued the dialogue as if nothing unusual had happened. "Ruth, knowing what you do now, can you really do what is needed to be of help to the heavenly host? It's better to be honest and admit if you can't, since whatever holds you back will make you more vulnerable to Lucifer. You seem to still have some strong mortal attachments…"

"I'm not so sure I couldn't do a better job down there than up here," Ruth said, her lips pressed together firmly. "You all might be created and all that, and I admit that being around for eternity changes things, but investing in children's lives is one of the most important things a mortal can do. I wasn't finished."

Miriam's earnest voice trying to convince Ruth otherwise was drowned out, for Sophia, by evil laughter. She tried to ignore it, but the sour mirth intensified.

"Yes, Sophia, wait and see how powerful you and your host of angels are when we get to that."

Sophia frowned, ignoring the Voice. While none of them could persuade Ruth to choose one way over the other, Miriam and Faras's words were compelling. Her attention was distracted by a summons from Gabriel, which made her stand up, relieved to be able to meet with him for reassurance and answers to the many questions she had accumulated already.

"I must meet with Gabriel. Please, continue without me," she told Miriam and Faras, searching Ruth's face to get a gauge of her feelings. "Don't worry. You'll be fine with them and I'll be back shortly."

As she drifted up to the Refreshing Room, Sophia sorted through the events that had occurred since she last met with Gabriel. For some still unknown reason, Ruth was important, and she was Sophia's first official responsibility as Senior Servant, but how could she guarantee a success? Her protégé seemed more concerned about the children she had left behind on earth than with submitting to the holy task she would be assigned here on the First Level of heaven. And what about Miriam and Faras, the two angels she should trust and depend on most? When would she start feeling as if she was really a part of their team and not just a tolerated observer?

12

In the Refreshing Room, she gratefully settled into Gabriel's presence. Despite their easy relationship, there were things about him that impressed her anew each time they met. In repose, his face was like a portrait of eternity, reflecting all the emotions and events that had taken place since the beginning of creation in the set of his mouth, the cast of his blue eyes, and the tilt of his head.

His size was striking too. Compared to the angels in the heavenly host, archangels were giants, easily as tall and massive as the original Nephilim. Unlike those evil creatures, Gabriel had a gentle strength. He was big enough to be imposing if angered, but more importantly, substantial enough to comfort during times of struggle.

This was one of those times.

"I feel like I've failed already, Gabriel. I know this is my first big assignment, but Ruth seems very fixated on earth, and on the children she left behind. She can't let go."

"Can you?" he asked, not unkindly.

"What do you mean?"

"Can you let go of your concerns and believe that all will be well if you trust and obey?"

She dipped her head, instantly aware of her failure to do the very thing she encouraged in others. How could Ruth be expected to submit with total abandon when Sophia, her role model, struggled herself?

"You've heard the voice of Lucifer, trying to raise questions," Gabriel said, coming over to hold his hands above Sophia's head. "Let us pray that both you and Ruth might receive additional strength through the love of the Almighty Divine."

"How…how did you know?"

"I didn't, but the Almighty Divine did. He knows Lucifer has spoken to you before and that you've resisted him."

Sophia buried her face in her hands. "I suppose that's something I should have confessed right away, but it makes me feel like I'm somehow to blame. Why does Lucifer target me?"

Gabriel shrugged. "You were the one who didn't listen to him in the beginning. He hates to lose. I suspect this won't be the last time, but it might not be such a bad thing to know what's going on in that cunning mind of his."

"Gabriel, you have confidence in me, but if you're the reason I was selected as Senior Servant, perhaps you don't know me as well as you think. Maybe I didn't say anything about the monster on the Earth Viewer, but I was just as disgusted by what happened to that child as Ruth. Being a prayer angel isolates you in some ways…"

He waited, knowing she needed to say more.

"We get so caught up in our inner existence, constantly interceding for mortals, but rarely focused on the specifics of a terrible situation." She sighed. "I guess when I prayed, I felt like I was actually contributing something to the battle between good and evil, even in a much removed way."

"Yes," he responded. "You were very devoted, which is why you were chosen as Senior Servant. Single-mindedness is very important in a Senior Servant, but expecting perfection from yourself after such a short time in this role is a bit excessive, don't you think?"

She looked at his quizzical expression and couldn't help laughing. "You may be partly right…okay, completely right, but I sense that Miriam and Faras are just waiting for me to make a horrible mistake, and I heard the things some of the heavenly host said when I was out there among them: 'Quiet Sophia, our Senior Servant?' and 'Such a little thing to hold such a big job!'"

"Isaac taught us all a lesson about appearances," Gabriel said gravely.

Sophia took a long breath in. "Why can't I know what happened to Isaac, Gabriel? Did Lucifer talk to him as well?" she asked. Instantly, she sensed that even if he were to tell, it was information she was better off not knowing.

"That's not something any of the heavenly host can know right now, Sophia. For you and the Selected Servants, part of the challenge is to trust and persevere with what you are assigned to do, no matter what the circumstances. Have confidence in yourself."

Sophia thought about the few efforts she had already made to try to gain acceptance by the heavenly host, and Miriam and Faras in particular. No doubt they would continue to have reservations about their waiflike leader for a long time after the charismatic Isaac was gone, but she would just have to persevere.

She sighed and brushed back a strand of hair that partially covered her face, leaning so that she rested against Gabriel, and feeling a steady flow of energy from him to her. Being so close to him gave her new hope.

"Sophia, let go of these doubts. You're the one who believes in mortals and understands how desperate Lucifer is to win this war."

"You're right, but compared to you and Michael I seem so limited… almost mortal!"

Gabriel laughed, raising her up so they were face to face, and he kissed her cheek. "Don't be so hard on yourself. The Almighty Divine isn't. We never said you would automatically be perfect when you were chosen as Senior Servant, but you're already making progress." He released her and leaned back on the fleecy cushions of blue behind him. "I know you have many questions, and we need to talk about Ruth, so you can start."

It felt like she was quizzing a student on the basics of the First Level, but she wanted to know as much as possible in order to do an effective job. Taking a deep breath, she started.

"Will Ruth get to be an angel?"

Gabriel folded his arms behind his head and closed his eyes, seemingly unaffected by a question that carried such weight. "I don't know. That will be the Almighty Divine's decision, but there's never been a mortal who somehow transformed into an angel. That doesn't mean it can't happen, though. What matters most is Ruth's motivation: if she only wants to assist us because she sees a personal reward ahead, we'll have to replace her."

"I guess the same answer might apply to her question about seeing the Almighty Divine directly?"

Gabriel opened his eyes and grinned at her. "What a fast learner you are! I'd like to take credit for some of that, but unfortunately, I can't. That's just the way you were created."

"And the Refreshing? Will it work for Ruth?"

"It will—better than the food and sleep she is used to."

She licked her lips, preparing for the question that concerned her most.

"Gabriel, Miriam said angels don't worry, but you know I do. Is there something so wrong with me that I'm anxious about doing the right things and pleasing the Almighty Divine?"

He sat up and put his hands on her knees. "It's what the Almighty Divine loves about you, Sophia. Miriam may not worry, but she has other issues that she wrestles with, as you've already observed. So does Faras."

She sighed in relief. "Why is it that I always feel better about myself when I'm with you?"

"Because, as you said, I believe in you absolutely," he said, a broad smile splitting his face. "As does the Almighty Divine. Now, we must talk about Ruth's assignment. She has been especially chosen from among mortals to perform a special task—to work with Miriam and Faras as a third Selected Servant, assisting you."

"Oh my! I don't think Miriam or Faras will like that at all, and it's hard to believe she's really ready."

"Sweet one, subservience—"

"—is the way to peace," she finished, before he could.

"That's right. Can we ever tire of saying it? All mortal struggles relate to humility in some way, but on the First Level, every angel can learn to overcome the desire for his or her own will—and you know the result of that. Sophia, some day you will see Him again."

"Really?" Her joy quickly gave way to dismay. "But Gabriel, you're an archangel. Being subservient and humble comes naturally to you."

"Don't be so sure of that. In some ways, being an archangel is harder than being a regular angel. Don't you remember how long and hard Michael struggled before he was able to cast Lucifer out the First Level of heaven so long ago? And look at how often the battle between them has replayed." His expression momentarily saddened, but then he took her hands in his. "Nonetheless, we will be victorious. Come, before we part, let us sing a prayer song of triumph, and know that I will continue to request special blessings for you."

As always, their voices blended perfectly as they praised the Almighty Divine, extolling His power to conquer evil with good. As the last notes

hung on the air, Sophia wished she could stay in the Refreshing Room forever, her hands and voice joined with Gabriel as they lost themselves in
sweet songs of praise and delirious happiness.

Unfortunately, their singing did come to an end, and after an additional blessing, she found herself back in the Guidance Room of Operations Central. Seeing the Selected Servants and Ruth made her feel as if a
heavy yoke settled down on her shoulders.

"I know this is much to try to understand," Miriam was saying. She
had one arm around Ruth and gave Sophia a cautionary look over her
shoulder. Faras continued randomly spinning the Earth Viewer, as if oblivious to the women standing next to him. Ruth was craning her neck to
look at the complex arrangement of buttons and switches on the control
panel.

Pressing her hands together, Sophia tried to recapture the sense of
tranquility she had just felt and even to infuse a sense of joy in the others.
She tilted her head toward the recliners and invited them to join her there.

Ruth fixed her eyes on Sophia and announced: "You're right about the
whole good and evil thing. It's what went wrong with JoJo—his foolishness
over drugs is all about thinking he's somehow entitled to a life free of suffering, although I sure don't know why. I see it in my oldest daughter,
Tamika, too. She was such a good girl, but now she's sliding into a bad way
herself, hooking up with one man after another because she thinks each
new one will make her happy. I couldn't figure out why God, I mean the
Almighty Divine, would allow that, but now I see it isn't His doing at all."

"The Almighty Divine is inviting you to join us here on the First Level.
Our purpose is simple: to love and serve Him," Sophia said. "If you can let
go of the past and focus on that mission, we should progress, even if you
still have some questions. I promise the answers will soon be less important."

"Less important?" The Voice laughed softly. "What wishful thinking
you angels engage in, Sophia. You just admitted your own doubts about
your ability to be Senior Servant. Why not give Ruth her wish and allow
her to come back to earth? I assure you, she will soon be mine, and you
could join her. We would work well together, Sophia. I would give you
special powers as one of my chosen helpers."

What was stirring in the energy of the First Level, giving Lucifer the ability to hear some or all that was said? Sophia looked at Ruth, whose presence had changed things in ways both subtle and more obvious. Was she the reason for the Voice speaking so often after a long period of silence, or had Lucifer just begun to target her as Senior Servant? He never intruded when she was a prayer angel.

"Gabriel gave me directions for all of you," she said. "Ruth, you can tell we each have assigned tasks. I'm the only angel who meets regularly with Gabriel, although he does appear to the entire heavenly host on special occasions. Miriam and Faras have special abilities too: Miriam can increase the good intentions of mortals and bring out that of the Almighty Divine which resides in each one of them. Meanwhile, Faras has the opposite gift: he diminishes harmful impulses every mortal struggles with, as Lucifer tempts them to put their own selfish desires first."

Miriam couldn't resist breaking in. "Faras and I complement each other's efforts in that way to help all mortals, while Hector, another angel you will meet, makes sure the heavenly host is on track with the bigger mission. You might consider Hector the general in command," she said, and then with a sidelong glance added, "Some of the angels call him 'Hector the Director.' "

Faras pressed on. "We never give up! Look at your life, Ruth. Didn't you ever feel us around you, guiding and protecting you?"

Ruth thought, then shook her head. "Maybe a few times, but not as often as I needed!"

Miriam raised her eyebrows. "Think of all the nurses and doctors at the hospital who helped you at different points, and those mysterious members of your congregation with a special message or gift that came at just the right time. Even some of the children who came your way briefly were my doing—angels who took on mortal form to help you."

"What about you?" Ruth turned to Faras. "Remember that cat, Trouble? It's true I never seemed to be able to get away from trouble."

"Of course you see it that way," Faras said in agreement. "What you didn't know is how many times your husband came looking for you over the years. Each time he got close, his eyes were closed until, eventually, he gave up. There were many other situations: dangerous people in the neighborhood where you lived who thought of robbing you, mothers or fathers of the children you cared for who became convinced you were taking money they deserved...all of them were deflected from harming you through my efforts and the angels on earth who were guarding you."

Sophia stood. "When you volunteered to come here to the First Level, we accepted you. Now, Ruth, you must accept us by surrendering what's left of your mortality, with all its flaws and limitations. Then you'll become our third Selected Servant, which is a great honor."

There was no missing the tightening of Faras's jaw or Miriam's startled look. Sophia placed one hand on each of their shoulders.

"Ruth's appointment doesn't reflect negatively on either of you." She smiled at them in turn. "You must admit, it's going to be very helpful to have another Selected Servant helping us in this never-ending battle."

How simple and certain she made it sound!

"Let us offer a prayer song for Ruth," she concluded.

They joined hands, knelt, and sang a simple prayer song. Eventually, their newest member joined in, her expression gradually becoming more radiant. Her body relaxed and, for a moment, her eyes drifted shut. Then they fluttered open and she smiled at the others.

"I'm ready. I still don't understand everything, but I believe what you've told me," she said, raising her hands to the delicate features of her perfectly oval face and then feeling down the length of her body again. "This old body has already been given a new life, and it's ready to work for the Almighty Divine!"

Sophia lifted her eyes to meet Ruth's. There was something there that bothered her—a haziness that prevented them from connecting their spirits in one look. Usually, when angels gazed on each other there was an instant connection, but Ruth's liquid brown eyes seemed all one color, like a shield protecting her inner spirit. Perhaps that was just the way it would be with any mortal, but for an instant it unsettled her.

"How about this?" Ruth seized Sophia's hands. "Let my first job be to go back and help JoJo. I know if he sees my spirit, I can convince him, and if I don't, that boy will end up in hell."

"He's already in hell," Faras said. "He doesn't realize it, but he is. Drugs are his false god."

"So let me go convince JoJo and my other kids that they need to change their ways. I know they'll believe it when they see me looking like this!" Now she grabbed Miriam's and Faras's hands. "I saw the looks on your faces when Sophia told you what I'm here for, and you can't fool me about this Selected Servant business. You don't really think I'm qualified, and I can't blame you. Sounds like the kind of position you work your way into, like when I was supervisor of the hospital."

Sophia, Miriam, and Faras exchanged an uneasy look, but of course, Sophia was the one to answer.

"Ruth, we are First Level angels. We don't come up with our own plans. It's our job to minister to mortals in whatever way we are guided by the Almighty Divine. His will is for you to work with us as a Selected Servant, in ways yet to be revealed. Try not to worry. Many others are helping all your children, including JoJo."

Sophia nodded at Faras, who went over to the control panel and pressed a few buttons. Briefly, they saw a picture of JoJo in his jail cell, weeping bitterly.

"See. He's penitent, Ruth," she said softly. "That's the beginning."

"I know I have to let go of JoJo and Tamika and the others," Ruth addressed Sophia. "But my heart feels just like it did back on earth when I lost my breath and this big invisible fist would wrap itself around my chest and squeeze so hard I couldn't move."

"That's the bit of your mortality you still carry," Sophia explained. "Your physical body is pure now, and eventually the heavy burden of your human sadness will be washed away too."

Miriam and Faras welcomed Sophia's suggestion to refresh in their separate chambers, hurrying out of the room with their shoulders touching and their heads bent toward each other. Sophia guessed they were trying to make sense of what had just happened, and she turned back to Ruth, who was already in a deep and apparently peaceful slumber. After leaning over to kiss the woman's forehead, she curled up on one of the other recliners and allowed herself to truly let go of her worries—if only temporarily—and sink into a blissful state of refreshing.

13

She stirred to find Gabriel sitting next to her on one of the other vacant recliners. Startled, she checked for Miriam and Faras, who weren't anywhere in the room. Ruth was still sleeping peacefully next to her.

"What is it?" she asked, reading the look of distress on his face instantly.

"We've had two angels defect since Ruth arrived here."

Her hand partially stifled the gasp of horror. "No, that can't be!" She looked at Ruth. "Lucifer told me she would soon be his. Do you think—?"

"That's not a question I can answer, but I can tell you that my predictions of what would happen to this point have been mostly wrong. So much for the intuition of archangels." His eyes were fixed on Ruth too, and a small line of concern creased his normally smooth forehead. "Clearly, we need to occupy Lucifer more with the affairs of earth. He's defeating mortals so easily he has time to focus on us."

"Is Ruth really ready to be part of this new plan? Her family and especially JoJo seem like such vulnerabilities. Can mortals ever truly let go of such attachments? It would be like me erasing you from my life." *Or*, she thought, *like what we did to Lucifer*.

"Sophia, dearest." He laughed softly but did not look away from Ruth. "I never tire of saying this: the will of the Almighty Divine is always right."

He shifted his eyes to the Earth Viewer and watched its lazy spin for a time, then sighed and gestured for Sophia to join him at the control panel. On the wall screen before them they saw thousands of Nephilim gathered next to the River of Fire, acting out every atrocity imaginable.

Just as each angel was uniquely beautiful, each Nephilim was hideous in a different way. Some were still giants, grotesquely proportioned with human features. Others were physically deformed, breathing out clouds of red smoke, or dripping a disgusting green fluid from their eyes and ears. Among them wandered the ones who worried Sophia most—those who had mutated to almost mortal form, with nothing to distinguish them as Nephilim but a certain hard look in their eyes or the mocking set of their mouth.

"How many more are there?" she breathed, unable to look away.

"Legions. The first Watchers and other fallen angels have multiplied at least a hundredfold."

"How does Lucifer control them all? We exist to serve, but the Nephilim only exist to inflict suffering. How can anyone be an authority over such evil?"

Gabriel looked at her sideways with a knowing smile. "Exactly: how can he control them?"

On the screen, Azazel appeared, calling out for the crowd's attention. "Our Lord and Master will soon arrive. Please, supreme ones, prepare yourselves for what he has to tell you."

One Nephilim, with glowing red eyes and a mouth breathing fire, pounded the ground with his long arms, causing a minor quake. "Lucifer better have a good explanation for why we haven't taken over the world yet. He promised mortals would be long destroyed by now."

Suddenly, Lucifer was behind the Nephilim, his clawlike hands gripping the creature's neck and snapping it with an easy twist. As the beast dropped to the ground, Lucifer hissed a cloud over him and within an instant, there was no sign the protestor had ever existed.

"Now," Lucifer said to the silent crowd. "Does anyone else have objections to my leadership style?"

Azazel ran to his side and straightened out Lucifer's heavy black cloak, motioning for everyone gathered to bow down. Everyone did, although some were less enthusiastic in their groveling than others.

"You know the angels are our enemies too, my friends," Lucifer said, stepping up on a boulder covered with soot. "So our battle is complex, but would you have it any other way? An easy victory would be boring, would it not?"

There were murmured assents from the crowd, but also a few glares. Lucifer chose to ignore them, continuing his speech: "We must lure more angels to our side. Brother Azazel has recently had two victories in this area. Mortals must suffer more; surely you can become more creative in your torments of them? Remember, these are the beings who stole the love of the Almighty Divine from you and me."

"Turn it off," Sophia said, both repulsed and uneasy. "It's hard to imagine he was once an archangel."

"That part of Lucifer faded when he fell, Sophia. Sometimes, I wonder if a little fragment of it may still be there, deep inside, nagging at him to give it all up, but hearing what he just said suggests the opposite."

"Seems like mortals are stronger than he thought," she said, raising her eyebrows.

"Deep questions, but not ones I came to answer." Gabriel turned back to check on Ruth, who was still sleeping. "You're right about her role here being special. There's something else I couldn't tell you until now. Ruth wasn't our first choice to be the third Selected Servant, but the other two candidates were tempted away before they even reached the Portal."

"You mean Lucifer has access to the Community of Resting Mortals? If it's come to that, what can we do?" Sophia asked, stricken.

"Michael and I are trying to figure that out, but in the meantime, remember that we were all created for good, not evil. Don't doubt or allow yourself or the others to be disheartened, and keep your faith in mortals."

He touched a few of the steady blue lights on the Earth Viewer, revealing scenarios of mortals quietly but steadily ministering to those in need, others studying to find solutions for continuing global poverty and war, and still more who lived in large colonies dedicated to worshipping the Almighty Divine. Nodding his head with satisfaction, he turned back to Sophia. "The Almighty Divine recently gathered the Council of the Elect to consider the issues we've just discussed."

Sophia considered this—another rare precedent. "If the Second and Third Levels came together, something big must be about to happen."

"Yes. From now on, we're going to be taking better and closer care of the heavenly host, yourself included. Focusing on mortals has left the First Level vulnerable to spiritual attacks, but it's also clear to the Almighty Divine that we need mortals to help fight the battle waging all around them that they cannot see. There are many who have strayed from their faith, not by actively rejecting it, but by not pursuing it with all their energy. Look at how few places of worship remain, even in the holiest of sites."

He touched a button and she saw the ruins of churches in Rome, collapsed temples in Asia, and abandoned mosques and synagogues in the Americas. Some had been neglected, while others were bombed or burned.

"Therefore, I am announcing a new strategy." Gabriel turned from the screen and looked down at her with a twinkle in his eyes. "One that only the Council of the Elect could devise."

"A new strategy? Praise be to the Almighty Divine!"

"Yes. It's called the Testings of Devotion. It will involve activating mortals who have drifted away from their faith. We know that the obvious saints and religious figures instantly attract persecution from Lucifer, but this will be more subtle: ordinary people, but ones whose lives could impact and unite others in a big way. I can tell you Ruth has been chosen to help test and temper a group of carefully chosen mortals so that they join our ranks as holy warriors, even though they won't realize that's what's happening."

"It sounds risky. When testing and tempering are involved, mortals have a tendency to crumble quickly, no matter what's at their core." Sophia glanced back at the still-unresponsive Ruth. "But still, there are many who grow stronger...this will be very challenging, very delicate, I think."

"Yes. It will be upon you, Ruth, and the Selected Servants to help carry out this testing by supporting the chosen candidates in any way possible. Lucifer can use the past to manipulate mortals, just as he did with Ruth, but he cannot know the future, so we will have that advantage. I will be working closely with the Almighty Divine in order to give you the best guidance possible in this mission."

She began to walk back and forth as he elaborated on the Council of the Elect's discussion of the Testings of Devotion, only half listening. If this effort succeeded while she was Senior Servant, it might have benefits for her too—like advancement to the Second Level. From what Gabriel was saying, though, much depended on Ruth. Who could predict whether she was strong enough to carry out such a special charge?

Miriam and Faras would also be part of the equation: they were used to working together and seemed to join forces effortlessly. How would she and Ruth blend with them, especially if they rebelled against taking direction from someone so new in such an important mission?

Something Gabriel said caught her full attention: "Sophia, what I'm about to tell you is a closely guarded secret that no one else can know."

He drew her close, knelt so their eyes were on the same level, and searched her face until he seemed satisfied she was listening carefully to what he was about to say.

"There's more to the story of the Nephilim. Lucifer has two groups of demons: those fallen angels who either left with him originally or were lured away later, and the Nephilim, who are part mortal and part angel. While it's not so different here with mortals and angels, we are bound by love. Lucifer's followers have different degrees of power and ability, which creates, as you saw, envy and hostility. Evil turned against evil creates chaos—"

"While good united with good creates order," she finished. "But the result of good against evil will not be manifest until the Almighty Divine wills it."

"Very good." He smiled. "You remember your lessons well; if we were on earth and you were my student, I'd give you an 'A.'   But my point is, the more unity we can create among angels and mortals, the more vulnerable Lucifer becomes. That's why we're so safe here, but also why he's interested in breaching our stronghold."

Yes, and I seem to be a particular target, she thought, with a slight shiver he seemed not to notice. She said: "So in order for the Testings of Devotion to succeed, we need to keep Lucifer as distracted as possible? It sounds like his own followers are helping with that, whether they realize it or not."

"That's right." Gabriel thought for a second, then inclined his head. "The Testings of Devotion aren't intended for the Ruths of earth who are already living their faith, but for mortals who have the ability to be like her, perhaps on an even larger scale." Gabriel waved one hand toward the Earth Viewer. "This woman is the kind of person we're thinking of. Her name is Lydia."

Sophia took in details of the scene: an animated middle-aged woman with short, curled prematurely gray hair and dancing blue eyes was talking into a phone balanced against her ear by her shoulder, scrolling through e-mail projected on the desktop, and clearing file folders out of her briefcase simultaneously. The one-piece work suit she wore was cut in a flattering style and her jewelry tasteful, giving the impression of a person well put together but not attempting to impress. But there was something contradictory about her. She moved and spoke with energy and passion, yet projected a sense of great calm and inner peace. Angels filled the room: behind her large desk, on both sides of the doorway, and immediately behind her, two stood with their hands resting on her right and left shoulders.

Gabriel explained: "Before she turned forty, Lydia led a good enough life as mortals go, attending church and doing her part to make the world a better place in ways that were convenient to her." Gabriel lifted his hand again, and in Life Review style, a slideshow of different scenarios from Lydia's life were projected on the screen of the Earth Viewer.

"She had two daughters and she was a good mother, but her husband was addicted to gambling. He ended up in such serious debt he couldn't pay the bills, although he kept thinking the next bet he placed would be the one that won and changed their situation. When that didn't happen, the only solution he could see was to abandon his family. One day, Lydia discovered she was literally penniless, and without any prospect of gainful employment."

Sophia saw a younger version of the woman opening the trunk of her car and discovering dozens of envelopes from bill collectors, hidden there by her husband.

"Her mother also died very suddenly after this, which, as you can imagine, demoralized Lydia further."

"I have been so protected from how deeply mortals suffer," Sophia said, looking away from the pictures of the distressed woman trying to console her two daughters.

Or perhaps you've willingly shut your eyes to the truth, Sister Sophia," the Voice taunted. "How can you believe in an Almighty Divine who not only allows but glorifies such suffering?"

Gabriel grabbed Sophia's hands. "Lucifer is speaking to you right now, isn't he?"

When Sophia nodded, the archangel began to move rapidly around the room, singing a prayer song of exorcism that gradually changed the climate from tense to peaceful. Sophia almost sighed in relief until it occurred to her that her own negativity may have given Lucifer entry into the situation.

She looked at Gabriel in horror. "Was that was my fault, Gabriel? Did my doubts allow Lucifer to attack my spirit?"

Her desire to please the Almighty Divine and perhaps even ascend to the Second Level suddenly seemed completely unrealistic until Gabriel gathered her up in his arms, much as a mother might a distressed child.

"Stop. You can't question everything you do, Sophia. You have so much wisdom and yet so much insecurity. The Almighty Divine has appointed you Senior Servant, and you are the one who will guide the heavenly host. Of course Lucifer targets you, but you must have confidence so we can use his own attempts against him and discover how he is able to reach you here."

"I can't imagine how it is for the others, but Gabriel, you know I was there with you when we sang praises over the creation of earth and wept when Lucifer fell. As a prayer angel, I poured my energy into interceding for terrible situations, just as I was directed, and many times I felt my insights actually helped." She turned and pointed at the image of Lydia sobbing in distress, with no one to comfort her. "But this is already wearing me down. Earth is just one sad story of suffering after another, except now I'm seeing it firsthand. Do we really make any difference?"

"Sophia."

It was not Gabriel who spoke, or his light that suddenly surrounded them. The mixture of rebuke and tenderness in this voice drove Sophia to her knees. Shaking with both terror and awe, she bowed her head and begged for forgiveness, understanding instantly that she was in the presence of the Almighty Divine. At her side, Gabriel sang a mellow song of adoration, clearly more comfortable than she.

The light burned brighter, boring into the core of her spirit with a whispering noise that sounded like the word "submit, submit, submit." She felt a melting warmth fill her being and went limp with total surrender. It was then that the light disappeared as suddenly as it had appeared.

"That was amazing," she said, lifting her head to look up at Gabriel when her strength returned. "I feel…so blessed, and so forgiven."

He smiled knowingly. "It is a miracle each time we are given His presence, but you should understand now that whether you feel capable or not and whether you like it or not, for the time being, you are to be the Senior Servant."

She did know. Questioning her appointment further would be the angelic equivalent of a mortal sin. Clenching her fists, she stood up as straight as possible, which still only brought her to the height of Gabriel's waist.

"From now on, everything I do is going to be focused on showing the Almighty Divine how much I love Him and want to serve. I'm even going to forget about my aspirations of being promoted to the Second Level," she declared.

Gabriel laughed. "Noble intentions, Sophia, and I've no doubt you'll accomplish the first. As for the second...I can't imagine you setting aside your longing for the Second Level. It's actually rather endearing."

Or frightening, she almost said out loud. *Committing myself to the First Level is keeping me closer to Lucifer than I prefer.*

14

R uth stirred, distracting her and Gabriel from the blissful reverie that remained after the Almighty Divine's appearance. Sophia looked at him, wondering if he would leave too, but he shook his head.

"No, we have important business to discuss. I have to stay, and I want Ruth to hear about this. She needs to know what's about to happen."

Sophia suspected Miriam and Faras would be upset when they discovered Ruth was permitted to be part of Sophia's meeting with Gabriel while they were not. She couldn't help laughing to herself. She was overflowing with dedication and determination, yet questions were already on the tip of her tongue. How much she still had to learn about obedience—and yet it was strangely exciting to think she could do so.

Sophia went over and brushed a tiny ebony curl back from Ruth's forehead. The woman's dark eyes fluttered open and fixed first on Sophia and then on Gabriel.

"W-who are you?" she whispered, her mouth resting in open position and her body tense.

"I am the archangel Gabriel, sent to speak with you and Sophia about the reason you have been allowed to come to the First Level."

Ruth scrambled out of the recliner and fell to her knees in front of him, burying her face in her hands and visibly shaking.

"No." Gabriel's voice was stern as he drew her to her feet. "Angels are not to be worshipped. We exist to serve the Almighty Divine, the only One worthy of praise from both mortals and angels."

Sophia put an arm around Ruth's still-trembling shoulders. "It's easy to be intimidated by Gabriel when you've never seen an archangel before, but he is our messenger, bringing directives to us from the Almighty Divine, just as he is sometimes sent to earth with important news."

"Come." He beckoned for them to join him at the screen, returning to the story of Lydia. "Sophia, please tell Ruth what you know about the Testings of Devotion, and what has happened to Lydia until this point."

As concisely as possible, Sophia gave Ruth an overview of the spiritual warfare waging on earth and Lucifer's rationale for wanting to destroy mortals. Then she proceeded to outline the rationale behind the Testings of Devotion and ended by explaining that Gabriel was sharing scenes from the events of Lydia's life as an example of the Testings of Devotion.

Gabriel took over when Sophia brought Ruth up to date, and proceeded forward in the story. By the time Lydia's daughters became teenagers, she had married a good man who provided both financial and emotional comfort to the fractured family. For a few years, there was peace in her life.

"Despite all the difficult times she had passed through, Lydia continued in her faith much as before, attending church but giving little more than an hour on Sunday mornings to the Almighty Divine," Gabriel said, studying an image of Lydia and her family leaving a red-bricked church with tall stained glass windows. "In fact, she held on to some anger, believing He was the one who somehow brought all the hardships into her life. Of course, she couldn't know the many ways she had been protected, or that we intervened to bring her new husband into her life and help her get a well-paying job she wasn't really qualified for.

"She thought the Almighty Divine had been punishing her for some unknown sin. Her new husband, however, was a believer who insisted they attend church every week and go to their pastor for counseling."

Gabriel hesitated before advancing the scene, his face tender at the sight of the couple on their knees, praying for the health and happiness of their family. It was at moments like these that Sophia found him most mysterious, the expression on his face one of sorrow, but his body braced as if for battle.

"Unfortunately," Gabriel said," Lucifer was instantly on the alert, and already planning new ways to try to destroy Lydia."

The three of them saw the touching scene of Lydia and her husband fade away, replaced by an image with a totally different feel. Lydia's older daughter was in a dusty room with a cracked window and little more than trash covering the floor. In one hand, she held a syringe with an expert grip, probing to find a vein that wasn't scarred and collapsed like the other telltale tracks up and down her arm. Her teeth were clamped on the end

of a worn jute belt that served as her makeshift tourniquet. As sh[...]
into unconsciousness, she murmured, "Mama.'"

Gabriel cleared his throat and said simply: "This is the overdose that will kill her."

The girl moaned in pleasure, then slumped down on the dirty floor. Her breathing grew ragged, as if she were trying to grab back onto life, but eventually it slowed and then ceased completely.

Gabriel went on as the pictures changed. "All the trauma took a toll on her younger sister, who developed a serious eating disorder that brought her close to death several times."

Now the angels and Ruth saw another girl who looked much like her older sister, curled over a toilet and trying to vomit up whatever food might be left in her concave stomach. After she was finished, she stumbled to the sink and splashed water on her face.

"I hate you," she said to her reflection in the mirror. "You were the one who should have died." There was no emotion whatsoever in her voice, and the look in her eyes was empty.

"Trisha?" From outside the locked bathroom door, Lydia called to her daughter. "Trisha, hon, please come out and talk to me."

Ruth, Sophia, and Gabriel could see Lydia leaning against her husband as if drained of energy.

"Lydee," he said softly, "She's got to go inpatient again."

Gabriel broke in to explain that the girl still lived with Lydia and her stepfather, who didn't understand the special power of anorexia or drugs over young people. Although it was old news to Sophia, Gabriel told Ruth that in the beginning of time, Lucifer had worked diligently to discover how he might take control of humans and win them away from the Almighty Divine. Azazel was the one who suggested a substance that would take away their free will, and thus alcohol addiction began.

"From then on it was easy to progress to the other addictions: sex, gambling, eating—anything that a mortal desires more than the Almighty Divine will work," Gabriel explained, although the vigorous nodding of her head suggested that Ruth understood all too well what he was talking about.

Sophia turned to Ruth. "That's what Miriam and Faras meant earlier.

People like Lydia's daughters haven't disavowed their faith, but they both allowed something else to come between the Almighty Divine and them. Lucifer considers that a win."

Ruth nodded. "Believe me, I get it. Just like JoJo, they need to surrender the importance of food or drugs in their lives and make serving the Almighty Divine their priority."

Surprised by the astute insight, Sophia looked up at Gabriel, but he was watching the screen. It occurred to her that, as a mortal, Ruth might understand the Testings of Devotion better than any angel. Hadn't she gone through plenty of trials herself?

Gabriel continued: "What matters most is how Lydia responded to this time of crisis. For her, it became a time of great change. She drew closer to the Almighty Divine because another mother included her in a prayer group. The pastor of her church had once struggled with drug addiction, and his story helped her realize the challenges that her older daughter faced were Lucifer's work. Both she and her husband began to pray more and learn more. Their faith grew.

"Lydia created a foundation for parents like herself and now touches many lives every day through public speaking and outreach on the Internet. We keep her surrounded by angels, because although she addresses a secular audience, she always manages to mention the Almighty Divine as her way of survival."

"A soft evangelist," Sophia murmured, watching Lydia speaking passionately to the American Congress.

"Soft, but powerful. She's considering running for political office—nothing high level, but significant enough to expand her sphere of influence. If there were many like this woman, they could create a serious grassroots resistance to Lucifer and his demons."

"So you want to cultivate a modern-day group of Jobs, right?" Ruth piped up.

Sophia bit back words of rebuke. As a newcomer and a mortal, it didn't seem right for Ruth to add commentary to Gabriel's words. Miriam and Faras certainly weren't going to be eager to collaborate with her if she took the same attitude with them.

Gabriel, however, seemed amused by Ruth's comment. "Yes, in many ways, you're right, Ruth, and you don't even know what happened after Job's sufferings, since the best part of his story isn't known among mortals. Your Sacred Writings don't describe how he became even stronger and more devoted as a consequence of his testing and used the riches he was given to help other families going through the same difficulties he had. Job didn't become a king or a great leader, but in his own way he defeated Lucifer on several levels—with the help of the Almighty Divine, of course. That's why we're helping Lydia prosper spiritually, so she can spread the news of the Almighty Divine's constant love, even in the face of suffering."

A sudden blaze of red lights on the globe and a persistent beeping alarm drew their attention to the Earth Viewer. Sophia rushed over and tapped it; a scene on a tropical beach replaced the picture of Lydia.

"Mommy, look!" A small girl was saying, pointing her shovel at the tide, which had receded to expose a great expanse of the ocean floor. Further out, a tall wall of water was gathering strength as it charged toward the land.

Her mother, stretched on a lounge chair with her face tipped toward the sun, waved off her daughter's observation until an angel swooped down and whispered in her ear: "Grab your daughter and run!" Puzzled, the woman looked around for the source of the voice, then leaned up on her elbows, glanced out at the tide, and screamed.

"Look out!" she shouted to the other sunbathers as she scooped up her child and sprinted inland, leaving her belongings behind.

Sophia and Gabriel saw angels everywhere, whisking small children to safe places, subtly guiding adults to higher ground, and pushing against the force of the wave itself, only able to slightly slow its progress and intensity.

"Mortals have wrought so much destruction to the earth's environment that Lucifer can now use all kinds of natural disasters to bring despair and suffering." Gabriel's expression was angry as they watched the tsunami descend in an explosion of water that blew apart houses and buildings with one enormous crash. "Hard to believe it was once a perfect world."

Sophia turned from the screen as Gabriel flew away from them, advising Sophia to summon the entire heavenly host for prayer. His final words were, "We can continue our other discussion about the Testings of Devotion later."

Leaving Ruth behind, she met Faras and Miriam in the hallway, hurrying toward her with shocked looks on their faces.

"I just saw what happened—" Faras began, but Sophia cut him off.

"Tell Hector to gather the heavenly host. Now."

When the heavenly host was assembled outside Operations Central, Hector led them in a period of prayer song as intense as the disaster they just witnessed. In the Guidance Room, the Selected Servants and Sophia saw mortals instantly responding to the crisis. From poor to privileged, men and women mobilized, contributing manpower, food, health care, and money.

Gabriel was right. If there were more mortals like the ones they now watched organizing relief efforts, the battle between Lucifer and the Almighty Divine would be no contest at all.

Looking around, Sophia realized Ruth was missing.

"Do either of you know where Ruth is?" she asked.

Miriam and Faras halted their efforts, searched the room, then raised their eyebrows in unison at Sophia.

"No," Miriam said, turning back to the control panel and tapping several keys. "But we better find her. Even in the Community of Resting Mortals, newcomers need to be kept with others until they're stable, and Ruth is not, if you ask me."

"Maybe she went outside to join the singing," Faras said, leaning his head toward the front of Operations Central where the songs of the heavenly host could still be heard. Then he returned his attention to the screen in front of him.

"I agree we need to find her, but I can't leave. Gabriel may have instructions for me to act on here," Sophia said. "The two of you will have to go."

Miriam sighed loudly and slapped both hands on the console. "Honestly, why would she choose a time like this to go exploring? Faras, why don't you check outside and I'll search the rest of the building?"

As they went out the door, Faras hesitated and turned back for a moment. "Sophia, are you sure you'll be okay here?"

It went without saying that she was new too, and perhaps floundering as much if not more than Ruth. She shifted her shoulders back and lifted her chin. "Yes, yes, of course, I'll be fine. Now go quickly."

After they left she went to the podium, frowning as she looked down on the scenes of destruction and suffering. The small patch of civilization that had managed to survive as a vacation colony was not likely to recover from this tragedy. Homes that were substandard to begin with were now little more than splinters of wood. A small local clinic—the only source of health care in a sixty-mile radius—had collapsed on itself, and food from the tiny local market floated on the water along with garbage and a few domesticated animals struggling to stay afloat. Angels and mortals were in place, encouraging and strengthening rescue workers and comforting the brokenhearted with small blessings, but their interventions seemed miniscule in the face of such disaster.

Sophia studied the screen, noting how many children were either injured or separated from their parents, weeping in fear and pain and desolation. It wasn't her job to directly intervene in the lives of mortals, but she couldn't help leaning closer, her spirit stirring with grief. Checking to make sure the Selected Servants weren't within sight, she reached out her hand tentatively. The Almighty Divine would certainly want her to heal those she could, wouldn't He?

Swiftly, she touched the images of the children before her, beginning with the youngest ones who stood alone. To each, she sent comfort that flowed from the deepest part of her being.

"Bless you," she whispered, knowing that each time her finger rested on one of their pictures, a small miracle would occur.

She had only reached out to a dozen children when a sickening heaviness overwhelmed her. Not knowing why, she persevered in her interventions, leaning against the podium until a great surge of energy knocked her away from it so violently, she fell to the floor.

The Voice was laughing with a mirth that vibrated through the room, gaining intensity until she thought she would be broken by its unspoken accusation. There was nothing to say—she had betrayed Gabriel and now intervened in areas that were not under her providence. In her weakness, she couldn't even cry out for help.

"Sophia!"

Faras and Miriam rushed in, the concern in their voices overpowering the sound of the Voice's obscene laughter.

"Please…pray," she gasped.

"Which prayers?" Faras, ever the pragmatist, asked.

Sophia felt completely paralyzed as she realized how seriously she'd transgressed. Hadn't she cautioned Ruth against focusing on her own wishes rather than those of the Almighty Divine?

There was a good reason for angels to attend to only the duties they had been assigned during their orientation to the First Level long ago. The task they were given was theirs to carry out completely and unquestioningly, and if anyone chose to take on other responsibilities, it would undermine the ability of the heavenly host to work together in helping mortals. They might well end up in a state of near chaos, just like Lucifer and his followers.

Crumbled on the floor with the cool white marble pressed against her cheek, she knew the right thing to do would be to confess immediately to Miriam and Faras and then ask Gabriel and the Almighty Divine for forgiveness. Instead, Sophia heard herself request a prayer song for strengthening. The two Selected Servants instantly joined their voices in a moving entreaty.

No sooner had they finished when Gabriel's voice spoke to all three of them: "Salvation through submission, Sophia. Submission."

"What does that mean?" Miriam's eyes searched the room for the archangel, her forehead wrinkled. Faras, equally baffled, helped Sophia to her feet.

"Submission," he said. "Who doesn't know that?"

Sophia leaned on him until the ache of her body slowly receded. Gabriel was right. She needed to humble herself rather than try to justify what had just happened, but now the opportunity had passed and there were more pressing problems to deal with.

"Are you sure you're okay?" Faras looked at her with concern.

"I'm fine." Forcing herself to concentrate, she thought about the disaster. "Did you find Ruth?"

"No," Faras said, rubbing his forehead. "I can't imagine where she would be."

"We did speak with Hector," Miriam offered.

"Tell me what's happening."

For the time being, Ruth was forgotten as they reported that many angels were volunteering to return to earth so they could assist mortals, even offering to assume human appearances if needed. It was no small thing to give up their angelic form, even temporarily, but this crisis was of epic proportion.

"Perhaps it isn't wise to allow a large contingent of the heavenly host to leave right now. I'm not sure I should even relay that offer to Gabriel. What do the two of you think?" Sophia couldn't reveal all of her thoughts to the two Selected Servants; with the heavenly host's ranks at an all time low, could they afford to risk such an intervention? It would be just like Lucifer to figure out their numbers were down, creating an ideal opportunity for him to try to storm the First Level. She had a suspicion she knew whom he would look to capture first.

"Maybe we should consult Hector," Miriam said.

"Just the thing," agreed Faras.

Hector answered their summons promptly, his normally jolly expression sober. He was as short as Sophia, with a smooth bald head and brilliant blue eyes, moving and speaking with an easy manner that made him much loved by the heavenly host.

After Faras explained their dilemma, Sophia said, "Ultimately, it will be the Almighty Divine's decision, but your input would be valuable. Knowing that any angel will be more vulnerable to the temptations of Lucifer the second they leave us, I feel uncomfortable sending so many—it could even be a trap. Do you remember when New York City was devastated by the terrorist attack a few generations ago? Gabriel told me the angels who went to earth to help were very demoralized."

They all nodded. More than a few angels had strayed then, either because they were overcome by the sadness of the situation, or because they were somehow persuaded by Lucifer and his followers that mortals deserved such punishment.

"I agree," Miriam said. "I want to see more angels help increase the good, but we can accomplish that in other ways and allow those already there to continue with their regular jobs. Still, it's very generous—I don't think we've ever had such a large number willing to go back." She shuddered. "I'm not in the least tempted to volunteer."

Hector was silent after they spoke, studying the many scenes of rav-
aged homes scrolling across the screen in the Guidance Room. Even when
he wasn't directly interacting with others, his compassion and openness
were palpable. Now, his hands clutched each other in a gesture of frustration as he took in the details.

"Every part of me wants to keep the angels here where they're safe, but
this situation is more than I can handle." He looked at Sophia, the blue of
his eyes dark. "I think we will have to rely on divine guidance, which is
where you come in."

15

When all three of them looked at her expectantly, Sophia allowed her eyes to drift shut and she sank to her knees, not caring how they reacted. Most likely Isaac had been a more theatrical Senior Servant, giving long talks of reassurance and acknowledging the difficulty of their mission, but she had just learned the consequences of trying to do things that weren't her talent.

After an extended period of silent prayer, the directions she sought pieced together in her mind, almost as if they were written on a scroll and delivered directly from the Almighty Divine. When she opened her eyes, Miriam, Faras, and Hector leaned forward eagerly.

"What should we do?" Hector asked.

She said: "You must tell the heavenly host to stay here, and for the time being, continue with their prayersongs. Miriam and Faras, please find Ruth."

The three of them departed, discussing her directions in low voices. The tenor of their conversation was heavy with disappointment, which was understandable, given their desire to do something dramatic to help the mortals. Ruth must have just missed them, because no sooner had they left than she entered, glowing with happiness. The difference between her and the grieving members of the heavenly host was jarring

"Where have you been?" Sophia asked. "We've been looking everywhere for you because we were so worried."

"This is incredible! I've never felt this good in my life," Ruth laughed, brushing the question aside as she danced around the room.

"We need to go find Miriam and Faras—I just sent them to find you. What have you been doing?"

"I went back to try to find that Portal, but just like you said, it wasn't there anymore. Still, I laid down under one of those beautiful trees with the fancy flowers and fell sound asleep again. Didn't think I was so tired, but there you have it."

"You were sleeping all this time?"

"Yes, but I had the most incredible dreams. I saw everything happening to my kids back on earth. I saw JoJo in prison, and Tamika, my oldest daughter, with her three kids." Ruth shook her head in disbelief. "She's jobless and husbandless again, and Leidel, the next to youngest, is back on drugs. So many problems." Ruth's eyes filled with tears momentarily, but then she seized Sophia's hands. "And then I realized I can help them! I can change their lives from here, and they can be just like those candidates Gabriel described, ready to fight for the Almighty Divine. They're good kids underneath it all. You have to talk to him about this."

Miriam and Faras walked in just as a flabbergasted Sophia was trying to frame her response to Ruth's request. How different the mortal mindset was from that of angels!

"Ruth came in just as you left," Sophia said, grateful for the distraction. She asked them for any other updates they might have heard from Hector on the tsunami crisis, and as Miriam and Faras filled her in, Ruth, overwhelmed, turned to focus on the Earth Viewer for the first time since returning to the room. Horrified, she began to pepper them with questions about why an "Almighty Divine" would allow such a terrible thing to happen.

"Just like that woman Gabriel showed us, remember?" She turned to Sophia. "Poor Lydia. She didn't do anything wrong either!"

Miriam froze in place, staring at Ruth with a look much like jealousy. "You were alone with Gabriel? How can that happen?"

"It was purely a matter of circumstance. She was refreshing here while you two were in your chambers, if you remember, and Gabriel came to check on her. Ruth woke up just as we started discussing the project all of us will be working on next. As soon as we stabilize the situation on earth, we'll all discuss it."

Miriam's face stayed openly sullen. Before becoming a Selected Servant, she had been an adoration angel, devoting herself to full time worship and praise of the Almighty Divine. In many ways, Sophia found these angels to be the happiest of all, since their attention was always directed upward toward the Almighty Divine, rather than downward toward the spiritual warfare on earth.

It was Miriam's ability to constantly adore the Almighty Divine that had led to her being appointed as the Selected Servant who increased the presence of good on earth, planting angels in certain situations where they were most needed and stirring the spirit of holiness within mortals so they would turn toward the way of faith. Gabriel had told Sophia that, initially, Miriam was humbled to be chosen for such a position.

Something changed, though. Just as Sophia found herself struggling with doubt in unguarded moments, already she had seen a fleeting expression on Miriam's face that suggested she longed for something different. Perhaps she wanted to return to her time of continuous praise and worship, or maybe she coveted the position of Senior Servant.

Faras sat down, his expression troubled but not affronted by news of Ruth's special treatment. Before he came to Operations Central, he was an earth angel, the most difficult of all angelic jobs. He roamed earth under divine direction, "putting out fires" and "delivering messages," as Gabriel described it. Assuming mortal form quickly drained the spirits of angels, and their capabilities were limited while on Earth, so those who functioned as earth angels could only make short visits, punctuated by long periods of refreshing.

"It's dangerous to be anywhere in the kingdom of Lucifer," Gabriel had said. "You're under direct assault from demons, subject to discouragement over the state of mortals, and worst of all, battling the confines of the corporal body you're forced to take on."

Faras lasted longer than most earth angels, but Gabriel said he had been grateful to return to the First Level on a more permanent basis. His appointment as the Selected Servant in charge of reducing evil in any situation was no doubt a kind of reward, but given his longstanding tenure in the position, it would be logical for him, like Miriam, to question why Sophia and Ruth appeared to be receiving preferential treatment.

Facing the two angels she should trust most, Sophia instructed them to proceed with the plan she had outlined to keep those angels on the First Level in place, but to shift their efforts to focus on the tsunami victims for a short time. Hector could also temporarily divert as many earth angels as possible to help. She held up one hand to stifle their protests and went to her chamber.

Kneeling next to the recliner, she lifted up her spirit to the Almighty Divine, asking for correction if her inclinations were misguided. When no response came, she finished with a prayer of thanking the Almighty Divine for being given the chance to lead the heavenly host in helping mortals as Senior Servant, rose to her feet, and returned to the Guidance Room to inform Miriam and Faras of the plan. They went to work instantly, while Sophia indicated that Ruth should sit on one of the recliners and observe.

"Don't forget what we talked about," she whispered to Sophia before obeying.

When the worst of the catastrophe had been settled, Miriam and Faras sighed and gave each other a tired hug.

"Bless the Almighty Divine. I believe we've done our best and helped many," Faras said, then inclined his head toward Sophia. "It was a good plan."

"Do you have the strength to discuss our new project?" she asked, wondering how to graciously inform them that Ruth, a newcomer and a mortal, would be part of a special mission that required all of them to work together? Before anything more could be said, Ruth did the worst thing possible.

"It's like this," she told Miriam and Faras. "Gabriel and the others have come up with a new strategy, and I'm the one who's going to be in charge of it."

"Excuse me?" Miriam said, her back stiffening.

Sophia broke in quickly, silencing Ruth with a warning look. "It's not quite that simple, but since Ruth is new, it might seem that way. Please, come and sit down." She motioned toward the empty recliners and blanked the screen of the Earth Viewer so they wouldn't be distracted by continuing scenes of the tsunami. Once they had all settled in, she came to stand in front of them and smiled enthusiastically.

"Do you remember when the position of director was created and Hector was appointed to work more closely with the heavenly host?" She addressed the two Selected Servants, who nodded reluctantly. "Gabriel told me you thought that meant you had somehow disappointed the Almighty Divine, but that wasn't the case at all. It was just a new approach." She checked their faces and saw they weren't convinced. "Given the status of earth, the Almighty Divine has consulted with the Council of the Elect and come up with a new plan. Even if we all tried our hardest, we could never have come up with such a wise and holy idea." She lifted her eyes upward in both appreciation and supplication. "Praise be to our beloved Almighty Divine who constantly intervenes on the behalf of both mortals and ourselves."

She didn't need the Voice to remind her that she was hardly a perfect role model, but that wasn't what was important now. Her first remarks were directed at Ruth.

"We all need to stay humble. Faras and Miriam have been here in Operations Central much longer than either of you or I, and without their help, we'll never succeed with the Testings of Devotion. I suggest we join in a prayer song of penitence before we go any further, so you and I in particular can submit completely to what we are being asked to do."

She started the praise portion of the prayer song and the three of them joined in, reluctant at first, but then joy took over, uniting them in adoration and love. By the end, it was hard to stop, but they had business to address, so she signaled that they must. The process had the effect she hoped for. Both Miriam and Faras looked less tense and Ruth had moved to sit closer to them.

"I couldn't even carry a tune on Earth," she said. "Couldn't read music, either. I pitied the poor people who sat next to me in church, because that didn't stop me from singing loud and proud!"

"That will change here," Faras assured her. "Each time an angel joins in prayer song, he or she gets better at it. As Senior Servant, Sophia is, of course, the most accomplished."

"Yup. She has the voice of an angel," Ruth said, waiting to see if they would smile, which they did.

Maybe this will work after all, Sophia said to herself. *I must believe that, and trust Gabriel and the Almighty Divine to guide us, rather than relying on my abilities. I have a feeling Ruth will be sure to keep us on our toes.*

She returned to the point of previous conversation, now focusing on Miriam and Faras. "As I was saying, this is a time of great tribulation on earth."

"Is it the final tribulation?" Miriam asked.

"Quite honestly, I don't know," Sophia admitted. "But there's no doubt it's a time of enormous turmoil. Both mortals and angels are succumbing to Lucifer's efforts despite our best efforts to prevent it."

"You mean earth angels, I assume?" Faras asked.

"Lucifer knows how to tempt angels on the First Level too. He hasn't been able to breach the Portal, but his spirit preys on any angel or mortal he thinks is vulnerable."

Now was the opportune time to illustrate her point with a complete confession of what she had done, but then a more persuasive mindset took over and she held back. Only Gabriel could pass a judgment on her, after consulting with the Almighty Divine, so why bother the Selected Servants with one more problem? Anyway, her actions had helped several children—were they really so wrong?

Sophia went on with her presentation. "That brings us to Ruth and this new mission. It isn't an easy one, but then none of them are, really. She hasn't had a period of preparation and seasoning as you had, so she'll really need all of your support, and together we will succeed."

She didn't say that Ruth was also still subject to mortal failings, but the looks on Miriam's and Faras's faces suggested that's exactly what they were thinking.

"You're talking about a new and different strategy?" Faras sat forward. "I confess, I've been praying for that. Defeating Lucifer will take more than reassigning angels to different duties like we tried last time."

"Yes, but before I share the details, Gabriel wanted to make absolutely sure you both know that your skills are the only way to make this approach successful. You're both in high favor for your diligence and collaboration." She paused to give the compliment extra weight. "Ruth's assistance will be of a different nature. She was selected because she is mortal and understands what it's like to live on earth and face temptations. Her strengths will perfectly compliment both of yours."

"So, if we're in such high favor," Miriam protested, "why do we need her? It's not that I mind extra help, but we've never had a mortal on the First Level before."

"You *are* in high favor," Sophia reassured her. "But you have no idea what it's like to be a mortal. We all know Lucifer is advancing his kingdom on earth in new ways. These floods and hurricanes and earthquakes are just one example. Destroying parts of the earth creates continual havoc. But in addition, even with our constant interventions, mortals are turning away from the Almighty Divine in anger or despair. We're losing too many. That's why we need Ruth and the Testings of Devotion."

Her words led Miriam to take Ruth's hand and squeeze it in encouragement. Faras was clearly excited, pressing Sophia for details. In an attempt to illustrate the plan, Sophia provided a summary of Lydia's story. This time, Ruth didn't add any commentary.

"Lydia wasn't like those mortals who know from a young age that the only way to survive the hardships of earth is through with faith," Sophia concluded. "She had grown complacent, which is not to say she was evil or even a bad person, but had her sorrows not changed her focus to others rather than herself, her Life Review would look completely different. As it is, she has done great good with the great sorrows that came her way."

"But we're not allowed to take away mortals' freedom of choice," Miriam protested.

"I don't think that's what Sophia is talking about." Faras ticked off points on his fingers. "First, she's talking about helping certain mortals who have the potential to become stronger through adversity. Second, the candidates will be people Lucifer normally wouldn't focus on because they don't have a high profile. Third, they still have the potential to touch many lives. It's brilliant—a grassroots effort."

"You mean I'm going to be the Angel of Adversity?" Ruth deadpanned.

With a slight smile, Sophia countered: "Adversity is already a part of life on earth. You'll help mortals grow stronger because of it, and as they grow stronger, they will persuade others by example. It will be a slow but steady effort to build our spiritual forces on earth."

"Balancing the good and evil is going to be tough," Miriam said.

"Exactly. That's why you and Faras need to be with Ruth every step of the way, teaching her what you know, and making sure there's enough blessing and encouragement for the candidates to persevere."

"Yes, and I've got some candidates in mind already," Ruth said, straightening up in her seat and holding up her clenched fists with a small shake. "I think—"

"Gabriel will be giving me the names of the candidates," Sophia said with a warning look at Ruth.

Seeing Ruth's Life Review revealed all the strength of character that helped her persevere through adversity, but what had been an asset on earth could become a liability in heaven. Somehow, Ruth needed to let go of her single-minded desire to help her own family over others once and for all before the rest of them were too frustrated to work with her. With these thoughts, Sophia felt the long-awaited summons from Gabriel.

"Faras and Miriam, Ruth needs to continue with her orientation. I must meet with Gabriel, so this would be a good time."

"You mean she's not going with you?" Miriam sniped, then clapped her hand across her mouth. "That was uncalled for. Forgive me."

It was a tense moment. Sophia waited for other signs that the Testings of Devotion would be undermined by dissent within their ranks, but then Faras straightened slightly and lifted his chin.

"Whatever it takes, I'm committed to both the new strategy and Ruth," he said.

"Miriam?" Sophia asked.

"Of course. We must help mortals. I'll do whatever the Almighty Divine tells Gabriel to ask of me," she said, but with less conviction than Faras.

The two Selected Servants took Ruth to the Earth Viewer and began to share their wisdom with her. Not surprisingly, they hadn't gotten far when Ruth peppered them with questions, but at least they were questions focused on her role in the Testings of Devotion, and seemingly prompted by her desire to do a good job.

"Sophia, let us be silent together," Gabriel said by way of greeting when she rose to his Refreshing Room.

"How much I prefer meeting here than in the Guidance Room," she said.

On the First Level, it was easy to be reminded of the many difficulties of mortals and the constant threat of an assault from Lucifer, but in the Refreshing Room there was a sense of peace and safety. Lucifer would never find her there, and if he did, Gabriel was on hand to immediately come to her defense. Her feet rested on a floor of fleecy white that was both soft and solid, surrounded by a light brighter than any on the First Level. The air was sweet, and in the far distance she could hear the chorus of the adoration angels, which never ceased.

She knew this was the moment to confess her wrongdoing; in fact, Gabriel seemed to already be looking down on her with forgiveness and a trace of sorrow. Yet, as she stretched out on the welcoming blue chair, her reluctance took on a presence of its own.

Finally Gabriel spoke. "How did Miriam and Faras receive the news of Ruth's appointment and the Testings of Devotion?"

"They took it well, I think. They're committed to doing whatever it takes to overcome Lucifer. We all are." Her words sounded hollow in the holy space. "I was waiting for direction from you on how to handle the tsunami crisis. I wasn't sure what to do."

Did she sound defensive? It occurred to her that perhaps she could justify her direct interventions under the guise of uncertainty, but then Gabriel sighed and she knew he understood everything that had happened.

"As Senior Servant, you serve by guiding others. I felt you knew enough to develop a strategy for a situation that obviously required our efforts. We believed you and the others would function as you have been assigned."

Did she imagine a special emphasis on his last words? His expression was grave as he waited for her to say more, and when she looked away, she could feel him continuing to watch her. Still, Gabriel would never force her to confess, so when she didn't, he handed her two scrolls bound with gold string. She absorbed herself with unrolling the first, knowing that, at least for the moment, her transgression was being set aside.

The delicate paper contained descriptions of the first four mortals chosen as candidates for the Testings of Devotion. The information about each was factual but brief; when she looked up to ask for further explanation, he had vanished.

Stunned, Sophia called out, much as the children on the beach had cried for their mothers after the tsunami, but Gabriel didn't answer. He had never departed so abruptly or refused to answer questions, but of course, she had never held back important information from him. Guilt swelled inside her, but it was too late to do much about it.

Her dismay worsened when she opened the second scroll and read what it contained. How she wished Gabriel would come back and assure her this would all work out, but despite her eager searching for his presence, there was nothing. Without warning, she found herself gently deposited back in the Guidance Room.

"Sophia, is there a problem?" Miriam was staring at her.

"No, of course not," Sophia said, trying to compose herself as she rejoined them.   "No, of course not," the Voice mimicked, chuckling as she struggled to appear normal to the others. "There are no problems at all, Sophia. You're doing exactly what I want you to do."

16

Faras left his position at the Earth Viewer and came to stand next to Sophia. He touched her hand, and without thinking, she pulled away, still overwhelmed by the truth of the evil Voice's taunt.

He looked at his still-outstretched fingers and said, "Are you sure you're okay?"

"Sorry, I'm just distracted." She held up one of the scrolls and offered it to him. "Gabriel shared information with me about the mortals selected to be the candidates for the Testings of Devotion. Here's a description of the first three. Perhaps you could do the honor of reading it?"

As he unrolled it and looked it over, she ran her delicate fingers through her pale blonde hair, then rubbed her temples. She desperately longed to refresh, but there was too much to do.

"You might as well get comfortable," Faras suggested. He adjusted his robe and waited until the women had settled themselves into their seats.

Miriam was graceful, carefully sitting on the edge of her recliner and settling the folds of her robe around her before swinging her legs up and crossing her feet at the ankles. Ruth bounced into the third seat, stretching out her arms and moving this way and that to get comfortable. Sophia sank down into her place and curled up, holding the second scroll against her chest with both hands, and closed her eyes briefly. For a moment, she saw the look on Gabriel's face right before he left her, and she realized how disappointed he must be with her.

Faras began to read from the scroll. "Each mortal selected to be a candidate is unique, yet they have something important in common—an early and positive experience with the Almighty Divine that opened their lives to a possibility for more. Unfortunately, as adults their faith became a matter of convenience. Now, with the right plan, each will change and grow, gaining influence over people in different areas of the world."

He crossed over to stand near the Earth Viewer, which was still pulsing with red lights, and turned it in different directions until he found an area of greenish yellow, and pressed a button on the podium. An attractive young man wearing khaki pants and a blue denim shirt jumped to life on the screen.

"This is Anthony Davis." He paused to read from the scroll. "He's just beginning his career in politics on a very low level, but he is expected to do well in the future because he's a very gifted speaker with good connections. The law firm where he's an associate has a long history of launching politicians; he's the one they're grooming for bigger things. His family is comfortable financially because his wife's father was a banker who made many wise investments. They have two young sons."

The angels watched a profile of Anthony's life. He was a devoted father, coaching his older son's peewee soccer team, and attending church most Sundays with his family. Although he prayed with his children every night before bed, his life had fallen into a routine more focused on the rewards of earth than heaven: a new car, tailored suits, and expensive jewelry for his wife—who begged him for the gift of his time, instead.

Faras shook the scroll so that it rolled open onto the floor. "Anthony is just the kind of person we're looking for, not too well-known but with the potential to become a prominent spokesperson. With the right amount of testing, Gabriel believes he will have a gradual but growing influence on his colony. We don't want to see him achieve anything too high profile, though."

"Why not?" Ruth quizzed. "That seems like a sure way to win converts, to me."

"Any person with great power on earth is like a magnet for Lucifer," Miriam explained. "It's very hard for mortals to maintain their integrity with so many pressures from every side, especially those in the ministry and politics. A few have been able to do it, but many have not."

Faras went on. "Anthony has never failed at anything significant, so a life crisis of the magnitude the candidates will experience will be new to him."

Miriam and Sophia were looking at Anthony with soft eyes, but Ruth's expression was hard as she crossed her arms over her chest.

"I'll say," she harrumphed, shaking her head. "It's going to take a lot of work to refocus his priorities."

Sophia's forehead wrinkled as she turned to Ruth. "Ruth, it's our job to love every mortal equally and show compassion for all. This man is no less worthy of the Almighty Divine's blessings than you are."

Miriam nodded. "There is that of the Almighty Divine in every mortal, since they were created in His image. Some may hide it better than others, but Anthony's faith—such as it is—means no more or less than yours."

The three angels exchanged a glance, taken aback by Ruth's outburst. It crossed Sophia's mind that, up close, mortals were more challenging to love than from a distance. Did Faras and Miriam already realize this, or were they as surprised as she? Their expressions revealed nothing, but they both continued to study Ruth as if she were a puzzle still scattered in many pieces. If Sophia told them Ruth actually believes that her own children would be better picks as candidates for the Testings of Devotions than the ones chosen by the Almighty Divine, there would probably be open rebellion against her.

She touched the sleeve of Ruth's robe lightly. "It isn't our place to pass judgment on mortals, Ruth. We believe there is always good inside every person waiting to come out."

"Of course, you all would feel that way up here in your heavenly home. You're angels, which means you're perfect," Ruth said. "I'm sorry, but I still think I'm partially right. Some folks are just a waste of your time and energy. They get everything they could want and they still don't feel any gratitude or obligation to help others." She looked unapologetically at the others. "I think I understand why the Almighty Divine wanted me or someone like me to come here just to prove how narrow-minded we mortals can be, even when we're well-intentioned. Men like Anthony did me or my kids wrong all the time without even realizing it. No wonder it's impossible to earn your way into heaven."

Miriam looked ready to agree, but Faras intervened before she could. "Ruth, you're comparing apples and oranges—isn't that the human saying? Mortals and angels are different, but neither is better than the other, according to the Almighty Divine."

Sophia leaned her head back and closed her eyes for a second, sifting through what had just happened. Were the Testings of Devotion about angels rather than mortals? So far, the biggest challenge was to see if they could really continue loving human beings up close and in person. Opening her eyes and squinting slightly at Ruth, she thought of how faithful and good this woman had been during her time on earth. Yet here on the First Level, her fixation with JoJo and the rest of her family made her seem stubborn and self-centered.

There was an uncomfortable silence, then Faras cleared his throat. "Shall I go on?"

"Yes, please," Miriam and Sophia said in unison.

He swallowed hard, rereading the scroll to make sure he hadn't missed anything, then Anthony's grinning face faded from the screen, replaced by the slight figure of a young woman with straight dark hair that curved in to frame her oval face and a perfect bow mouth that rested in a half smile. As they watched, she flipped through pages of a thick textbook, tapping information into a paper-thin laptop computer every now and then.

"Kim Lee is a senior at the University of Eastern Asia, studying nuclear engineering. She was especially selected for this highly competitive program and has done well throughout her four years in school. She's just about to take her final exams and begin a career with a top secret agency for the Eastern Asian states. She was exposed to the Almighty Divine as a child when a group of Christian missionaries came to teach at the small rural school she attended. Despite the disapproval of her parents, Kim was baptized and took an active part in the life of the church the missionaries started. In fact, the same people who introduced her to faith were instrumental in helping her qualify for the position at the university. Once she got there, however, things changed. Her religious values became a liability, so she drifted away from them, especially when she began dating a young man who is an avowed atheist."

Faras shook his head in regret and flipped to the next candidate. A rough-looking fellow appeared on the screen sitting with a group of friends in a smoke-filled café. His hair was unruly and his face unshaven as he grabbed a bottle of vodka and tipped it to his lips, then passed it to the man on his left.

"This is Gustaf Chernoff, who lives in the Central Asia states. His family used to attend the Russian Orthodox Church, until it was outlawed. Interestingly, in his youth, Gustaf was so serious and passionate about his faith that he thought about becoming a monk."

Gustaf had one arm loosely draped around a girl who much younger than he; a cigarette dangled from his hand, dangerously close to her long blonde hair. In between sips of vodka, he used his other hand to gesture as he spoke, clearly in charge of the conversation.

Faras consulted the scroll before going on. "Oh dear. After his parents were killed in the realignment of the Central Asia states, Gustaf became bitter and frustrated and joined the government police. He works as an undercover officer and has been quite successful in preventing violent outbreaks like the ones that took place during his youth, but increasingly, he has been attracted to a radical faction of his colleagues who favor an attack on the nearby states that used to be part of their union."

As the angels studied Gustaf, Ruth made a loud "tsk," then covered her mouth with her hand and gave a muffled apology. Faras seemed not to notice, rerolling the scroll and tapping it against his hand restlessly as Miriam stared pointedly at the other unopened one, which now rested on Sophia's lap. Before anyone could speak, Ruth grimaced and gave a long sigh of discontent.

"I'm not sure how I'm supposed to transform these folks into leaders for the Lord. I confess I don't really see a lot to work with here. I think my kids have more potential to advance the faith than these folks. I'm feeling like you all are going to have to take the lead on these testings." Sophia gave her a stern look and Ruth dropped the subject.

"Ruth, the Almighty Divine chose you out of all those who volunteered because he knows you understand better than most what it's like to struggle with your faith while confronted with mortal challenges. *How* the three of you succeed will require a joint effort, " Sophia said, rising with her back to the screen before the Miriam and Faras could say more.

Ruth shook her head slightly, pressing her lips together. The fingers of her hands were pushing down on the sides of the recliner, and her feet crossed and uncrossed restlessly.

She's afraid, Sophia realized, and her spirit softened. It would be terrifying to come here and have so many expectations placed on you as the first mortal, in addition to whatever hopes Ruth had for making a difference. She came back and knelt at her side.

"I know this must be a bit scary for you," she said, stunned when Ruth burst into tears and threw herself at Sophia, sobbing.

"It was a terrible mistake to volunteer to come here," she said, weeping. "How could I think I would have any ability to help angels when my motivation was so small-minded?"

While Sophia held her, Miriam came over and patted her shoulder, making soothing noises. "It will be okay, Ruth. Really."

Eventually, Ruth wiped her eyes dry with the sleeve of her robe and hugged Sophia and Miriam. When the two of them stood up, they looked at each other in amazement. Neither of them had witnessed anything like Ruth's outburst before.

Faras, more seasoned, was less moved.

"I thought there were four candidates?" he said, checking his scroll. "I don't have any information on the last one here."

Sophia cleared her throat and extended her hand toward his recliner, indicating that he should sit down. She got back up and went over to the podium, slowly unrolling the second scroll and scanning it briefly even though she was already aware of its contents.

"The fourth person is controversial, so I wanted to prepare you. As you saw, the first three candidates haven't really confronted great failures or unusual challenges, even though their lives are hardly what we would like them to be right now."

"So the last candidate is different?" Miriam asked, squinting at the Earth Viewer as if it contained a hidden message.

"Yes," Sophia said, "he is. His life has been marked with failure in recent years, but there's still potential."

She lifted one hand toward the screen, knowing that behind her JoJo's face would appear.

17

Miriam jumped out of her recliner, put her hands on her hips, and lowered her chin. Her face was frozen with fury.

"That's not right. This will just keep Ruth pining after her son. You just saw how emotional she is."

"You know the Almighty Divine's forgiveness knows no limits, but in this case one of the basic commandments has been broken," Faras added. His expression was grim as he turned toward Ruth. " 'Honor thy father and mother.' Look what he did to Ruth. The others might not be saints, but they're not murderers."

"Gabriel must have misread this one. You need to go back and confer with him and get things straight." Miriam took a step toward Sophia, reaching for the second scroll.

"There's no mistake," Sophia said, holding it behind her back. "Gabriel knew JoJo might cause dissent, but he was clear on the selection."

"Here's the problem, Sophia," Faras said, "I've been on earth as an angel. It's going to be tough enough to intervene in the lives of people who haven't already broken the commandments in a big way, let alone for some-one like JoJo, who has committed a universal sin. There's no religion on earth that sanctions killing the only mother you've known. I can't imagine what the Almighty Divine could be thinking. It's a terrible message to send: sin and you can still be one of the chosen ones."

"Faras, that's already the case. All mortals sin, and all can be forgiven," Sophia said gently. "May I remind you that it's not our place to question? We are asked only to submit and obey with joy."

Even as she spoke, an image of herself breaking that very rule with a simple touch of the Earth Viewer screen seemed to blaze in the air in front of her, but she reasoned it away. Hers wasn't really the same kind of sin mortals committed, since her intentions had arisen out of compassion.

Ruth held up one hand, as if asking permission to speak. "Excuse me, but you all don't get it. JoJo's a good boy underneath—that's why the

Almighty Divine chose him. He *can* turn his life around. He doesn't have any priors, and if his lawyer can just show he wasn't in his right mind when he…when he pushed me, maybe he can get off."

"He *murdered* you," Faras said, glowering at Ruth. "I for one have a hard time elevating a murderer to a position of glory. Forgiveness is one thing, but rewarding his behavior is another. You forget that I spent time on earth. He's part of the drug crowd that is one of Lucifer's strongest weapons against mortals. Most of them are probably Nephilim, determined to destroy each other, as well as any men, women, and even children they can throw into the mix."

Ruth stood up, her hands clenched and planted on her hips. "My boy is no monster."

Sophia crossed over to stand between them, ready to intervene, but Faras shrugged. "It doesn't matter anyway. It would take one of us going down to earth to save him, and believe me, that angel won't be me."

So much for angels not experiencing mortal emotions. Faras's reaction was like a hard blow to the tender area where Sophia's human heart would be if she had one. She winced when Ruth made a small sound of distress and ran to a far corner of the room, turning her back to them and leaning against the wall.

Miriam crossed over to stand next to Faras, clearly as angry as he was. The silence stretched out until Sophia felt her spirit was calm enough to address them. "Fine. Faras, you and Miriam can work with Ruth to develop the others. I'll be responsible for JoJo."

Giving Faras and Miriam a look of defiance, she moved closer to Ruth, thinking that in some small way, this could be her penance for the secret "sort-of" transgression she'd committed with the children devastated by the tsunami. Anyway, she tended to agree with Ruth: thanks to her, JoJo seemed to have the strongest grounding in faith of any candidate.

Trying to deflect the energy in the room, which was still as sharp and dangerous as the furious red lights on the globe in front of them, Sophia made another appeal for them all to rethink the situation and find a way to work together. If Gabriel were there, she would have asked him how she could possibly deal with so much dissent from within her own circle of helpers.

Faras wasn't interested in reconciliation. "This is too much. I need to refresh before we go any further." He looked at Miriam. "I don't know about you, but it was hard to face those angels who just volunteered to descend to help with the tsunami catastrophe and tell them that, instead of going down to earth, they could help by praying more. Now we hear about a mortal who is a known murderer being chosen as a candidate for this new project."

"I agree," Miriam said, sweeping out of the room.

Gabriel said it was rare but not unheard of for the Selected Servants to refresh separately, but never were they to do so without Sophia's permission. Faras hesitated, looked at Sophia, and then followed Miriam out the door. So much for precedent.

Sophia rolled the scroll back up and tied the gold thread around it, pacing back and forth in front of the podium. The Earth Viewer continued its slow spin, and Ruth busied herself examining her fingernails and fluffing up her curls.

"Was that my fault?" she finally asked in a small voice. "I thought angels all got along."

"We do. This is the first time I've ever had a disagreement like this with another angel. We debate different points of view sometimes, but never to the point of anger."

"I'm sorry. Maybe my idea about JoJo and my other kids wasn't such a good one after all."

Sophia didn't have the energy to explain that Ruth's wishes weren't the real cause of Miriam and Faras's upset. This angel-mortal experiment wasn't going very well, in her opinion, because the two groups were at cross purposes. Angels wanted to help mortals, but it was beginning to seem as if mortals were fixated on themselves. Wearily, she sank down into a recliner.

"You know, I think you and I could refresh too," she said.

It took some effort to push the aftershock of what had just happened out of her mind, but eventually she drifted into a lovely state of relaxation, wondering if she needed to take a lot more time for them all to refresh. Maybe she was rushing things and not allowing enough opportunity for them to recharge. During her orientation, Gabriel had warned her about that very thing.

In fact, that was probably why she intervened with those children when she wasn't supposed to. Her guard had been lowered and she gave into temptation. Anyway, what she had done now seemed like a mild misstep in comparison with Miriam and Faras's open defiance.

I'm going to put this all behind me, take more time to refresh, and get back to my regular routine of personal prayer, she decided in her last moments of consciousness. Gabriel and the Almighty Divine will forgive me, and then, when we successfully complete the Testings of Devotion, it will all be forgotten.

She awoke from her rest to find Faras kneeling in front of her.

"Sophia, I'm ashamed of how I acted just now. Please forgive me," he said, looking toward Ruth, who was still in deep repose. "I've hurt both of you and I didn't mean to. Should I offer prayers of penitence?"

"No," she replied, beckoning to Miriam, who was standing just inside the doorway. "Please, come join us. If Gabriel were here, I would ask him for a prayer of exorcism, because only Lucifer could be the cause of such a division between us. I know Isaac was a different kind of Senior Servant, so maybe this is my fault, but whatever the reason, we must not be divided, or doubtful of the One we serve."

At first, Miriam seemed ready to stay where she was, but then her face changed. She came over, fell to her knees, and bowed her head to Sophia and Faras.

"I'm sorry too. The Testings of Devotion are about expanding the kingdom of God on the earth, not about me, or Faras, or Ruth. It was selfish of me to be upset."

"We need to pray before we go any further," Sophia told them. "There has to be total agreement about this or we will fail. Our unity is what gives us strength."

"But she's so...mortal," Miriam said, wrinkling her nose at Ruth. "How will we ever be unified with her? That outburst was too much! If I have to settle her down all the time, I won't be able to concentrate on the testings."

"Try harder. Faras can help both of us understand mortals," Sophia said.

He cleared his throat. "I don't know about that. I've observed a lot, but understand? Can't say I do."

"Well whatever the case, we must work as a team. This effort cannot fail." Sophia touched Ruth's arm lightly to wake her and then the four of them stood, joined hands, and sang a long prayer—part song and part spoken petition.

When they finished, Faras was recharged and energetic, wanting to discuss the details of the plan to transform JoJo first. Miriam had settled down and had her hands folded together as she waited to brainstorm with the others. Ruth was once more cheerful and funny, making a performance out of settling herself on the recliner and arranging her robe.

"I have to clean up my act and start looking angelic, now that I'm an 'official' part of the God Squad," she explained.

Sophia went to the Earth Viewer and switched it to real time. Their moods quickly turned somber as they studied JoJo lying on his bunk in his jail cell, the look on his face inscrutable. He had lost weight but built muscle and had several homemade tattoos decorating his arms, neck, and calves. One across his chest said: "Trouble," and another, "Ruth 17: 'Where you die, I will die.' "

They watched JoJo's cellmate lift one wiry arm out and up from the bunk below, slowly exploring until his fingers curled around and stroked JoJo's exposed thigh. In an instant, the scenario changed.

"Faggot!" JoJo screamed, flying off his bed.

Yanking the man onto the floor, he pummeled him mercilessly until all his victim could do was shrink into a fetal position, trying to deflect the worst of the blows. Eventually, the clatter of hard shoes against cement floor signaled the arrival of two guards, who quickly unlocked the door and restrained JoJo.

"Kid, when are you going to learn your lesson?" one of them asked.

The other knelt and checked the man on the floor, who was moaning in pain but able to stand up with help. "You okay?"

"And that's a sign of penitence?" Faras raised his eyebrows as the screen blanked.

"Not a very convincing one," Sophia agreed. "But since you saw him last, he's found a way to get drugs on the inside, and he got roughed up a few more times. Being around men who constantly tempt him back toward his old lifestyle will make his testing tough. Still, there's hope. Pastor

Ephraim comes to visit twice a week, and although JoJo refuses to see him most of the time, sometimes he doesn't."

"Now, that man's an angel," Ruth commented. "You sure he's not one of you?"

"He's not," Faras assured her. "When an angel goes to earth, he or she can only stay for a short time, especially in mortal form."

"It looks bad, I know, but if Gabriel believes there's a chance for JoJo, so must we," Sophia cautioned.

She waited for Faras and Miriam to challenge her again, but they didn't. Instead, all four of them sat down to think through a plan. She asked if JoJo should be tested differently than the other candidates, and if so, how?

"I say we go with Pastor Ephraim," Miriam began. "He's our best chance. If we build him up, maybe get him some money to hire a good lawyer for JoJo, the door might open."

"Good thought," Sophia said.

"We need to work within," Faras suggested. "We should cut off his contact with the bad influences in the prison, and Miriam can bring more positive people to him—people he'll see day to day, hour to hour. Maybe a guard, or someone who could be a role model. Then Ruth can try a small testing and see where it goes."

"No." Ruth stood up. "I want to go back. That boy needs an angel, and I'm the next best thing to one. You know I'll be able to convince him better than anyone else, and it seems to me he does require something special."

Seeing tension flicker across Miriam's and Faras's faces, Sophia folded her hands together so the tips of her fingers touched her chin. "Those are all good ideas to discuss with Gabriel, and they aren't mutually exclusive. In the meantime, what about the others?"

Each Selected Servant came up with ideas on how they could test the candidates in ways that would both break and build up their character, running their thoughts by Ruth for validation. As suggestions were debated and prayed over, the group finally came to agreement on how to begin.

Anthony's wife and one of his sons would be in a car accident that left her in a coma. Although she would eventually recover, her health would be precarious for an extended time. Angels would come in the form of nurses and doctors who took good care of her and comforted him, but Anthony would quickly find that attending to his sick family forced him to make hard choices between his career and the wellbeing of his wife and sons. It would also, hopefully, lead him to renew his relationship with the Almighty Divine.

Gustaf would meet and fall in love with a woman who was a devout Christian and committed to reunifying the fractured countries of Central Asia. His loyalties would be tested as his colleagues pushed him to join them in secret operations that would wreak destruction on his enemies. At the same time, his girlfriend would pressure him to leave his job and join her in efforts to reconcile the divided countries. The ultimate test would come when his colleagues asked him to mastermind the abduction and murder of a group of peacekeepers.

Kim, the gentlest spirit of the group, would be accused of cheating on an important exam by a jealous classmate. Although she wasn't guilty, the university would expel her anyway, bringing great shame to her sickly widowed mother. Kim would be left without a future, as her boyfriend abandoned her and her mother died of a heart attack, presumably brought on by the stress of her daughter's disgrace.

"It's terrible to think of inflicting such suffering," Faras said as they finished sketching out the preliminary phase of the project. He looked at Sophia. "You're right. This really is a test of our own devotion, and I'm not sure how dedicated I can be."

Miriam added: "Having Ruth here has really helped me understand mortal behavior. I'm glad she's the one who will be spearheading this instead of one of us."

Sophia couldn't help questioning Miriam's intent. If she truly was grateful for Ruth's presence and not just looking for a scapegoat, should something go wrong, they were making progress.

May that be so, she prayed, dipping her head in a brief moment of prayer. How she longed to stay lost in an ongoing state of adoration and petition as she had throughout the majority of her existence. Now, however, a more daunting job confronted her. Hopefully, it would bring similar satisfaction.

18

All eyes were on her when she looked up. Despite their comments, Faras and Miriam both had wrinkles of concern on their foreheads, while Ruth was leaning against her recliner, her brown eyes dreamy. Sophia took a deep breath in and focused on the Selected Servants.

"I know this seems to go against everything we've always done, but think of it as strengthening, not causing pain. Great athletes train relentlessly for their competitions, so this is our plan to get these mortals into fighting shape," she said. "At least we're privileged to see the bigger purpose in this situation. If we had to inflict all this sorrow without knowing there was a goal of eventual good, it would be worse."

They looked skeptical as she felt a slight stirring and heard the archangel whisper her name. She stood up and suggested this might be a good time for them to check in with Hector and show Ruth to the chamber that would be hers.

"Gabriel wishes to meet with me," she explained.

After they left, Sophia prepared herself for the meeting. Overall, she was satisfied with the plans they had developed, and with Miriam's and Faras's eventual acceptance of JoJo as a candidate. As she mulled over the status of the Testings of Devotion, she sensed that she had been waiting longer than usual. Although her life was not oriented to hours and days, Gabriel usually drew her up to his Refreshing Room soon after summoning her or else appeared at her side. Her thoughts grew uneasy, and the Guidance Room grew larger and emptier as she waited.

Too many "never befores" were happening. Sophia began to sing her favorite prayer song of sustenance, but her voice sounded flat and even a bit harsh.

Nothing could harm Gabriel, of course, but he had called to her, indicating he wanted them to meet. Now, he failed to appear, and the last time they were together, he vanished abruptly. What was going on?

Her singing turned into a plea for strength and courage as she sensed Lucifer's readiness to take advantage of the kind of fear she felt. After centuries of silence, he was targeting her for special temptation, when she was one of the few angels who felt sorrow rather than anger over the choices he had made. Why couldn't he ask her to help him repent and return to heaven, rather than try to lure her into the place of pain where he must dwell every day?

The song turned sweeter and louder as Gabriel's voice joined hers. Looking around, Sophia finally saw him far above her, so transparent she could barely make out the features on his face.

She laughed nervously. "Gabriel, please come closer so we can speak easily."

He remained where he was. "There is a strategy for the Testings of Devotion?"

"Yes, and a good one, I think." Sophia swallowed hard, hoping he would descend next to her so she could see his face clearly. When he didn't, she described the plans for each candidate except JoJo, explaining that there was, as predicted, controversy over his candidacy. Throughout, Gabriel remained almost a vapor in the distance.

"Which of the proposed plans for JoJo seems most appropriate to you?" Gabriel asked when she concluded.

"Each has its merits, I guess...but I'm inclined to agree that, in his case, someone must descend to earth and minister directly to him. Of course, Ruth didn't hesitate to say she would go back, but her motives are complicated."

During the long silence that followed, she grew to understand the meaning of Gabriel's distance, the lengthy time he had given her for preparation, and her own general feeling of discomfort. When he finally spoke, she heard a different turn in his voice than before—he was chastising her!

"Yes, you have come to the correct conclusion, Sophia. Someone must go to earth, but not Ruth." The last three words pierced her spirit with a sudden, painful understanding.

"It's me, isn't it?" she asked, her voice barely a whisper.

The archangel floated down to stand before her. Sophia expected his expression to be angry or disgusted; instead, his eyes were soft with compassion and his face lined with sorrow.

She seized his hand. "Oh Gabriel, no! Anything but that! I'm not that strong, and the Voice has come so often recently . . ."

"Sophia." He gathered her into his arms tenderly and began to sing a prayer song rendered all the more special by his soothing voice. Gradually, she gained strength as his spirit filled her with a strange combination of resignation and anticipation.

When they finished, the confession spilled out of her.

"I know I used my power for things I was not meant to, Gabriel. If I help all those in need according to my own will, I won't be able to concentrate on supervising the heavenly host. I didn't trust that the Almighty Divine, in His great wisdom, had a plan that was better than mine."

"Yes, Sophia, you took on a responsibility that was not yours, but is that truly why you've felt such guilt and anxiety?"

She waited for him to explain further, but then realized on her own that her bigger sin was not the inappropriate intervention but the failure to acknowledge it. On two different occasions she could have confessed and asked forgiveness, but she didn't.

"My mistake would have been forgiven and forgotten if I had shared it with Faras and Miriam as soon as they came in the Guidance Center right after I intervened, wouldn't it? And then later, I didn't acknowledge it to you, either."

"Why did you keep it to yourself, Sophia?"

She lowered her head, but he tipped her chin up so she was forced to look at him.

"You must tell me."

"I don't know! I was embarrassed, I guess, and disappointed in myself for doing something so wrong after being named Senior Servant." She shut her eyes. "Please, dearest Almighty Divine, forgive me, even though I don't deserve it."

In the distance, she heard the sweet song of the prayer angels, floating through the silence as if the music was a message meant specifically for her.

"We've been interceding for you, Sophia," Gabriel said kindly. "We all know the paradox: our greatest challenge and greatest strength comes through submission to the wishes of the Almighty Divine, whether we think He is right or not. That's what faith is all about."

"I feel so mortal, lecturing Ruth about being too focused on her own family and what she wants for them and why that's wrong—then I go and do something similar myself." She leaned against him for comfort, wishing there was an easier way to repent for her behavior.

"Sophia, despair is also failure to submit. You know the Almighty Divine is above all and over all, so be uplifted by His strength, and know that there are many reasons for you being selected to descend to earth. I can't come to you again before you leave, but know that many of us will be watching over you. Now, consider your apology to the heavenly host as the first step in your own Testing of Devotion."

Gabriel left before she could ask for guidance about the specifics of what she was to do next, but this time his departure didn't upset her. She called for Miriam and Faras, and asked them to gather the heavenly host immediately.

In an instant she was standing on the wide portico in the front of Operations Central, facing an audience of angels that extended into infinity. Hector was in the first row, smiling encouragement. If only he knew what she was about to say!

She raised her hands so they might all begin with a prayer song. The music flowed through her being until she felt as if she was being lifted up to the Almighty Divine along with the sweet familiar notes of praise. When it finished, she stepped forward and spoke out, her voice magnified so all could hear.

"Dearest angels, I called you together to make a confession."

There was a collective sound of surprise and then busy murmurs of dismay. It was unheard of for the Senior Servant to speak about his or her struggles, although every angel shared them, to a degree.

She persevered. "I have transgressed, and because I transgressed, I must ask for your forgiveness. This is my wrongdoing: after the last disaster on earth, I used my powers to comfort many children directly, when as you know, the Senior Servant is not an angel blessed to watch over children or one to take action on behalf of specific mortals. Further, I was ashamed of my sin, and when the Selected Servants came to me, I didn't tell them what I had done." She turned to look at Miriam and then Faras. "I need the pardon of all of you, for if I cannot be a Senior Servant who is steadfast in carrying out her responsibilities, how can I expect any of you to do the same?"

The heavenly host was completely still until Faras and Miriam held up their arms and began to chant, "The blessings of forgiveness are upon us all."

Sophia knelt down and bowed her head.

"Dear ones, thank you," she said when they finished. Still on her knees, she asked them to continue praying for her in the future. "In a short time I must descend to earth on a mission, where we all know the temptation to stray will be even greater."

A gasp swept through the crowd, but before anyone could question or protest, she signaled for Hector to meet with the heavenly host privately and reassure them. As the crowd dispersed, she turned to the Selected Servants and asked each of them to pardon her for correcting them, but failing to be open to the same treatment for herself.

When she turned to Ruth, she discovered the woman's brown eyes were filled with tears. "Sophia, I wasn't even there! You didn't wrong me. If something like that is so bad, I'll never make it here."

"Oh, but I did. You and I met shortly after I transgressed, and I didn't mention that I had done the very thing I was warning you about. It would have been an ideal opportunity, and it would have lessened the seriousness of my actions." Sophia brushed away the tears that had spilled onto Ruth's cheeks. "We all make mistakes and are all forgiven as soon as we repent. That's how much the Almighty Divine loves us."

Unbidden, the memory of Lucifer came to her, defying the Almighty Divine and attempting to defeat Michael. Could *his* mistakes ever be forgiven?

Ruth pulled her thoughts back to the present. "Ever heard the expression, 'Let's let bygones be bygones?' That's how I survived on earth, and it seems like a pretty good rule up here. If it's okay by the Almighty Divine, it's okay by me."

"The Almighty Divine always forgives. Still, we create our own consequences for the transgression." Miriam hesitated, then hung her head. "It was long ago, but I was sent back to earth for failure to submit to my calling, and I never want it to happen again."

"I'd *like* to go back to earth," Ruth said. Then her expression changed from determined to surprised. "That's transgression, isn't it? I always want my own way instead of devoting myself to the job I've been given."

"Exactly." Sophia nodded.

Faras looked at Sophia, clenching and unclenching his hands. "What will happen to us while you're gone?" he asked in a hoarse voice.

"My descent to earth will be a Testing of Devotion for all of us. You three must work together to guide the heavenly host while I'm gone. Don't forget that Hector is also working to fulfill the Almighty Divine's directions. You've come up with a plan to start the Testings that Gabriel approved, so you should proceed with them."

"But we're not allowed to see Gabriel for further instruction. How will we know what to do if there are problems?"

Although Sophia had briefly wondered the same thing when she learned she was going to earth, she gave his shoulder a reassuring squeeze. "Faras, you'll know what to do. Trust that if you don't, you'll be given the guidance you need."

"Yes, of course you're right." He smiled sadly at her. "There I go with *my* lack of faith. It'll be difficult to witness what you're going through on the Earth Viewer—but we'll be vigilant, so we can help if you need us."

"We'll all be fine. How can we fail?" Sophia turned to Ruth. "Your thoughts about JoJo were correct. He does need something extraordinary, and that will be my mission on earth, although I don't know exactly what I'll be doing for him."

"So, you'll get to see JoJo?" Ruth asked.

"Not in the way you think," Miriam answered swiftly. "It's torment to travel back. None of the forms we assume on earth are pleasant. Just moving around down there is exhausting, which is why we do it for such short times."

"So what about JoJo? What will you do?" Ruth still hadn't looked away from Sophia.

"That is my Testing. I have to go without knowing what will happen once I'm there, and you must keep yourselves strong while I'm gone. It will be a time of great danger both here and on earth."

"Lucifer will know the instant you enter his territory," Faras said. "I'll be sure to counteract those who act on his behalf to harm you, and Miriam will send believers who can uplift you when you need them. It will be important to refresh often so we keep our strength up."

Yes, thought Sophia, *you'll be able to take time out, but not me. I must complete my mission without pausing to rest.*

"You're right, Faras. Please, once I'm through the Portal, come back and let the heavenly host know all is well. Now, we must go."

Their trip to the Portal was a quiet one, marked only by the distant singing of the praise angels, which drifted on the air like the scent of perfume. Sophia could sense what each of her companions was feeling: Ruth, who didn't understand how challenging it was to return to earth, was probably hoping JoJo would be instantly and easily redeemed. Miriam's downcast expression suggested she was commiserating over what was about to happen. Faras, the most experienced in earth descents, seemed weary on her behalf. Oddly, she felt confident and even ready for whatever awaited her on earth.

Once they reached their destination, they joined hands and Sophia gave them an encouraging nod. "You'll do well, and I'll return quickly with great victory. Blessings upon you."

"And blessings on you, Sophia," they said in unison, stepping forward to kiss her cheek and give her a hug of encouragement.

After each of them said good-bye, she turned toward the Portal. Without pausing, she stepped through it and felt herself flying away from the First Level of heaven and all the safety and security she had known throughout eternity.

19

Descending was worse than the agony Miriam described, but Sophia remembered Faras's advice and offered up every prayer song she knew and allowed her wings to flutter out. Briefly, she thought she heard Gabriel singing along with her, which bolstered her spirit, but the confidence she demonstrated before stepping through the Portal evaporated as the burden of mortality grew heavier and heavier.

Mercifully, her exit from the descent was an unconscious one. She awoke in complete darkness and felt a bare wood floor beneath her that was slightly cold. Gradually, her eyes adjusted, and she felt her way toward a large bed set against the far wall. When she stood up, she saw Ruth's pastor, Ephraim, snuggled next to his wife, Anita. Both were sleeping soundly despite the mighty snore he made with each long breath in.

Entering his dreams, Sophia encouraged him to continue ministering to JoJo even though his efforts seemed unappreciated. She suggested ways he could pray to alleviate the boy's overwhelming guilt, as well as interventions to help Tamika, Ruth's oldest daughter and the only sibling who continued to visit JoJo in prison.

After finishing with Ephraim, she passed her hands lightly over Anita until she located the cancerous mass that had been recently diagnosed in her left breast. Resting her hands on the hard lump, Sophia drew it out, feeling the sickness enter her own spirit with a dull pain. She continued to pull the disease up through her fingers until the tumor was gone, along with the cancer cells that had invaded other parts of Anita's body.

Sophia lingered to watch the couple sleep, thanking the Almighty Divine for allowing her mission on earth to begin with such a positive task. A small dog she hadn't noticed before wiggled out from under the covers, wagging its tail. Delighted, Sophia patted the creature's head and it yipped with pleasure.

"Ephraim, the dog needs to go out," Anita murmured, elbowing her husband. "And you're snoring to wake the dead."

"Mmm...ten more minutes. Come here, sugar," he murmured back, wrapping one arm around her and pulling her close. They cuddled back together and dozed off again.

It was now morning, and the heaviness of time was tearing at Sophia as she traveled to the prison, understanding what she must do next. When she arrived at JoJo's cell, he was staring at his breakfast tray, half awake. He was still in solitary, which made it easy for her to take on the form of a male prison official, and open his cell door.

"What the—?" He looked up, momentarily surprised, but then his expression quickly turned hard and calculating. "Who are you?"

"I'm one of the prison chaplains, here to see how you're doing."

"At this hour? You must be one hell of a worker." He scowled and shoved the tray aside. "Get me some better food, if you're so important."

"JoJo." Sophia spoke in a way that made him look up at her in surprise.

When their eyes met, his defensiveness fell away, and she saw the chubby curves of the face Ruth loved so much. It was easy to imagine him as an enthusiastic little boy, singing louder than anyone else in the church choir.

"I know you far better than you think."

"Are you kidding? What kind of chaplain are you, anyway? Nobody told me about anybody coming to visit, let alone someone who thinks he has special information about me," JoJo snapped.

"My name or position isn't important, but what I have to say is."

"You don't have nothing to say to me. No man of God wants anything to do with someone who kills his mother, even if they pretend otherwise."

"The person you really are didn't kill her. The crack you used that night was laced with PCP. That can make the most peaceful person violent."

"That's bullshit!" He jumped up and banged the wall of his cell with his fists. When he faced her, tears were clearly visible in his eyes as said through gritted teeth, "I-killed-my-mother."

"JoJo, stop." She put one hand on his arm, waiting for a blow to come her way, but instead, he collapsed against her, weeping. "Listen to me."

She pushed him gently back onto his bunk, stilling his spirit as she did so. "My message to you is that today is a new day and a new chance. You can never undo what's been done, but you can start making better choices this very moment."

"I don't believe a word you're saying," he said, glaring up at her, his eyes still wet with tears. "I deserve to burn in hell."

"That's not your decision to make, and not at this time. Soon your attorney is coming to see you, and I want you to tell him about the drugs and give him the name of your dealer. Tell him you heard about it from someone on the street or another prisoner—I don't care how you put it, but do that much."

With that, Sophia left as she had entered, instantly invisible once she was safely in the hallway. She saw JoJo rush to bang on the door and summon a guard, who listened to his story about a mysterious visitor.

"You kiddin'?" the guard asked. "Nobody gets back here without my say-so, not even a chaplain. Other than the kid who delivered your breakfast, no one's been here. Eat your breakfast. Your lawyer's coming by with some papers for you to fill out."

Sophia's next destination was Tamika's apartment. Tamika barely resembled the girl who spent hours rocking JoJo through the worst of his tremors, or protecting him from bullies on the playground many years later. Even after her mother's death, she couldn't let go of her love for the only sibling she considered a "real" brother.

The tiny apartment where she lived with her three children had layers of clothing piled on the dirty carpet, and unwashed dishes littered throughout the kitchen and living room. Next to the shabby sofa where Tamika was dozing, a huge ashtray overflowing with cigarette stubs sat on top of a stack of magazines. Her youngest child was curled up against her, drowsing through a television program about mischievous baby raccoons. A space heater on the floor was aimed in their direction, providing a meager beam of heat in the cold room.

"You see how mortals really are?" the Voice teased. "She's too lazy to go get a job to support her kids. Instead, she'll let them starve while she collects a check that she spends on cigarettes and booze. Go ahead, try to save her. She'll be a nice challenge for you."

Sophia braced herself, knowing the Voice was likely to speak often during her sojourn on earth. Trying not to stare at the obvious thinness of the child and the half-empty bottle of whiskey within easy reach of Tamika's limp arm, she entered the young woman's dreams. She appeared as a glorious angel complete with dazzling white robes, a set of white feathered wings tipped in gold, and a blazing halo over her head, the image Faras told her most often impressed mortals.

"Tamika, your brother needs your help, and if you don't change your ways, your life will be ruined too."

She gave Tamika a vision of the near future: a social worker alerted by one of the older children's teachers would come to the apartment. Seeing the disarray and noting the bruises Tamika's latest boyfriend had inflicted on the youngest child would make the case for foster care. All three of her sobbing children would be removed as Tamika remained passed out on the sofa.

"I can't," Tamika argued in her sleep. "I can't change anything. No one will give a welfare mom with three kids a job, no matter what I do."

"Unless you stop drinking, you will lose your children," Sophia said, persisting. "You're an addict, no different from JoJo. You understand where he went wrong, so get help for yourself now, and then you can help others around you."

Tamika stirred, as if trying to escape the dream, but she couldn't. "Go away and let me alone. I'm doing the best I can."

"No, Tamika, you're not. This is not what God intends for you," Sophia continued, willing herself to glow brighter. "Your mother thought you were the one who would be most like her because you had so many talents. That can still happen."

As a knock sounded at the door, Sophia released Tamika. The knock repeated louder as Tamika shook herself awake, still in a state of shock. She climbed over her child and opened the door to find Anita standing in the hallway, frowning.

"Tamika Miller, what are you doing asleep at this hour of the morning? Anyway,   praise the Lord! I was hoping you'd be home," the pastor's wife said, sweeping into the apartment without waiting for an invitation.

Tamika made a halfhearted attempt to clear away some of the debris on the sofa so Anita could sit down, but quickly gave up. "I'm sorry it's such a mess, Miss Anita. I've been…" Her voice trailed off. "I guess there's no excuse for dirt, like Mom used to say."

Anita sat down on the arm of the sofa and lightly rubbed the head of the child, who had woken and was sucking his thumb. When her eyes fell on the whiskey bottle and the ashtray, she slapped her hands palms down on her thighs and squinted up at Tamika. "There's no excuse for booze and cigarettes, especially when the heat's turned off." She scooped up the boy and wrapped him inside her coat. "Girl, what are you thinking?"

"Miss Anita, do you believe in angels?"

Anita gave Tamika a hard look. "Are you fooling with me?"

"No, I really mean it. Do you believe people can see angels? 'Cause I just had a dream where I did."

Anita's eyes flickered around the room and returned to rest on Tamika. "I don't know if you really saw an angel, but you sure had one act on your behalf today." She unsnapped her purse, took out an envelope, and held it toward Tamika. "Last Sunday, the congregation took up a special collection on account of my cancer and all the treatment I was going to need. This morning I went to the doctor and guess what? That darn lump is gone! He rushed me over for some tests and they couldn't find any sign it was ever there. 'Course, he wants me to come back for more tests, but I told him the Lord is my physician, and He has healed me."

"That's wonderful!"

"It's more than wonderful; it's a miracle! When I told Ephraim, he said right away that we needed to give you the money from the collection plate so you could pay your bills."

Tamika looked dumbly at the envelope, which was stuffed full of cash, then tears filled her eyes. "Shouldn't someone else get at least part of it?"

"It's not that much!" Anita chuckled. "But Ephraim insisted on it; in fact, he woke up in the best mood and said right away that you were on his mind." She shook her head. "Hmm...I'll be blessed, I think you did see an angel."

"Why?"

"I've been meaning to come by this week anyway, because Miss Lila told us a few days ago that she's moving north to be closer to her kids, so we'll have a job opening for a church secretary. It isn't much, but it'll get you started, and you can put Caleb here in the church nursery while your other kids are in school, and work for us." She touched Caleb's arm lightly and frowned. "You have to get rid of that boyfriend, though. I heard bad things about him through the grapevine, and your older kids don't need to see you get beat up every night."

Tamika blinked away the tears in her eyes and looked away from Anita. "You're offering me a job *and* daycare, even though I'm such a mess?"

"You're a smart girl, Tamika. I remember how your mom always told me that, and you got good grades in school. Anyway, Ephraim's been trying to get Miss Lila to learn to use the computer, but she's as stubborn as a mule when it comes to that. Come to think of it, her leaving might be part miracle too, 'cause between you and me, the church records are a mess. Didn't you take a night course in computers one time?"

"I got started, and I learned how to type, but I didn't finish," Tamika's voice trailed off. "Caleb got sick and the other two had so much homework, I couldn't keep it up."

Sophia left, believing Anita's considerable powers of persuasion would convince Tamika she could do the job. Hopefully, Tamika would take her dream seriously and start to change her lifestyle even if she needed a lot of support, but Miriam and Faras were probably working on her behalf already.

As she drifted away from the scene, she realized she had yet to encounter another angel. Were they invisible to her too? Since she had never visited earth it was impossible to know, but the absence of even one other heavenly visitor seemed strange. Weren't they all spiritual warriors fighting the same battle?

As the hours passed, Sophia felt her spirit grow sicker and slower. The wings Faras encouraged her to use were hard to navigate as she moved toward the office of JoJo's attorney.

Thy will be done, she repeated over and over, wondering how long she would be able to persevere. She arrived to see the lawyer at his desk, shuffling through file folders as his law clerk stood attentively to one side.

"It's just about lunchtime for me, kiddo, but there're some cases I want you to work on." He selected several folders and handed them to an attractive young woman in a tidy suit. He summarized each one, then picked up a stray file and flipped through its contents. "I might as well give you this one too: JoJo Miller—up for homicide, odds against him, no priors."

As Maria took the folder from her boss, a piece of legal paper fluttered free. When she bent to retrieve it, Sophia touched her shoulder lightly and whispered in her ear.

"What's this about PCP?" Maria asked, straightening up and tucking a strand of loose hair behind one ear. Her eyes were fixed on a few sentences scrawled across the bottom of the page.

"Kid told me this morning he got bad coke the night he offed his mom."

"Hmm...there was something in the paper about that not too long ago. The city hospital ER had a bunch of overdoses come in all at once. If he really did get bad drugs, could that reduce the charges? Maybe temporary insanity."

"Alvarez, that case has 'loser' written all over it. You do anything extra you want on it, but it's your time."

"My boyfriend's an undercover cop," she said, adjusting the armful of files he had already given her. "I might be able to get a little free advice on this one."

The senior partner shrugged, his way of dismissal.

As Maria walked out of the office, her heel caught on the carpet, and although Sophia eased her fall, legal documents scattered everywhere.

"Damn stilettos," Maria said, her face reddening as another attorney rushed to help her gather up the papers. "This is the second time I've tripped wearing these shoes."

"Yeah, but they're pretty easy on the eye," the other man said with a wink, handing her a page with JoJo's picture stapled to it. Before she could slide it back in place, his eyes widened and he grabbed it.

"Is this JoJo Miller?" he asked.

When she nodded, he said, "I'll be darned. He goes to my church, or I guess I should say he used to. His mom was a real saint. You might have heard of her—she started a clinic for crack babies." He snorted. "Ironic, huh? He was her first patient and then he ends up hooked and violent. I always got the idea he was basically a good kid, but it just goes to show you never know. You on the case?"

"I just got it."

"Well, see what you can do for him, and let me know if you need some help. His mom deserves a break, even if she won't be around to appreciate it."

Sophia felt herself suddenly jerked out of the law office and dumped into an apartment even more decrepit than Tamika's, crammed with people. One woman was dancing slowly to the harsh beat of music blasting from a portable player. As Sophia settled down into the room, it felt as if her spirit was being stabbed over and over by the sound. On a filthy mattress wedged in one corner she saw JoJo, laughing uproariously. It took her a few seconds to figure out, but she realized she must somehow be in the past.

Submit, she told herself, wondering what she was meant to do in such a terrible situation. Every adult was using some kind of drug: several were shooting heroin and nodding off, others passed a crack pipe back and forth, and a lone couple danced in the center of the room, taking turns inhaling from a thick joint. Eventually, they stumbled toward the mattress, shedding their clothes and laughing crazily as they nearly fell on JoJo.

"Want to join us?" the woman asked, trailing one hand down the side of his face.

JoJo shoved it away and pushed some buttons on the boom box so the music changed to the voice of an enraged man screaming obscenities. With a mellow smile, he tapped his fingers against the mattress in synch with the beat until another young man jumped to his feet, screaming. He grabbed the boombox and threw it against a wall.

"It's killing me; it's killing me!" he shrieked.

"That's my box, man!" JoJo snarled, smacking the boy full in the face. The kid crumpled to the floor and didn't move as a few of the others slowly applauded.

Without the music distracting her, Sophia's attention turned to a small girl cringing in one corner of the mattress, sucking her thumb and clinging to a shred of blanket. In the next room, a baby was crying, clearly in distress.

"Somebody shut that kid up," one of the men said.

Grinning, the woman who had been dancing stood up, clad only in her underwear, and retrieved the child, jiggling it up and down as she settled back on the mattress. It continued to cry until her partner pressed his big hand across the little face. Although the baby's body thrashed hysterically, the sounds it made grew muffled, and then stopped all together.

"Asshole!" the woman screamed. "If you killed that kid, we'll all be in a shitload of trouble."

Sophia felt as if she might cease to be. It was one thing to watch such horrors on the Earth Viewer and another to be a few feet away when they happened. She restrained the urge to knock the man over and breathe life back into the baby, shutting her eyes in the hope of guidance.

"Yes," she heard Gabriel say. "Wait."

A second later the baby gave a weak whimper.

"Be cool," JoJo crooned to the little girl crouched next to him, trembling as she watched the baby struggle to move. "Big daddy'll make you feel real good." He hooked her ankle with one hand, picked up a crack pipe, and pulled her closer.

"Nice people, huh? You really want to get this guy out of prison so he can go right back to corrupting others? What is your 'Almighty Divine' thinking? You saw him beat his mother to a pulp. Why save scum when you can help innocent children?"

The Voice was a hiss that penetrated to the core of Sophia's soul, just as the music had. She knew the words were meant to trick her, but she couldn't look away. The girl tried to free herself from JoJo's heavy hand, eyes fixed on Sophia.

"Please help me and my brother," she pleaded silently. "I know you can."

20

The child was so delicate and clearly terrified that Sophia nearly whisked her away to freedom. Would anyone even notice? JoJo continued teasing, pulling her closer and pushing the pipe in her mouth as she struggled to free herself. The tiny baby in the sodden diaper began to wail again.

"Save those innocents. You can do it. She's only ten years old," the Voice urged. "And the next time, that baby will die if you don't intervene. Sophia, you can rescue them."

The little girl was crying. Sophia felt herself drawing closer and closer to the situation, considering alternatives. She could assume the form of a police officer, burst through the door, and end it all. If JoJo was arrested, that might save Ruth's life too. Perhaps this was the reason for her return?

Submit, submit, submit, she prayed, but what was she to submit to? Faras and the other earth angels she had spoken to never mentioned being taken back in time—that must mean she was there to prevent something in the future from happening, right?

"Hey man, let her be," one of the other men drawled, but JoJo was just warming up. The more hits he took from the pipe, the more possessed he became, ridiculing the girl for her tears and snatching her blanket away.

"You're too old to suck your thumb, sugar. Suck on this instead," he said, pinning her head against the wall and bringing the pipe close to her lips.

Sophia couldn't endure any more. Just as she moved forward, the apartment door exploded open and a tall black woman swept into the room.

"Mommy!" the little girl wailed.

With a glance, the woman who had just arrived took in the situation, advanced on JoJo, and gave him a hard kick in his ribs.

"Are you crazy?" she snapped, gathering up the girl and hugging her on one hip. "You told me you would watch them while I went for cigarettes." She crossed over and grabbed the weeping infant as well, glaring at the man and woman who had laid it on the floor between them. "Don't either of you two touch my son again."

"Hey Selma, give me some cash," JoJo drawled. "I know you got it."

"Forget it, JoJo. You're a great guy when you're straight, but I'm done supporting your drug habit. Find someone else." With a final glare in his direction, she sat her daughter down long enough to wrap her jacket around the baby. Then, gathering the girl back up and balancing a child on either hip, she wrestled the door open and stalked out.

"Thank you, Miriam," Sophia whispered. Was this a second chance for her to show that she could witness the suffering of children without taking action to change the situation?

"If you intervened, those children would have been safe for the moment and their mother wouldn't have removed them from the situation," Gabriel's voice said to her. "Seeing her children in such danger finally gave her the motivation to leave JoJo and change her life. You see how far-reaching the consequences of your actions can be?"

She sighed, a mix of relief and fatigue; how she longed to refresh and feel the wonderful lightness of angelhood, which was, of course, impossible on earth. The existence of time and its impact on her spirit concerned her. Some angels claimed there was a "point of no return," when it became impossible to shed a mortal body. Was she in danger of that?

Wait for direction, she told herself with a shudder. Wherever she was now, it was completely dark—another strange thing. How comforting it would be to see another angel's friendly face or know that success in this mission would bring her closer to the Second Level of heaven.

Suddenly, she was surrounded by such loud music it made her spirit tremble. Why was music so different on earth? On the First Level it was always a source of calming, but now, what she was hearing made her feel jumpy and afraid.

She was in the midst of a crowd of young people who were dancing in an odd way, bumping roughly against each other so that she bounced from one person to the other. On a stage in front of them, a thin man with long unkempt hair was gyrating and singing, pausing to lick the microphone in a lewd sexual parody while the crowd cheered. For a moment, Sophia felt overwhelmed by the uninhibited nearness of so many mortals.

Not wanting to draw attention to herself, she began to move with the rhythm of a new song with a slower beat. Vibrations swelled out of the speakers, so sensual and raw that a strange euphoria coursed up from her earthly feet to the tips of her fingers. Like the others writhing around her, she closed her eyes, leaned her head back, and moved in time to the music.

"You must be from heaven, because you look like an angel to me." An attractive boy grabbed her and hugged her so closely, she could smell the sweat that had soaked through his shirt.

In spite of his behavior, he had the look of someone who paid attention to his appearance. The oxford cloth shirt he wore was heavily starched white cotton, and his khaki pants were clearly expensive. A flat gold watch was clasped around his wrist, and his hair, although disheveled, was styled rather than cut. Although a bit stale, the odor of cologne clung to him. At the same time, his eyes were so out of focus that he had trouble looking at her directly.

Sophia pushed free of the embrace, but he continued to clench her hand.

"Hey Sophia, don't you recognize me? It's Thomas!"

She tried harder to pull her hand away but he continued, and because there was something familiar about him, she relented for a moment and let him shout into her ear.

"Isn't this great? I've got everything here. So much better than heaven. Why don't you join me?"

"Maybe because you betrayed all of heaven," she snapped back. "If you and the original Watchers hadn't followed Lucifer, mortals would be better off."

"Better off!" He threw back his head and roared with laughter. "How much better does it get than this?"

The music picked up speed again and he let go of her hand, dancing so spasmodically, he seemed about to spin out of control. As the last note sounded, he screamed with joy and hopped crazily up and down along with the people pressed in around them.

A swell of applause sounded, and he took her by the wrist again, pulling her close. "What are you doing here, Sophia?"

"I've been sent on a mission for the Almighty Divine, but I'm hoping to return to the First Level soon. I'm starting to feel so weary. How can you stand to be trapped in a mortal body, Thomas? Why don't you repent and come back?"

"You get used to these bodies; in fact, they start to feel pretty good. You just need to loosen up."

He dug into one of his pockets and pulled out some tiny white pills, then pressed his closed palm against Sophia's free hand, motioning for her to swallow them. She looked at the small white discs, fascinated, while the music twisted deeper into her spirit.

"Take them. There're more where they came from, and believe me, mortals pay a lot of dough for them. I'm living the good life," he said, close to her ear. "Why would I ever want to come back to heaven and be just one more angel of no special significance when I'm 'somebody' here? I control a big part of the drug traffic in my region, and have more money and prestige than you could imagine."

"But that's temporary, Thomas. Please come back."

"Nah. Not for me. Take the pills, Sophie, baby. You'll find out that being mortal isn't so bad after all."

Would it hurt to have a positive experience on earth? Could she survive if she didn't take his little white pills? She felt heavy and sick, while Thomas looked ecstatic, reveling in the next set of the band's frantic music. Maybe the chemicals would help relieve the feeling that bags of garbage were heaped on her shoulders.

She lifted her cupped hand to get a closer look at the pills when a man with the physique of a bodybuilder shoved past her and grabbed Thomas, handcuffing him and dragging him off through the crowd. His buddy grabbed Sophia and followed.

The angel-turned-mortal struggled and kicked, scattering dancers as his captor, who turned out to be a police officer, wrestled a path through the crowd. When Thomas finally jerked free with a roar, Sophia's guard let go of her to help his buddy.

As she drifted away, she suddenly understood that Thomas was the one who had sold JoJo the PCP-laced cocaine that led to unusually violent behavior. Her last vision of him was ugly. He was in the midst of pandemonium, thrashing against the two police officers, his face twisted with hatred as he swore and struck out with all the supernatural energy his drugs and Lucifer provided.

"Heavenly Father, protect and defend me. Guide me in your way that I may carry out your will in perfect obedience," she chanted over and over, stunned by how close she had come to taking the drugs. Lonely and afraid, she knew there was more to do, because soon she was back in JoJo's cell, her spirit bruised by the heavy sound of the concert music and the grip of the drug dealer's fingers.

Ruth's son slept as Sophia hovered above him, fighting off the urge to fall down on the hard floor and get some rest. Again, she saw the child he had been, innocent and at peace.

"He's despicable," the Voice said. "Why don't you feel disgusted by him? You've met his mother. Think of the good she could have done if she had lived, and how many babies she might have saved. Sophia, you have the ability to make a difference! We've both known that since the beginning. Why stay in heaven when you can rule earth with me?"

I must obey the Almighty Divine without question, she told herself. This was not much different than the invitation Lucifer had extended on that long ago day when Michael cast him out of heaven. With new energy, she assumed the angelic form she used with Tamika and descended to touch JoJo's shoulder. He woke, instantly scrambling upright with his hands cocked.

He shook his head, pressing his eyes shut, then looked again. "Man, this must be one hell of a drug flashback."

"JoJo, I'm not here to harm you," Sophia said. "I've come on behalf of your mother, who wants me to tell you she forgives you and still loves you. More than anything, she wants you to return to the ways she taught you and become a person who uses his life to help others."

"Yeah, right. You tryin' to tell me she's in heaven or something?"

Sophia came closer so he would absorb the details of her appearance. Mortals were always persuaded by a blonde haired, blue eyed angel dressed in white and surrounded by a bright glow. For effect, she spread her wings wide open and tipped her head so he could see the blazing circle of her halo.

JoJo was hesitant, but then he stretched out one arm and passed his hand through the hem of her robe. When he touched the edge of one of her wings, his jaw dropped.

"Heaven is exactly where she is."

He snorted. "I'm here for the rest of my life, lady, however long or short it might be. No one can save me."

"Nothing in the future is certain except your eventual death. God has a plan for your life, JoJo. Confess your sins, and ask for forgiveness. It's the only way."

"Who are you? Is this some kind of trick?"

"See?" the Voice chided. "He's hopeless. You've missed the point, Sophia. You were supposed to save that little girl and the baby, who will be right back in the same situation tomorrow, thanks to your misunderstanding. No matter how many angels you send, their situation here on earth won't change for more than a night or two, and you know it."

"There are always angels," Sophia retorted, ignoring JoJo. "We can make something good result from even the worst circumstance you create."

"Ah yes, but you can only remain on earth for a limited time before you become mine. You are almost there, Sophia, and then there will be no decision to make because you will be weighted down and filled with all the transgressions you believed you came to earth to remedy. Do you think Gabriel or the Almighty Divine even remembers you exist?"

It was true that the longer she remained in mortal form, the further away the First Level of heaven seemed to recede. Sophia sank down until she was in front of JoJo. He glowered at her, oblivious to the conversation with Lucifer.

She tried for what she decided would be the last time. "JoJo, you had a cat named Trouble. He ran away after your mother died and there was no one to take care of him. Don't try to find him again. That's what your mother would say if she were here: 'Let go of trouble, JoJo. Be the good boy I taught you to be.' "

Sophia moved closer and waited. After a time, JoJo hesitantly reached out and this time, his fingers touched her hand. She felt as if something dirty and wrong splashed over her spirit.

"You're real," he said in a soft voice. "A real angel sent to give me a message."

"Yes," she said.

The second she said the word, she was sucked away by a great force that pulled her down through the floor and into a cold darkness. She struggled like a swimmer caught up in a deadly current, but the harder she wrestled against the emptiness, the faster she traveled through it.

Her sense of dread grew as Lucifer's voice sang in her ear: "Come to me, sweet Sophia, come to me."

The sound of her scream exploded into flames of fire that snapped toward her, gaining fury as she continued to fall. Tongues of searing heat licked at the remnants of her human body, searing the tender flesh away. As she continued to plummet into nothingness, she felt her only way of escape might be to surrender to Lucifer.

"No! I will not!" Although she spoke out loud, the words were quickly lost in the roar of heat all around her.

Suddenly, what she needed to do became completely clear. With a mighty shout of joy, she stopped fighting and allowed what was left of her mortal body to go completely limp. As soon as she surrendered, her spirit rushed free, floating up into the strong arms of the ready rescuer who had been beside her the whole time.

21

Gabriel held her until she felt strong enough to sit in one of the Refreshing Room's chairs on her own. She looked up at the intense blue of the high ceiling, which faded upward into pure white, and relaxed, sighing with contentment and letting her eyes drift shut. Each deep breath of the pure cool air revived her further.

Gabriel settled her on the recliner and sat near enough to hold her hand, both protective and comforting. The two of them had never touched in this way, but as he surrounded her with love, the flurries of turmoil still churning within her eased and then gradually subsided. Each note of the new prayer song he sang pulled free the last bits of earthly iniquity clinging to her spirit. When finished, he gently released her, and the balmy blue mist reserved for soothing during difficult discussions drifted in to surround them.

"You were there the whole time, watching over me, even though I couldn't see you. Thank you," she said, opening her eyes to smile at him.

"Yes," he said, his eyes downcast. "It was hard to see someone I care for so much go through that kind of experience."

As she silently reviewed the details of what happened on earth, she balled her hands into fists and pressed them against her forehead, grimacing at the ugly memories of mortals who acted hurtfully, and innocents she hadn't been able to help. The descent had turned out to be every bit as difficult as Miriam predicted, and with questionable results.

"It seems I failed both you and the Almighty Divine. I'm sorry."

"You didn't fail us, Sophia."

Gabriel stood, a giant but unimposing figure, slightly transparent yet visible enough to reveal a look of approval on his handsome face. "You succeeded."

"I...I succeeded? It certainly didn't feel that way."

"No, I imagine it didn't, but you accomplished everything expected of you. Sophia, you were sent to earth as penance, but that was only part of the reason."

"Was it because of JoJo? He seems so resistant to changing. I can't imagine he'll ever turn into a successful candidate unless—"

"No," he cut her off. "It wasn't about JoJo, although the Almighty Divine is pleased with your intercessions for him."

"Then what?" she persisted, disappointed by Gabriel's curtness. "I couldn't convince Thomas to repent either." Surely she deserved some kind of explanation, but the guarded look in his eyes suggested she shouldn't push further. After a brief silence, she guessed, "That must be another one of those things I'm not supposed to ask about, right?"

The archangel gave her a long look, then bowed his head. "I will tell you a few things, although you can't speak about them to anyone. Had you not just gone through such a testing yourself, you might not be strong enough to hear them." He paused, as if framing an argument, and drifted back and forth in the Refreshing Room, either deep in thought or anxious. "Any angel could have gone to minister to JoJo, if that was all we needed. You were chosen because a Senior Servant has never gone to earth."

"I thought I became Senior Servant because Isaac went down and somehow didn't come back."

Gabriel's face clouded with an emotion she couldn't quite describe. "We don't know exactly where Isaac is, Sophia, but while it is true he went through the Portal and vanished, he was not sent on any kind of holy mission." He seemed to reflect on whether to say more about that situation, but then changed the subject. "Your descent has nothing to do with Isaac, though. We picked you to tempt Lucifer, just as he tempted you."

"Really?" She found the thought almost pleasing until she remembered how the interaction had played out. "But it almost worked. I was on the verge of surrendering to him."

"While on earth, you were only able to see events as they took place right before you. I can assure you, Lucifer's inability to recruit you away cost him dearly," Gabriel said. "He invested a lot of his own resources to follow your every move on earth, and ultimately, he failed at something that meant a lot to him, whether you were aware of it or not. After I reclaimed you, he was as frustrated as I've ever seen him." Gabriel chuckled. "We're letting him know he's in for a fight."

"Are you saying I went down as bait?"

"Not bait—a test of his intentions. As you know, all divine things are complicated, but consider this: you learned many things about yourself during your time on earth, and you gathered valuable information for us."

"Can you tell me what that was?"

"Yes, in fact it's important that I do. Sophia, I've been sensing that something isn't right on the First Level of heaven for some time. It's subtle; a notion that Miriam or Faras isn't fully invested in being a Selected Servant, and the way Isaac had of appearing to agree so totally with everything I said, but then subtly undermine it. Without you overseeing the Selected Servants, I thought whatever was worrying me would become clear, but that didn't happen." He frowned and examined his large hands, flexing his fingers several times. "Among the things I did learn from your descent, one was especially odd. There weren't any angels around you."

"I noticed that too!" The possible implications of his words made her drop deeper into the blueness that surrounded them, taking refreshment from the cool mist that had begun to float in around them. "Are you thinking one of the Selected Servants is…well…a traitor?"

He was still looking at his hands as if a secret message was written there, making it impossible to read his expression. "Much has been revealed during your descent, but I can't elaborate on it all right now. However, you're back, so it will be important for you to find out whether Miriam or Faras or even Ruth have been hearing the same Voice that tries to tempt you. You also need to find out why there weren't angels there. There could be many reasons, all of which trouble me. However, we've come up with a plan to explore all these issues further. You can rely on Hector to help you, of course. I'm quite sure he's not the problem."

Sophia nodded, thinking fondly of the cheerful angel with wavy dark brown hair and twinkling eyes a few shades lighter. She sometimes wondered why he, projector of such a bubbling good humor and ready smile, hadn't been chosen Senior Servant in her place.

As if her thoughts had been spoken, Gabriel said, "Hector has been kept with the heavenly host because he desires it, and because the Almighty Divine wants to keep a senior angel among their ranks at all times. He has been faithful in his duties, which is why I trust him completely, but when you return to the First Level of heaven, charge him in my name to search the spirits of every angel in the heavenly host. He should look for even the slightest sign of problems, just as you should with the Selected Servants. Hector will report to you and only you in this mission."

"What about Ruth? I know you said you've had suspicions for a while, but she definitely has a different perspective than any of us. It makes me see the wisdom of keeping the Community of Resting Mortals separate from us."

Gabriel pondered for a moment. "Actually, I'm hoping Ruth will help us uncover the problem. Not intentionally, of course, but because Miriam and Faras act differently with her around." He crossed his massive arms over his chest and sighed. "Although I hope I'm wrong, it seems one of the Selected Servants is the source of my worries. As you discovered, deceit and disobedience can be hidden very well. Once a mortal or angel acts according to Lucifer's ways, it becomes a barrier between him or her and the Almighty Divine."

"So, you didn't really know what I had done when I helped those children after the tsunami?"

"I knew there was an obstacle between us that hadn't been there before, but not the reason why." He touched the top of her head in a sign of blessing. "Let's put that behind us now, and prepare for your return to the First Level of heaven. Do you feel ready?"

"Hmm…let's see. I could stay here with you and enjoy eternal bliss or go back to the First Level where I'll have to constantly worry about sabotage. What a choice. Tell me, after all this, will I be even just a tiny bit closer to the Second Level of heaven?"

Gabriel laughed. "Sophia, when you're ready for the Second Level of heaven, you'll know it."

"How wonderful it would be to look upon the Almighty Divine." *And to be further away from Lucifer*, she thought.

Gabriel's entire form became radiant. "You have, Sophia. You see Him in the goodness of the angels, and when you were on earth, you saw Him in people too."

She grimaced. "When I was down there, I saw more wrong than right, which was shocking. You know I've always been a champion of the inherent goodness in mortals. Add to that the possibility of a Selected Servant who's actively betraying us and I think there's a grave threat to our ability to triumph over Lucifer."

"Right now, I only have suspicions," he cautioned. "If one of them has fallen prey to Lucifer's temptations, it's something subtle, which will become obvious in the future. It always does." Gabriel was moving away from her, his features melding with the blue mist until she only heard his voice. "Go back now, and remember the lesson you learned, dear one."

Instantly, she found herself just outside the Guidance Room, full of energy and eager to see the others. She prayed that Gabriel would be wrong and no one was trying to derail the Testings of Devotion. For her part, extra vigilance was warranted, and with the Almighty Divine's special blessings, perhaps she could play a small part in the triumph of good over evil, just as she had unknowingly done on earth.

She moved into the room with a smile on her face, discovering that Faras was the only one there. When he saw her, his expression went from relieved to somber.

"Sophia! Thank the Almighty Divine you're finally back," he said. "Let me get Ruth and Miriam."

Before she could reply, he scurried out, returning shortly with the two women. All three of them hugged Sophia briefly in welcome, then stood stiffly in a row before her. Was it Sophia's imagination, or did they look guilty?

Be careful not to treat them differently because of Gabriel's revelation, she told herself. Even he admitted it might be nothing.

"So, how was your time on earth?" Miriam began brightly. "I trust you accomplished your mission?"

"You must have seen everything that happened," Sophia said.

"Not everything," Miriam returned quickly, "and as you know, the Almighty Divine doesn't always reveal everything to us."

Sophia knew this was true, but still detected a note of defensiveness in the Selected Servant. "Things went according to His plan, I believe, but I'm incredibly relieved to be back with you. Please, tell me what's happened with the Testings of Devotion while I was away."

"Well...we proceeded just as you wanted us to; in fact, exactly as we discussed before you left," Ruth said, emphasizing the "exactly," and looking at the other two Selected Servants for support. They both nodded.

After a short silence, Faras stood up straighter and pressed his lips together before speaking. "It isn't going like we thought it would, Sophia. JoJo seems to be the only potential success story."

They looked at the screen behind the large globe and saw an image of Pastor Ephraim praying over JoJo. Tamika was there too, holding her brother's hand. The picture switched to Maria, who had connected the legal dots and convinced her bosses that JoJo's charges might be reduced to manslaughter due to his temporary loss of cognitive capacity after taking the tainted drugs. Even Thomas, disguised as the boy at the center of the drug hub, was playing cooperative and confessing to his drug dealing and addiction.

"Let me sign myself into rehab while I wait for the charges to be processed," he told his lawyer, a penitent look on his face.

"Amazing," Sophia said, debating whether to tell them the real identity of the criminal. Instead, she looked at Miriam. "Thanks for sending so many good people my way when I was down there. Faras, I'm sure you shielded me and the others from more harm too." She waited to see if either of them would mention the absence of angels, but they looked away, clearly uncomfortable. "So…what is it that you need to tell me about the rest of the candidates?"

When no one answered Sophia's question, she repeated it more forcefully.

"We don't know what happened," Faras said. "But the others haven't responded like JoJo…and in one case we've already failed."

"Failed? How can you say that? You've only just started," Sophia protested.

"You're right, but the theory behind the idea of turning 'trials into triumphs' must be flawed," Miriam said.

"How?" Sophia demanded, noting that each of them avoided meeting her eyes.

Ruth finally lifted her head and spoke, staring fixedly at the Earth Viewer as she delivered the news: "It's Anthony Davis, Sophia. He killed himself shortly after you left."

22

Sophia's disbelief turned to shock as she searched each angel's expression for some kind of explanation. Miriam looked embarrassed, Faras sorrowful, and Ruth sad; each seemed genuinely distressed.

"Tell me what happened," she said, turning away so they wouldn't see the concern on her face. No doubt Gabriel was furious that any angel would take his or her rebellion to the point of murdering a mortal.

"We didn't deviate at all," Miriam said, coming to Sophia's side. "We brought hardship into his life through the family crisis, but instead of growing stronger, he fell into a state of despair. I sent so many angels to minister to him, I had to deny other mortals, but Anthony was obsessed with the tragedy."

"Why wouldn't he be?" Sophia asked, refusing to look at Miriam.

"Of course it's understandable, but for Anthony it was more in a way of self-pity than concern for his family."

Faras gave a short, bitter laugh. "Then he started hanging out with one of his co-workers, a guy he knew from college, and that led to a lot of heavy drinking—and worse."

Sophia spun around to look at Ruth. "Maybe the testing was too intense. Did you go as slowly as possible?"

"Sure did. I made sure he came to terms with each challenge before I added another one. He seemed okay until Jack, that lush, came along. Faras is right—that one's bitter to the core, one of Lucifer's own. Every time it would seem things were starting to go in the direction we wanted, Jack would convince Anthony his life was hopeless, and that a drink was the best medicine. One drink always led to another, and you can guess it wasn't long before Anthony was depressed about that too. He stopped going home, never visited his wife in the hospital, and then one day, he just went to his father's house, got out a shotgun, and killed himself. We had no idea he was that bad off—you know we can't read minds, and without you here to guide us—"

A glare from Sophia stilled Ruth's attempt to justify what had happened, but Faras took up the protest. "We did everything we could, Sophia. I even made Jack lose his job so it wouldn't be so easy for them to see each other, but Anthony was drawn to him. I think Jack must be a Nephilim. You can't blame us for what happened."

Faras touched the control screen and a picture of Jack appeared, seated at a bar next to a woman they instantly knew was a prostitute, albeit an expensive one. He looked like the ancient giants, but was dressed in well-tailored clothes that outlined the bulk of his muscle-packed arms and thighs. Despite his well-kept hair and beard, the slack expression on his face and dull gleam of his eyes made his appearance sinister rather than suave.

Jack grabbed the woman's arm and jerked her from her seat. When she lost her balance and fell, her eyes filled with fear. Another man sitting nearby attempted to intervene, but Jack easily shoved him away.

"I've got plans for you and me." Jack pulled the woman up against him and led her, tripping behind him, out of the bar.

Sophia turned to Miriam. "You've had to help mortals deal with Nephilim before. You already know they have no feelings for human attachments. Expecting someone like Jack to feel compassion or sorrow for Anthony, or anything like remorse for his other actions, is unrealistic."

"We tried to work with that and hit him in the places that would hurt, but Jack had enough money to impress Anthony with cars, vacations, women, and success—all temporary distractions when there's such underlying angst. The day we arranged for him to be fired from Anthony's law firm, he was snapped up by another because of his ruthless professional life. No matter what I tried, Anthony couldn't be pried away from him, even when his family tried to intervene." Miriam studied the fingernails of her clenched hands, frowning slightly. "Because he left his kids with sitters whenever he could and went out drinking with Jack, the grandparents got temporary custody of the children. I guess Anthony couldn't live with the guilt and sadness—not many mortals could."

"We were so careful, but it seemed doomed from the beginning," Ruth chimed in. "As soon as the accident occurred, Anthony was angry. His first thoughts were about how this would influence his career, not how his wife and child would recover. She had threatened to leave him a few years ago because he was so caught up in his career that there was no time for family. They worked it out, obviously, but I guess he never really surrendered his anger about that or forgave her,"

"Miriam, you can save anyone with good people! I saw it happen when I was on earth. You sent that woman to save the children in the crack house—"

"I can't 'save anyone,' Sophia," Miriam snapped. "You give me too much credit. I saw the woman in the crack house—she was concerned about her children. Some mortals are truly good, remember?" The angry flush on her face faded and she looked down. "I tried with Anthony, Sophia, I truly tried. If I could have transported Pastor Ephraim to minister to him, I would have, but his own pastor wasn't so dynamic. I tried to use his favorite sister, who is a woman of great faith, but every time she tried to speak with him, he put up a wall in his mind. The only voice he seemed to hear was Jack's."

"Do you think Lucifer might have learned about the Testings, and interfered?" Faras asked.

Only if one of you told him, Sophia wanted to say, but she bit back the words.

Even if Jack was a purer form of the modern-day Nephilim, a true giant like the Philistines of the past, Anthony should have been able to resist his influence, given all the support the Selected Servants tried to provide. Was there something they had missed in their careful research, or was there a damning clue in another candidate's story that would resolve the mystery?

"What about the others?" she asked.

Again, the angels avoided her eyes.

"You mean it gets worse?" She pushed, careful to keep her voice level.

"Lord, no!" Ruth said. "How could it get any worse than suicide? Point is, it doesn't get much better."

The lightness that had buoyed Sophia up before her reunion with the Selected Servants was evaporating. Gabriel had known about Anthony when they met; why hadn't he prepared her differently or given her some idea of what to do?

"Gustaf and his buddies are just bad people, Sophia. I'm not sure we can reach him," Ruth said, referring to a projected scene of the man and his compatriots in a squalid shack. On the floor of the shack were two women, bound and bloodied. "Their prisoners are part of a Christian peacekeeping team, suspected of spying for sectarian rebels just across the North Asian border."

"Gustaf led the torture of this one in particular," Miriam said, enlarging the image of one of the captives. The woman was clearly broken physically, with a bruised face, split lip, and bloody cuts on her arms and legs, but she murmured a prayer of forgiveness for Gustaf even as he stood over her, preparing to inflict more pain.

"Where are the angels who should be ministering to this woman?" Sophia asked in a clipped voice.

"There are multitudes there," Faras answered, flinching as Gustaf pressed a lit cigarette against the prisoner's neck. "But they're not able to do much more than comfort the captives. Only one of Gustaf's colleagues disagrees with what he's doing, but that's not enough to change the situation."

As they watched, a bulky man the same height and size as Gustaf beckoned him aside and handed him a bottle of clear liquid.

"Have a drink, my brother, and think of what we are doing here. Since when do we torture women like this?" he asked softly, handing Gustaf the bottle. For a moment he hesitated, but then Gustaf took the bottle, tipped it back, and swallowed a generous slug.

"Karl, we have been friends since childhood, and you know this is war. A different kind of war, yes, but no less important. All will suffer."

"At least bring in a doctor and tend to their wounds," Karl urged, gesturing for Gustaf to keep the nearly empty bottle. For a moment, the candidate looked uncertain, then he relented.

"Very well, but that's it. Go fetch Boris and see what he can do."

"Boris? He's nothing but an attendant. How will he be able to help?"

"Then find someone else," Gustaf slurred, finishing the alcohol in the bottle.

Sophia closed her eyes, unable to watch, and said, "Before we go on, we need to offer a prayer song for these women, and all others who are being tortured because of their beliefs," she said.

Their voices quickly joined hers and continued with concentrated effort until she signaled they should stop. Just as their song ceased, they saw another man enter the room, carrying a small bag.

"Where's Karl?" Gustaf demanded, slamming the empty bottle down so hard it shattered.

The angels tensed.

"Karl told me you had need of help," the newcomer said, kneeling down and going to work. In his bag he had an abundant supply of painkillers and antibiotics, which he dispensed to both women, murmuring assurances as he did so.

"An earth angel," Faras guessed, watching the doctor's every move.

"Go on," Sophia said to Ruth. "Thank the Almighty Divine we only have one more candidate."

Kim Lee's picture materialized on the screen. She was alone in a dormitory room, pacing back and forth, wailing and pulling at her short black hair.

"She's just been expelled from the university. A classmate set her up by accusing Kim of having sex with her teacher in order to maintain a good grade." Ruth shook her head as the action switched to a tiny rural village where Kim's mother lived. "Unfortunately, a girl from Kim's village called home to tell her family about the story, and it reached Kim's mother, an elderly widow named Shu. For many years, Shu had a bad heart condition, but she wanted Kim to go away to school and make a better life for herself. Shortly after hearing the news, she had a massive attack and died within minutes. Kim had been so busy filing an appeal to reverse the university's decision that she didn't take time to call mother, never thinking the rumor would travel so fast. Now, Kim will never have the chance to tell her mother the true story."

Sophia didn't bother to ask if the others saw angels with Kim, because she knew what the answer would be. Instead she faced Faras, trying to control her anger.

"Couldn't you have stopped the rumor from spreading so fast? The plan you presented was for Kim to be expelled, not lose her mother as well!"

"I tried, Sophia. Every step of the way, I was unsuccessful. The university officials were all determined to act as quickly as possible, and the rumor monger couldn't wait to suggest Shu's daughter wasn't the brilliant scholar she thought."

"And you, Miriam? Why isn't there someone to comfort this poor girl?"

"She has a boyfriend who tried to be supportive, but soon his friends were laughing at him for her dishonesty. It's hard to find anyone who follows the True Way in China, Sophia."

Sophia couldn't contain herself any more. "There must be someone who can help her. Why aren't there angels with her?"

Her question was directed at Ruth, but all three angels stared at her, amazed.

"There are angels, Sophia," Faras said gently, waving his hand in front of the screen. "In every one of them." He quickly replayed the scenarios of Anthony, his wife, the prostitute trapped by Jack, Gustaf with his colleagues, and Kim. Sophia checked to see if he might be teasing in a misguided attempt to lighten the mood, but his face was serious.

"You see angels with each of them?" she asked, and they nodded energetically.

"Wait." Ruth interrupted the dialogue, gesturing toward the screen.

Someone was knocking on the door of Kim's room. It turned out to be one of her other professors, an American woman who held a visiting faculty position at the university.

"Kim, please come and meet with me and my husband tonight," she said when the door was opened. "I think we can help you, but this isn't the place to have a conversation."

"No one is to help me," Kim sobbed, pointing at the suitcase she was packing. "I am to leave university immediately. I do not even have a place to live."

The woman put one hand on Kim's shoulder. "Hear me out this evening. We'll meet with you if you're willing and want to see what can happen. I believe in you, Kim. You're a very bright young woman. You wouldn't need to do anything dishonest to pass a class."

While Kim didn't stop crying, she did shrug her shoulders. "I have no more to lose," she said, accepting a card with the women's telephone number and the name of a restaurant on the back of it.

"Seven o'clock," said the woman, closing the door.

"This woman's husband is a missionary. They can help Kim—maybe even take her to America," Miriam said. "We can send angels to help her succeed there and have a new start."

Sophia felt a small measure of thanks. At least there were promising signs for JoJo and Kim, but otherwise, the Testings of Devotion seemed so damaged, it would take more than a supernatural effort to turn them around.

"Perhaps we should refresh," Faras suggested, clasping his hands as he watched her study the screen.

"No! If anything, we need to work harder, Faras. We can't refresh every time you feel a need to," Sophia said, turning to the Earth Viewer with her lips pressed together. She couldn't stop replaying the scenes they had just viewed, hoping she had missed something.

"But if you're not seeing clearly, perhaps you're the one in need of restoration," Miriam said, watching over Sophia's shoulder. "Your spirit might still be exhausted from your descent."

"I'm fine—Gabriel and I were together before I returned to you, and I assure you, there's nothing wrong with me." Sophia clasped her hands together so the others wouldn't see them trembling. What was Lucifer engineering here?

"What we do need is a few minutes of prayer," she said, squeezing her eyes shut so she wouldn't be distracted by their confused faces. "Please join me so we remain united and strong in our efforts. We cannot allow ourselves to question or stray from our mission."

Gabriel, how should I repair this harm? she prayed silently. *And is it the Almighty Divine's will for the Selected Servants to continue with these Testings, even though it may cause more suffering for mortals?*

She was so lost in her request for guidance, she didn't know what Miriam, Faras, and Ruth were doing, since the room was perfectly still. Perhaps they were stunned into silence by her response, but at least for the moment, the four of them were connected—if only by a shared sense of quiet.

23

Gabriel did not answer directly, but the burden of worry slowly lifted from Sophia, and the peace of reassurance replaced it. The Almighty Divine had given Gabriel instructions about the Testings of Devotion, so He wouldn't fail her or any of the candidates, ultimately.

But what about the Second Level of heaven? It shamed her to admit it, but in her short tenure as Senior Servant, the possibility of advancing herself had become like a mantra pulsing throughout her spirit. The success of the Testings, distancing herself from Lucifer, and advancing to a level closer to the Almighty Divine had begun to seem like one inseparable goal in her mind.

"Might I suggest we refresh?" Thankfully, Faras distracted her.

"Not now," she answered gently.

The flagging of Faras's spirit seemed pronounced and suspicious. Although his face was perfectly alert and observant when he bowed his head toward her in acceptance, something in his persona seemed slower and weaker. Could he secretly be exhausting himself with a plot to derail the Testings of Devotion?

Surprisingly, Miriam moved to stand next to Faras in support, raising her eyebrows at Sophia.

"Are you sure?" she asked. "It's been some time since we rested."

Although she and Faras worked well together, their opinions on most matters usually differed, so Sophia was surprised to find them aligned against her.

"No, we need to press on."

Ruth said, "You're right, Sophia. We shouldn't get discouraged. There's still hope for the candidates we have left, some more than others. Who knows? Maybe this is a test to see if we'll stick to our task without questioning the wisdom of the plan. Maybe you forget how it felt to be mortal, but when things looked bleakest, if I kept plugging away, they got better."

Ruth isn't the deceptive one, Sophia decided. In fact, she might be the wisest of all of them, since she had proven her ability to submit to the Almighty Divine when she was mortal, despite the difficult circumstances of her life. But when Sophia glanced over to give Ruth a reassuring smile, she saw the woman fixated on the Earth Viewer, and her opinion wavered.

Was Ruth mesmerized by all the technology, or was she still hoping for a glimpse of her beloved JoJo? Who knew what her feelings for him might motivate her to do?

Miriam spoke. "There is an issue we need to deal with. We were given four candidates, but now we only have three. Gabriel selected the others, but while you were on earth, Sophia, I offered a prayer song and came to feel it was rightly ordered for me to select a new candidate."

Miriam looked at Sophia, and for an instant there seemed to be defiance in her deep purple eyes.

"You told us we would know what to do." she said, crossing over to the screen as the likeness of a handsome man appeared on it. "Ruth and Faras agreed that I should search for someone to take Anthony's place, so I spent much time looking for the right candidate. Here is the person I was led to."

"He sure is easy on the eye," Ruth said.

Miriam ignored the comment. "His name is Samuel Olsen, but he's different from the others in that he is already living a life of committed faith. His ministry began in Africa, but has spread to Europe, which we know is an area of great concern for the Almighty Divine. Samuel is so charismatic, his followers believe him to be a prophet. Not one of his ministries has failed, which means his influence is continuing to grow."

Sophia watched many scenes from Samuel's life flash by: long days of teaching and travel, endless fundraisers to build new churches, and relentless conversations with others as a way to spread the word of the Almighty Divine. As Ruth observed, Samuel was also attractive, tall, slender, and almost as beautiful as an angel, with burnished blond hair and penetrating hazel eyes.

"He has no family?" Sophia asked, wondering how such a charismatic mortal could fail to attract a wife or at least be surrounded by relatives who believed in his cause.

"No," Miriam shrugged. "His family was killed in an automobile accident and he's far too busy for romance." She sniffed as if Sophia's question was offensive, and continued showing scenes from Samuel's life on the Earth Viewer. The angels and Ruth saw him on television performing faith healings, speaking to large groups of delegates from different churches, and delivering riveting sermons from the makeshift pulpit at a theater auditorium. On one occasion, he held an outdoor baptism that lasted from dusk to dawn.

Sophia considered the proposed candidate for a long time, not sure why she couldn't feel instantly enthusiastic like the others, who were smiling at the screen in approval. Was Samuel too good to be true? Or was it the luxurious lifestyle he seemed to allow himself, justifying the purchase of expensive cars and clothing with the rationale that "God wants me to be blessed"? Certainly, the Almighty Divine didn't prohibit His children from acquiring material possessions, but something about Samuel seemed excessive.

"How will you test him, though?" she finally asked. "If this man is as engaging as he seems, Lucifer is no doubt aware of his activities already—we know evangels are one of his favorite targets."

It was Ruth who answered. "His next endeavor is to establish a ministry in Amsterdam, right near the most sinful district in the city. He has raised funds for a building he will convert into a church, so he can have a home base instead of traveling from place to place as a visiting preacher. From there, he wants to continue on, planting churches in the U.S. and elsewhere. The Testing of Devotion is this: the building he is using to build his church will burn down, and he will lose not only his following but all his other resources. There will be questions about arson, and an investigation into his use of the many donations he has received. That will challenge him to continue in his ministry and persevere in serving the Almighty Divine regardless of his external circumstances. As you can see, he has been well rewarded for his efforts so far."

"Perhaps now is the time to take a break and consider." Faras's suggestion was tentative, but finally appropriate. They had reached an impasse and Sophia needed guidance from Gabriel.

"There's some wisdom to that, Faras. I won't join you, but please, feel free to be together in refreshing, and I will try to sort through all of this. It's a lot to work through, and I'm uneasy taking on a task that wasn't directly requested from the Almighty Divine."

Sophia watched the three of them hurry off to their adjoining chambers. Even Ruth and Faras had participated in some way to help Miriam identify this replacement candidate without being directed to do so. She didn't want to sink into paranoid analysis of the Selected Servants and Ruth's behavior, but it was hard not to wonder. Still, her task was not to resolve the situation, but to carry out the instructions Gabriel had given, vague as they were.

Meeting with Hector was the first step. He would give her a better perspective on the information she just received. Kneeling before the Earth Viewer, she waited for a clearer understanding of what to say, but it was a long time before she felt ready to do what was required.

"Gabriel, if I'm going in the wrong direction, please stop me now," she whispered, but the Guidance Room was completely quiet, with no sign the archangel had even heard her request. That silence continued until Hector appeared as soon as she summoned him, robes swirling as he swept in the room, surrounded by a soothing blue mist. As soon as he saw her, he broke into a big grin and drew her into a hug.

"Sophia, we haven't been alone together since you became Senior Servant," he said. "It's good to see you." He clapped his hands together at the sight of the empty recliners. "And I always appreciate the opportunity to sit in one of your recliners. Why are they so much more restful than my own?"

She waved him into one, smiling. "Enjoy yourself, and thank you for coming so quickly. I'm sorry we haven't met sooner. Somehow, I never got to tell you how surprised I was to be chosen. Between you and me, I thought you were better suited to the job and confess I feel constantly challenged to be the kind of leader the Almighty Divine desires."

Hector gave her a calculating look. "Surely Gabriel told you my happiness in my current position led me to pray you would be selected rather than me. Even if that were not so, we can never fathom the wisdom of our Almighty Divine."

"Hector, you're with the heavenly host most of the time, and you know the state of their spirits well. Although the Selected Servants have secondary authority over the heavenly host, it is you the Almighty Divine wants to help with a special mission."

"I'm blessed! Whatever's needed, I'll do it."

"I'll be brief and then you can ask questions. It's no great secret that our battle against Lucifer is raging stronger than ever, and recently we seem to be losing ground. Mortals are either actively turning away from the Almighty Divine, or drifting into the false ways of Lucifer."

He frowned and reached out to take her hand. "It isn't just mortals. An unusual number of angels have fallen lately; in fact, enough to arouse my suspicion."

She dropped into the chair next to him, massaging her forehead with her fingers. "Are there signs they're struggling, or do they just suddenly disappear?"

"I've just started to watch closely. First, I noticed the earth angels seemed to be leaving us without warning, even ones I was sure would be strong warriors. Then I talked with some of the others, and it seems the defections are more widespread than I realized. You probably didn't know that Lara has gone."

"Lara? How can that be? She seemed so devoted…Is there a particular kind of angel among those who fall?"

"It's my sense that the earth angels are the greater part of those who leave. I'm sure, now that you've been there, you can appreciate how difficult it is to walk the earth, but that's always been the case. Why would we lose more now?"

She got up and paced around the room a bit, then stopped in front of the Earth Viewer. "Earth angels would make an especially attractive target for Lucifer. They know a lot about the First Level of heaven and how things operate here, as well as the ways of mortals. My return to earth convinced me Lucifer is gaining strength in new ways. I confess, at times it was even hard for me to resist his temptations."

"Even you, Sophia? Then we do need special help, since the Senior Servant should be stronger than any of us. "

"Should be," she said dryly, "but as you know, I went as penitence for a transgression. I second-guessed the Almighty Divine, Hector."

He made a sound of empathy. "I've done similar things myself and not suffered any consequences, Sophia. There must have been other reasons for your descent. Perhaps it was a test to see if you're ready for the Second Level of heaven! It's about time one of us went."

She took a slow breath in, remembering her own recent longings. Could Hector be right? Then the circumstances before her quashed any hope. For the foreseeable future, she was needed on the First Level of heaven, to continue carrying the burden of the Testings of Devotion and find the source of any deception that might undermine their efforts.

"How I wish you were right, but for now, we've got something more important to worry about. In an effort to build spiritual soldiers who can help in the eternal battle between good and evil, the Almighty Divine gave Gabriel a new strategy to pass on to me."

Moving to sit beside him, she provided a brief overview of the Testings of Devotion and each of the Selected Servant's role in carrying them out, omitting the tie-in to the Nephilim, the specifics of any candidate's test, or Gabriel's suspicions. Trying to sound upbeat, she laid one hand over his.

"Now, we need you to be part of the Testings of Devotion because Gabriel wants to make sure there are no problems among the heavenly host that might be giving Lucifer an advantage. He requests that you screen all the angels to make sure there's no dissention or disobedience coming from within."

"Of course, I'm honored and humbled to have such a purpose." He inclined his head, but when Sophia's fingers slipped away and she let out along breath, he looked up in alarm.

"Hector, some very unusual things have happened. First, I didn't see a single other angel during my time on earth. Then, when I came back and looked at the Earth Viewer with the Selected Servants and Ruth, they saw angels while I did not. It seems impossible, but could all three of them be right and I wrong? As you can imagine, it's caused some tension between us, but either they're not giving you the right directions for the heavenly host—or some of your angels are disobeying."

"You know I carry out orders, but the Selected Servants can always divert or recall angels after I've dispensed them if they think it's indicated, so I don't have a definite answer for you. It sounds very serious. Should I request more prayers for you?"

"No! I appreciate your suggestion, but none of the heavenly host can know about this. Gabriel was very clear that you and I are the only others to be included. Of course, as always, your personal prayers are welcome."

"So be it," he said gravely.

She waited for it all to sink in, then felt a spinning in her spirit that made her stumble backward and slide down into one of the recliners, covering her face with one hand.

"Are you okay?" he asked, dropping down next to her.

She gave her head a tiny shake. "There's more difficult news, I'm afraid. If we are to truly investigate whether the earth angels are carrying out their responsibilities, you may have to descend. I'm sorry, Hector."

His expression soured as the blueness of the air that had slowly arisen to circle around them darkened. "When you were selected as Senior Servant, Gabriel assured me I could continue doing what I am now. He knows I don't have the constitution to descend."

"None of us can say we'll never have to descend, Hector. I hated to go, but now I see why it was important, and both Gabriel and Michael go to earth frequently."

He sighed, clearly exasperated. "They're archangels, Sophia. They're so much stronger than we are, it's hardly a challenge for them to go."

"Remember the price I paid for failing to submit, and what's at stake. I encourage you to accept this. You might just need to get information Gabriel requires or observe the situation with Samuel more closely, but clearly, it's important." She was surprised by his reticence, and tucked her legs so he wouldn't notice the nervous shifting of her feet.

It took some effort, but eventually he composed himself and looked into her eyes. "They know I'll do it, of course. I'm always ready to serve, Sophia, no matter what it requires, but that doesn't mean I'm full of joy at the idea of going down to Lucifer's playground."

24

After Hector left, Sophia quieted, knowing she would soon meet with Gabriel. When she was lifted up to his Refreshing Room and he appeared, the blueness around them took on a strange sparkle.

"So, Sophia, do you have the same sense of a struggle among the Selected Servants as I do?" he asked, settling next to her.

"What else would explain what's happened with the Testings of Devotion so far, Gabriel?" She breathed in the blue air, trying to calm herself, but the image of Anthony in his final moments of despair seemed to hover before her. "Poor Anthony. He and his family suffered so much, and for what purpose? The Almighty Divine must be very grieved."

"I've been charged to review every detail of his Testing of Devotion, including the evil people who came into Anthony's life. Right now, I can find no fault with any of the Selected Servants, but my uneasiness remains."

"They've taken it upon themselves to select a new candidate, which concerns me."

She described Samuel Olsen and all that she'd been told about him, waiting for Gabriel to be displeased too. There was a long silence as blue tendrils of mist stroked their faces. When he finally spoke, there was a thoughtful look in his eyes as he rubbed his chin with one hand, over and over again..

"Of course I must share this with the Almighty Divine, but something tells me all is as intended." He seemed to be talking to himself more than to Sophia. "The Selected Servants shouldn't have acted on their own initiative, but while that's worrisome, it may help us discover the truth."

"If Miriam, Faras, and Ruth are joining their efforts, how can I possibly counteract them? I may be the Senior Servant, but I'm still just one angel."

"Sophia, haven't you noticed how much stronger you are since you came back from earth? Give yourself credit for the progress you've made, and recognize that by submitting you've gained greater power."

His comment made her realize suddenly that she did feel different; inside there was a new confidence about her ability to carry out the Almighty Divine's wishes, and maybe, in some small way, she was less motivated to put distance between herself and Lucifer by getting to the Second Level. Still, the notion that the Selected Servants and Ruth might be united against her was daunting.

"You're right. I have changed; I just hope it's enough." She waited for him to assure her that she had made significant improvements, maybe even Second-Level-worthy improvements, but instead he returned to the subject of Samuel.

"So, we should use him to replace Anthony. Continue on as you are, Sophia. Since angels aren't secretive by nature, it's going to be hard to keep your suspicions from the others. Give me your hand."

She held her right hand up, resting it lightly in the palm of his. Instantly, she was filled with a sense of supreme peace as every barrier between her and the Almighty Divine fell away. The delight ended too soon, but left her completely serene.

After a few more final instructions, she returned to the Guidance Room, which was empty. She went to the Earth Viewer and idly examined the lives of the original candidates one more time, both disappointed and reassured when there still weren't angels in any of the scenarios.

A thought occurred to her, and she flicked back to a scenario of Lydia, the first mortal Gabriel had mentioned when explaining the Testings. The woman was speaking to a large audience of legislators, surrounded by angels.

Swiftly, Sophia projected the lives of Kim, Gustaf, and JoJo, implementing the changes Gabriel suggested and sending a legion of angels to each. She was just finishing as the other three came in, instantly joining her at the screen.

"I thought I was in charge of the Testings of Devotion," Ruth protested when she realized what Sophia was doing. On either side of her, Faras and Miriam looked equally dismayed.

"Gabriel and I met, and he gave me further directions for the original candidates." Her tone left no room for discussion. "He also thinks we should proceed with Samuel Olsen as a replacement, as the three of you recommended. Gustaf has just watched his close friend and co-worker be arrested as a traitor, even though he's no more disloyal than anyone else in the inner circle of the secret police. When Gustaf spoke up in the man's defense, the guards at the prison threatened to torture him too. Seeing what happened to this man has finally made Gustaf begin to question his own behavior. I believe an old girlfriend who belongs to a church and is very faithful will come on the scene at any moment. Between her influence, the doubts of his friend Karl about Gustaf's tactics, and some time to think, we may see some repentance.

"JoJo continues to change. After Tamika started visiting, he began to listen to Pastor Ephraim and is now returning to prayer and reading his Bible and other religious books. The charges against him have been reduced to involuntary manslaughter, which brought his prison time down to about seven years. He'll have the chance to get out of prison and reconstruct his life, and can continue on with all that he's started in the real world."

"Praise be!" Ruth squealed, and clapped her hands.

"Finally," Sophia continued, "Kim is indeed on her way to the U.S., with many angels to heal and minister to her. Her rescuers have reminded her of the teachings she learned about the Almighty Divine as a child in the village school. I think her prospects seem good too."

"Can you see the angels with each person now?" she said. When she looked at each one of them and they responded with a nod, she felt an inner surge of relief. "So we're all on the same page with this?"

Again they agreed, but despite his half smile, Faras seemed emotionally exhausted and Miriam all but openly pouted. Only Ruth was beaming, singing an earth hymn about rejoicing and hugging each of the angels with all her strength. Studying the slightest lift of Miriam's eyebrows and the tug on the corner of her mouth, Sophia wondered if she might be sulking over what could appear to be Ruth's success at her part of the Testings of Devotion.

They had just refreshed, which usually led to a state of calm and even euphoria. Why weren't they happy to see such a positive shift in the direction of the Testings of Devotion, even if their efforts weren't the reason for it?

"Any thoughts on what could have been done differently the first time through, so we can be sure to succeed with Samuel?" Sophia asked, avoiding their eyes so they wouldn't guess what she was thinking. How much easier all this would be if there weren't secrets—secrets between her and Gabriel and Hector, and obviously, secrets inside within at least one of the group before her.

"You think it's my fault about Anthony, like I did something wrong." Ruth's lower lip trembled slightly. "Well, you're wrong. I stayed here and let you go rescue JoJo when every part of me wanted to be in your place. I just did for the others what you told me to before you left, and went along with Faras and Miriam. And look at the rewards of obedience. JoJo is going to make it, I know! We will come rejoicing!"

"Believe me, you wouldn't have wanted to be in my place, Ruth. Descending was very challenging." Sophia softened and stroked the length of Ruth's arm until their hands met. Lightly massaging the woman's fingers, she explained, "It's standard practice to review efforts that don't turn out as predicted. Sometimes we learn more from them than the ones that succeed."

"But of course, this has nothing to do with you, Sophia, does it?" Miriam moved ever so slightly closer to Ruth. "You're the superior angel, better than all of us put together. You survived a descent and didn't fall to Lucifer. You came back, found things in a mess, and because you don't trust us, you took over and 'fixed' the Testings of Devotion."

"I'm not superior to any angel," Sophia said, surprised by Miriam's rancor. "I just did what Gabriel asked me to do."

"Of course you're better than us. You're the Senior Servant." Faras joined the argument, suddenly animated. "I don't know every detail of what happened to you on earth, Sophia, but nothing I saw could explain why you've come back like this."

"Like what?"

"We've never disagreed before, but look at us now," he answered. "The three of us are like naughty children being punished for something we didn't even do, and you seem to consider yourself some high and mighty authority over us."

Sophia was ready to refute what he said, but as she opened her mouth, the serenity of submission she felt when resting with Gabriel returned to her, as if he was whispering cautionary advice in her ear.

She bowed her head before them. "What Faras says is true. We must stop bickering and stand together and cooperate, or we will fail. Please believe that you're each equally important, and if I've somehow suggested otherwise, I sincerely apologize. Maybe being on earth and realizing how bad things really are made me overly eager for the Testings of Devotion to succeed. Come, let me offer a prayer song so that we might reconnect with each other in love."

She sang sincerely, understanding that what had just happened offered direct proof of something wrong. As Selected Servants, it was forbidden for Faras and Miriam to speak so defiantly to her, and arguments never occurred on the First Level. As for Ruth—she was clearly hanging onto her attachment to JoJo for all she was worth.

Sophia realized what danger could result as the prayer song came to an end. The well-being of mortals was at stake, and if she—they—failed, it would be a crisis of universal proportion. Until proven otherwise, she had to trust Gabriel's instincts and consider both Selected Servants and Ruth her possible adversaries, without them knowing she did so.

25

When Sophia's song ended, each of the others spontaneously offered an additional prayer requesting forgiveness for being proud and disobedient. Which one wasn't sincere? Was it Miriam, with her placid violet eyes and dark hair swirled so perfectly around her oval face, standing tall and composed by the podium? Or maybe Ruth was the culprit. There was no ignoring the way her fluid brown eyes flitted back and forth from the Earth Viewer or her restless posture and the regular way she reached up to play with the circle of ebony curls that framed her face. Then again, it might be Faras, whose features still seemed fatigued despite the recent refreshing. The usually bouncy cap of his hair was flat and dull, his glistening brown eyes were drooping, and lines of fatigue pulled down the edges of his moist lips.

As they joined hands, Sophia willed a new energy to flow through them, hoping that whichever of them had wavered might reconsider his or her actions. At her suggestion, they recited the vows of commitment used when beginning a new mission, and every part of her spirit prayed for their pledges to be honest.

Then a scene on the Earth Viewer caught her attention. It was a horrific battle between two of many religious factions in a small African country, triggered by an unknown and most likely trivial incident. Thousands of people were fleeing from the fighting; mostly women and young children. Faras and Miriam broke free and moved as one to deal with the crisis. Ruth and Sophia stood alone, holding hands.

"I think I'm too preoccupied with these Testings of Devotion," Ruth said. "It really bothers me to deal out suffering after I spent my life as a mortal doing all I could to end it. Maybe it was a mistake for me to leave the Community of Resting Mortals. I think I might have been happier there."

"Things will get better," Sophia assured her, then wondered if this was an entrée to some kind of confession. "But if you need to talk more about how things are going here, we can do that. Would you like me to ask Gabriel if you can be released to go back with the other mortals?"

"Oh no! It's just that you all don't realize how hard it is to just forget about people you love."

"You're right. I haven't experienced that, but I know it's painful to hold onto any kind of attachments other than those the Almighty Divine gives us. He is ready to relieve you of that burden."

"Well, before those attachments are completely gone and I'm a care-free woman, I do want to thank you for helping JoJo and Tamika and Ephraim. Although I would have gone back to earth in an instant, it was dumb of me to think I could go in your place. I couldn't have done half the job you did."

"I only did what I was led to do by our beloved Almighty Divine, Ruth. How it works is a miracle. As an angel, I could never craft such a chain of events." She looked at the Earth Viewer, relieved to see that, with Miriam and Faras's intervention, the situation appeared quieter. "Now, do you need any help with Samuel, or should I leave you to begin his testing?"

"Miriam and I talked it through already, but maybe I should run it all by you again, just to make sure I've got it right."

Their proposed approach sounded straightforward and appropriate. A mysterious fire would break out in the building where Samuel's new church was meeting, which would lead to questions about arson. When he came under suspicion of setting the fire in order to recoup insurance money, Samuel would flee to the United States, discouraged but still long-ing to establish a ministry that would touch many lives.

That wouldn't be difficult, given his charismatic personality. Before long, he would build up a new following, but then rumors from overseas would follow him, and the new congregation would voice doubts about his use of their weekly contributions. In the end, he would triumph, but the testing had to be carefully balanced. Since Samuel was already living a life devoted to the Almighty Divine, Lucifer might escalate his attacks if too much success came.

"Faras will use angels rather than people to minister to him, and Miriam will bring a special spirit-filled woman to help inspire and restore him in his brokenness," Ruth concluded.

"A woman? Who?" Sophia frowned, trying to remember when they discussed that idea.

"We haven't decided. Maybe Kim Lee? They'll be in the same city, and she's already started to show great power in her faithfulness. She's devoting most of her time to reading about the Almighty Divine and meeting with other believers to pray and learn more. Miriam said sometimes brand new believers from atheist countries have a special influence on those who have never experienced religious repression. What do you think?"

"Hmm…appealing, but two candidates together might attract even more unwanted attention and reach a limited audience. Let's continue reflecting on it until I seek Gabriel's input again." Sophia gave Ruth a quick hug and kissed her cheek. "I must leave now, but don't allow yourself to become discouraged."

"Do I ever get to be just perfect and leave all the negative stuff behind? You know, the 'mortal' stuff, like getting all worked up about 'me instead of Thee,' as Pastor Ephraim used to say?"

Sophia smiled. "If it's any comfort, that's a question even we angels ask. Perfection is impossible for any of us. Still, it builds our faith to wrestle with the issues, and in the end, I think it makes us stronger."

"Or makes you decide you'd far rather spend eternity with me," the Voice said.

Ruth was looking doubtfully at Sophia. Would she ever stop struggling? Her inability to find contentment with just being on the First Level of heaven was bothersome, and Sophia couldn't help returning to her earlier doubts. If Lucifer managed to influence Ruth through her earthly attachments, he could gain direct access to the secrets of the First Level.

As if to protect her, she moved in front of the woman. "Don't worry about what's happening on earth right now, Ruth. Spend some time praying for all the candidates and let Miriam and Faras work on this."

Ruth grinned. "I'm bugging you, right?" she said, studying Sophia's face. "Remember, I'm a mortal, and even on earth that was one of my bad habits—questions. All through school my teachers told me I asked 90 percent of the questions they got in a day. I think even Ephraim got a little frustrated with me, but answers make me feel like I'm headed in the right direction."

"You're right, Ruth. A good question keeps us all on our toes. I should welcome them more. Now if you'll excuse me, I'm going to go talk to Hector."

Leaving Ruth to work alongside Faras and Miriam, she went to the Great Way, choosing to mingle among the heavenly host so she could get a sense of their spirits. As other angels passed by or paused in their prayers to greet her, she knew she had made the right choice. It was a relief to be out of Operations Central and away from Ruth—who was lovable but challenging—and the Selected Servants who might be actively undermining her. Instead, she relished the company of ordinary angels who went about their daily business, singing or rejoicing in each other's presence. One even stopped her, pulling her over to a group of angels where a woman with long silver hair and blazing green eyes was the center of attention.

"Sophia, please, you must come and hear Eve's new song. She's been working to perfect it for some time, but now it's ready to be shared."

Underneath the elegant ivory flowers of a tree with graceful drooping branches, Eve beckoned eagerly to Sophia. Although she was in a hurry, Sophia decided it was a good opportunity to set aside her worries about the Selected Servants and enjoy a celebration.

Once the group gathered, Eve sang her song, a tune that quickened Sophia's spirit and made her glad she hadn't declined the invitation. Even the breeze that stirred the lush green grass and made the tree leaves whisper seemed to accompany Eve's voice in a soft chorus. When the song finished, a brief moment of satisfaction kept them silent.

Sophia hugged Eve, resting her cheek against the other angel's as she blinked away the emotion that briefly blurred her vision. "How lovely—and the very thing I needed just now. Bless you all."

Reluctantly, she pulled away from them, wondering what her existence would be like if she requested to stay on the First Level, only not as Senior Servant? Would she enjoy the simple pleasure of a song more if she wasn't preoccupied with praying or otherwise intervening to protect mortals from evil? The heavenly host was blissfully unaware of what she alone knew.

I'm just like Ruth! she realized, stepping back onto the Great Way with a small laugh of surprise. She can't stop wishing to be on earth with JoJo, and I seem fixated on going to the Second Level. The insight filled her with renewed love for the Almighty Divine, who could correct her with a beautiful song.

As she continued on through crowds of angels, she marveled anew at how lovely they were; their physical perfection and emotional joy seemed striking. There was no note of discontent or unhappiness in the conversations she heard around her, and although as Senior Servant she was recognized by her special luminance, the angels rejoiced in each other's presence as much as they did hers.

"Sophia!" Hector was surprised and happy to see her when she entered the Director's House. He ended his discussion with a group of angels, dismissed them, and waved her to sit in front of his Angel Viewer, a replica of the Earth Viewer she and the Selected Servants used, but smaller and embedded into the surface of a table surrounded by chairs.

"Hector, I must tell you I feel incredible! Originally, I thought I would come to you myself so I could be among at least a small part of the heavenly host and get a sense of how things were going. Along the way I stopped to listen to a song of praise, and it filled my soul with true bliss. I can see why you love your work."

She must truly have been touched by the Almighty Divine, because Hector's look was guarded. "You're just finding that out now, Sophia?"

Seating herself and tracing the surface of the table, she shook her head slightly. "No, not just, but spending so much time in the Guidance Room has made me forget. Being Senior Servant removes you from some things...Anyway, how are your investigations going?"

He drummed his fingers against the table, as if unsure how to start. "In relation to the heavenly host as a whole, all does seem as usual. You must have noticed that as you passed: the angels are diligent in their prayers for mortals and praise of the Almighty Divine. It was a little harder for me to check in on all the angels on earth, but I believe they are carrying out their duties as instructed."

"So, there are still more earth angels returning to the First Level of heaven after their time on earth than staying with Lucifer?"

"Yes, no problem there as far as I can tell." He put his hand against the screen to illuminate it, and she saw what he meant. There was an incredible flow of angels between the First Level of heaven and earth. The earth angels descended through the Portal with brave and hopeful demeanors, but returned downcast and clearly in need of the comforts of the First Level of heaven.

"They look weary, but I suppose I did too, when I came back."

"But what about Lara? Did you figure out what made her leave? Or…" Sophia looked around to make sure they were truly alone. "Isaac? It's very mysterious that two who seemed so devout could be tempted away."

"I agree, but I haven't been able to find out anything about either of them." He rubbed his chin with one hand and touched the Angel Viewer with the other, flipping from one scene of Lara and Isaac to another. "These are all from the past. When I try to locate them now, nothing happens. There's also some kind of block around your candidates for the Testings of Devotion. Whenever I try to discover more about them or intervene, my Viewer stops working, or I'm overcome with such a heaviness I can't go on. All I can do is watch them from here."

Sophia pressed her hand to the Angel Viewer and focused on Samuel Olsen. An image of the man appeared instantly, poised at the lectern of a church packed with people who applauded and shouted "Amen!" at regular intervals. Samuel appeared relaxed and confident, but there were no angels around him. Quickly, Sophia checked on the other candidates and found the same situation. She studied the screen, trying to sort through the complicated chain of events and unsure of how much to say to Hector.

If Miriam was acting alone to sabotage the Testings, there would still be angels, since Faras would surely notice and compensate for the deficit, but maybe the two of them were working together. Then again, Ruth could be collaborating with one of the Select Servants to misrepresent the actual circumstances the candidates were in. And, although Hector hadn't uncovered it, there was still the possibility of rebellion from within the heavenly host.

Hector stood to look over her shoulder, increasingly upset as she progressed back through the candidates. "I couldn't even get to this point, Sophia. Each time I tried to pull up a picture, it wouldn't come, but this is worse. There aren't any angels there. It's as if I never sent any, yet surely you know I did. One of the Selected Servants must have called them back, or sent them elsewhere. That's a very bad sign. There must be something not right with the Selected Servants, or maybe it's the mortal. Does Gabriel know?"

"Yes, of course he knows, but for some reason we are to continue on without his immediate intervention." Her spirit felt as heavy as it had during those moments on earth when she stood helplessly before the small children who were captive in the drug users' apartment.

Despite Hector's help, she was no closer to resolving a mystery that could endanger everyone on the First Level of heaven. How wrong she had been to think that descending to earth was her most challenging assignment. Clearly, there were more difficulties to come, and Lucifer was almost certain to be at the heart of them.

26

B efore returning to Operations Central, Sophia asked Hector to refresh with her. The renewing she received from the Almighty Divine was exactly what she needed to free her spirit from concerns and ready her for action. She was the first to rouse, stretching her arms over her head and pointing her toes for a delicious second of tension, then turning on her side to watch Hector in repose.

As she watched the other angel continue to rest with a half smile on his lips, Gabriel's voice sounded as a whisper in her ear. His words were quiet, but their content made her sit up and clench her eyes shut for an instant, not wanting to see the innocent and carefree expression vanish from Hector's face. Why must she be the one to give him bad news?

"That was wonderful. Just what I needed," he said when his eyes finally flickered open and he saw her looking at him. Something about her expression must have warned him all was not well because he jumped to his feet. "What is it? What have you learned?"

When she shared Gabriel's instructions, Hector's hands curled into fists.

"You've both deceived me! Our last discussion was just a ruse so you could set me up for this, wasn't it? 'A possibility of descending,' indeed. I'm needed here far more than on earth. Why can't Faras or Miriam go in my place?"

"Hector, it must be you. It's what the Almighty Divine wishes."

She didn't explain the real rationale for sending Hector instead of one of the Selected Servants, although every part of her longed to as she took in the terror on his face. Hadn't she felt much the same in his situation? She bit down on her lip, frustrated. Even if Hector was told that his descent was going to help uncover duplicity on the part of Faras, Miriam, Ruth, or all three, it wasn't likely to change his attitude about going, and it might alter his behavior.

They were at a standoff. When she tried to touch his arm and encourage him, he pulled away, his face pinched in anger. It was difficult to see the one angel who was always good-natured and ready to rally the heavenly host despite any circumstance so flushed with anger.

"Hector, I'm sorry," she said softly.

He seemed about to snap back at her, but then his face changed, as if realizing the consequences of disobedience. He closed his eyes, and after a brief silence spoke without opening them.

"What will it involve?"

"Only Samuel Olsen. Since he's the newest candidate, you must stay with him, just for a while, and see how his Testing of Devotion is proceeding. Your presence will hopefully provide us with the answers we need, because you're strong enough to prevail against Lucifer. Hector, please understand that right now this is more holy than any of the other work you or I are doing. I can't share everything, but trust the Almighty Divine and submit to Him. You've always been better at that than I have."

"Maybe so, but this situation is unusual, Sophia. To be honest, I'm afraid. I see what goes on down there and I confess: sometimes I watch the earth angels with gratitude, relieved that I'm here instead of there. It's one thing to send others off to fight in a war you know is just, but another to go yourself."

"Amen," she said.

He looked at her quickly. "Tell me, were you tempted to stray during your descent?" When she didn't answer immediately, he pressed. "You were, weren't you?"

She thought of the pills cupped in her hand and the near-trance the concert music had induced in her, as well as her fight to resist falling downward into what she thought was hell. "I was."

"Terrific," he snapped, massaging his forehead with one hand. "If it's going to require this kind of effort to save mortals, maybe the old prophecy is true. I've heard it said that eventually the Almighty Divine will gather up all the angels and seal the Portal for good, leaving those mortals still on earth under the dominion of Lucifer." He grimaced. "I just hope I don't accidentally get caught down there if that happens."

She too had heard such talk but had never taken it seriously. Knowing what she did now, the battle for mortal souls was close to a climax. If the Testings of Devotion didn't work, how many other strategies were left?

"I don't know, Hector. Maybe those on the Second or Third Levels of heaven do, but until I'm directed otherwise, my job is to continue intervening to win the souls of mortals."

"Think of it, though. How many attempts have failed since we've been here? Even the descent of so many powerful holies didn't work completely; in fact, each one got dismissed with more and more hatred."

"This isn't a time to doubt—you have to descend with courage and conviction, and be thankful you won't have to assume a mortal body." She shuddered. "Those were the times when I felt the worst."

"You're right, of course. I should feel fortunate that I'm trusted to go on this mission." He nodded and lifted his chin. "I *do* feel fortunate. We are all called to be servants who do even the most unpleasant tasks with great joy."

"Blessings on you, Hector. Go now before we are noticed, and remember—Gabriel and Michael will be watching over you as only the archangels can."

They walked toward the Portal together, arms linked and voices joined in a prayer song of blessing, so no angel who saw them would suspect anything was wrong. When the Great Way divided, Sophia reluctantly turned toward Operations Central.

"You know I can't be seen with you from this point on or the angels will wonder." She gave a small laugh. "Ruth coming here has raised enough questions as it is."

He kissed her cheek as his arms wrapped around her shoulders a bit longer and tighter than usual. "Pray for me, Sophia."

"I will, dear Hector, you know I will. Now go, quickly. Gabriel promised he would be there to show you the Portal, and I know his presence will encourage you."

She put her head down and hurried away, assuring herself he would not fail. Relieved to find the Selected Servants and Ruth occupied in the Guidance Room, she retreated to her own private chamber, which, unlike the others, had an Earth Viewer set into one wall. Without looking away, she touched the screen and seated herself on her recliner, watching until she saw Hector appear as a pale form behind Samuel Olsen.

The candidate had just finished leading a revival meeting for hundreds of people, all members of his new church. Satisfied that at least Hector was in place and ready to follow all that happened to Samuel, she was just about to stand up and join the others when laughter sounded.

The pitch of the Voice froze her in place. On her Viewer, she saw that the church, an old school auditorium, was in the process of renovation. In one corner, stacks of lumber were piled next to cans of paint, while scaffolding and a large canvas took up most of the other. Clearly, Samuel was actively working to create a church environment that would draw others in: there were flyers announcing upcoming events tacked to the doors, and plenty of greeters to make sure each attendee got a personal welcome.

As the last of his congregation filed out, Samuel gathered his notes from behind the makeshift lectern and stifled a yawn. The paper coffee cup he picked up was empty, so he crushed it, and with basketball precision, popped it into a wastepaper can just offstage.

"How blessed is your Brother Hector now, Sophia?" the Voice asked slyly.

She gasped as a circle of fire closed around Hector, growing more violent as he struggled to free himself. His frantic attempts to escape reminded her of the absolute despair she felt during her last moments on earth; she winced and closed her eyes.

"Sophia, you forget I am the wisest of the universe! No sooner was your pitiful plan formed than I began to destroy it. One by one, your mortal candidates will all bow to me, should I want that. You've chosen badly, though, because none of them are even worthy of my smallest demon. They will all die as Anthony did."

She was about to reach out and touch the Viewer, willing other angels to the scene to help Hector, but stopped. If nothing else, she had learned to resist interfering when it wasn't her job to do so; instead, she watched helplessly.

Oblivious to the angel struggling next to him, Samuel climbed down from the stage and stretched out on one of the worn auditorium chairs whose seat was made of pockmarked velvet. Pulling out a cigarette, he lit it and took a deep drag, carelessly tossing his match so that it landed, not on the floor, but on the seat next to him.

How long could Hector last? Trying to block out the obscene glee of the Voice's howls, Sophia sang one prayer song after the other, so loud she was almost screaming. Samuel, lost in thought, continued to smoke carelessly. It was easy to foresee how the fire that would consume his hoped-for church building was going to begin. This was part of the plan she and Ruth discussed, but there was no suggestion that Samuel would be harmed during the tragedy.

"Hector, be brave, Hector be strong," Sophia chanted as Samuel dozed off. His cigarette fell onto a few tissue-thin pieces of music stacked below the seat where his match was still smoldering a hole into the cushion. Instantly, the papers caught on fire.

"Oh, I can do better than that," the Voice chortled.

In a flash, the auditorium was ablaze, burning as fiercely as the cage of flames around Hector. Samuel stirred, coughing, then awoke and ran to one of the exits, which was locked. After pounding on it and discovering no one heard his cries for help, he ran to each of the other doors and found them sealed as well.

Where were Miriam, Faras, and Ruth? Each of them had the ability to intervene in the situation, saving Samuel and possibly Hector.

Hector and Samuel collapsed at the same time, the angel almost invisible in the midst of the spiritual fire. Sophia gripped the sides of her recliner, tensing in an attempt to refrain from intervening.

Then everything changed.

A space cleared in the flames and Michael appeared, effortlessly scooping up Hector and Samuel. With a gentle breath, he sent them through the ceiling and outside the building where they drifted to the ground as slowly as autumn leaves dancing on a breeze. Then he stifled the blaze in the auditorium with a sweep of his magnificent sword.

The triumphant howl of the Voice began to falter, but then resumed in a roar of victory as a legion of demons charged into the auditorium. Each was hideous in a different way: some had the face of one animal and the body of another; others dripped bile and blood from every opening on their scarred bodies, and one contingent was clearly Nephilim, with over-sized bodies and misshapen heads.

The intent of the evil army was clear as they charged up the aisles and tore apart the lectern. Next, they leapt on top of the simple altar and jumped until it split into fragments. Every hymnal and Bible in the auditorium burst into flames simultaneously, which made the demons howl with approval.

The second wave of the fire was worse than the first, but Michael returned, his mammoth sword now sparking with white fire that vanquished whatever it touched. Energy radiated outward from it in bolts of pure silver, causing Lucifer's workers to fall back in fear when the light struck them. Whimpering, they began to retreat from the stage as Michael picked up a hammered brass cross that had fallen to the ground and set it upright between the parts of the broken altar.

"Begone!" he commanded as sirens sounded outside the church.

Shaken and relieved, Sophia hurried out to the Guidance Room, wondering what Miriam, Faras, and Ruth would have to say about what had just happened to Hector. As expected, they were busy at the Earth Viewer, each seemingly focused on helping firefighters save what was left of Samuel's church.

"Where's Samuel?" she asked.

"He found an open door and got out," Miriam said, without turning away from the screen.

No! Sophia wanted to protest. *He was rescued by our most powerful warrior—didn't you see it?*

"We made sure all the people in his congregation were out too," Ruth said. "No one was hurt, not even Samuel, thanks to that passerby who called for an ambulance."

Sophia could barely restrain herself from demanding to know why Ruth hadn't let Miriam and Faras know their help was needed when the fire first started. If Samuel hadn't been so tired, he and Hector could have been long gone before the building went up in flames.

"And don't forget all the angels who came to help the firefighters and the ambulance crew," Miriam added, without turning away from the Earth Viewer.

Faras was the only one who looked confused. He tapped his fingers on the furrowed creases of his forehead and shook his head.

"I don't understand it. The janitor responsible for locking up the building was supposed to pass out in the bathroom after one drink too many so Samuel would be sure to have an exit. Instead, all the auditorium doors were locked. I don't know how that could happen." He looked closer. "There're hymnals and Bibles everywhere too. I'm sure the janitor was supposed to gather them up, stop for a break, and then pass out. With so much paper lying around, it's no wonder the place caught fire so easily, but our plan was for Samuel to be long gone."

Was it an act? Sophia couldn't tell for sure, but his demeanor was convincing as he backed away from the Earth Viewer.

"Lucifer can lock doors like those without any trouble, can't he?" Ruth asked.

"Theoretically, yes, but there has to be more to it than that. Maybe I'm just overloaded. These Testings are harder than I thought they would be. I really must refresh," he said, still studying the Earth Viewer in disbelief.

Without asking permission or inviting the others to join him, he scurried off. Miriam watched him go, then rolled her eyes at Sophia.

"What's up with him?" she asked. "Seems like he's always worn out these days."

What's up with all of you? Sophia wanted to reply, but instead she watched him retreat innocently.

"I wish I knew," she said, "But he has a point. I didn't hear anything in your plan about Samuel being trapped in the building."

"Does it matter that much?" Miriam asked. "He got out, and if anything, the escape from danger will make him turn toward us even more. Faras is overreacting; the janitor is irrelevant."

"Do you two think Faras has been doing his part in the Testings?" She looked from Ruth to Miriam, trying to calculate which of them seemed more sincere.

"Of course," Ruth said, turning away from the Earth Viewer. She touched one curl of her hair and smiled at Sophia. "We all are, just as you told us to."

27

In the quiet blue cocoon of Gabriel's Refreshing Room, a gentle current of peace washed over Sophia, pushing the confusion and frustration out of her spirit. All the questions she had stored up to ask and reassurances she longed for floated away, no longer important. With great reluctance, she returned to consciousness when Gabriel softly said her name.

"I fear I've overwhelmed you with concerns about the Testings of Devotion," he told her, going on to share his concerns about Lucifer capitalizing on any doubts or uncertainties she might have. He leaned closer and asked if anything had happened to validate his feelings.

It felt like failure, to be honest, and yet she had learned her lesson on that account. "I heard him just now, and yes, you're right, I'm overwhelmed. Watching helplessly while Hector was tortured on earth is just as much of a test for me as the other things I've been through recently. What happened?"

He gave his head a small shake that made a few strands of his blonde hair brush against his cheeks. His normally chiseled features sagged with worry lines tracking across his high forehead. Even the corners of his elegant lips slanted downward. "I don't know. You and I were the only ones who knew Hector was going down to check on Samuel—or so I thought."

"Maybe Lucifer was already watching Samuel, since his ministry has been so successful. Hector might have been an unanticipated bonus. But why didn't he just kill Samuel like he did Anthony? Do you think he was hoping Michael would appear?"

Gabriel gave her a sharp look. "Hector doesn't know about Michael and Lucifer's battle after the scene inside the church."

He waved his arm across the wall and it transformed into a scene of the two enemies wrestling high above the earth, each blow shaking the clouds like a tremendous thunderstorm. Michael had been powerful in the makeshift church, but swept up into the massive canopy of the night sky, it was harder to vanquish his foe.

"I had to go help too," Gabriel said in a subdued tone as they watched the replay. "You know that doesn't happen very often."

Sophia glanced at the final image of Lucifer being cast back toward earth once more, and pressed her lips together. "He just won't give up. It's no wonder mortals are having such a hard time."

Gabriel turned away from the screen and stood up. "Hector's descent helped us in an important way, though. We now know that Lucifer *is* struggling, not only to capture the souls of mortals and negate our actions, but with his own legions. Azazel in particular has decided he is just as qualified as Luficer to lead the fallen." Behind the archangel, Sophia saw something on the screen that made her move to the end of her recliner for a better view. Lucifer was in front of his army of demons, a combination of Nephilim and the same angels who had once existed with her on the First Level of heaven. They were all so misshapen and ugly it was difficult to recognize some of them for sure, but Azazel stood out, clearly more hideous over time. His face was as rough as leather, and the beady black of his eyes had sunk deep into his head, shrouded by greasy black hair that spilled over his forehead. His body seemed to go in every direction: his arms spiraled outward, one of his legs bowed forward and the other backward, and his belly sagged out over a wide metal belt.

"Follow me, my brothers and sisters," he called to a crowd of demon warriors, but the dissention among them was so loud, his voice was quickly drowned out. The more he attempted to rally them, the harder they fought with each other, too busy to pay attention to him or Lucifer.

"Do they—can they—destroy each other?" she wondered out loud.

"Oh yes, and that's another part of Lucifer's problem." Gabriel sat down to look with her, pointing out the forms of fallen Nephilim in and outside the church. "The Nephilim don't hesitate to kill each other. The fallen angels can't be destroyed, which gives them a special power, resulting in almost complete chaos among those Lucifer claims as his own, but the Nephilim are a different story.."

While watching the screen, Gabriel told her there was talk of rival factions among the evil army: some wanted to broach an attack on the First Level immediately, while others thought it best to work on completely dominating mortals. So far, Lucifer had been able to maintain control, but it distracted him from other concerns.

"Poor Lucifer." She said it without thinking of the impact it would have.

"'Poor Lucifer'! What can you be thinking?"

She held up one hand apologetically. "I don't really feel sorry for him in the way that I feel sorry for mortals who suffer, Gabriel, but just imagine how hard it must be for him to see everything he gambled on falling apart. If he can't unify his followers, he won't be their leader. He's sacrificed everything for a possibility that doesn't seem likely to happen. Deep inside, he must feel desperate."

"Remember, his main goal is to annihilate mortals. He still seems to have a very good chance at that," Gabriel said bitterly. "But we need to worry about the situation here on the First Level too. Now that you've had some time to assess the situation, who do you think is betraying us?"

She shared the conclusions she had come to when she had weighed that same question recently: Ruth seemed to be the logical candidate because she was mortal. She might be using her new powers to help those she loved, or even believe she could go back to earth as some kind of superhuman and try to change things there. However, Faras and Miriam had motives too.

Sophia wrapped her arms around her waist and rested her head back on the recliner, eyes closed. "Miriam is all you said she would be: steadfast, determined, and right on top of the need to send angels to help mortals. The only thing that makes me question her commitment is her pride. It's been obvious she resents Ruth's presence, and having me chosen as Senior Servant rather than her could be all the bait Lucifer needs to convince her to join forces with him."

Gabriel clapped his hands together and adjusted his belt and tunic, as if preparing to depart. "So that's it, then. One or both of the women are the source of our problems."

Sophia opened her eyes and shook her head. "Unfortunately, no. For some time now, I've noticed that Faras seems weary, which makes me wonder if he's working so hard to be deceptive that it drains him. He seems to crave constant refreshing." She stood up and bowed her head. "I'm sorry.

I haven't been able to do what you asked of me."

He tipped her chin up and cupped his big hands around it. As soon as they touched, a delicious comfort flowed through her spirit.

"Don't give up so easily, dearest. The Almighty Divine has noticed many changes in you since your descent, although we both are sure your longing to come to the Second Level continues." He smiled to let her know he was joking. "We never thought it would be easy to find the betrayer, but you're making progress."

"So, you have an idea of who it is?"

"Not specifically, but I think we can say it's either Ruth or one of the Selected Servants. I'm satisfied with Hector's evaluation of the heavenly host."

"Do you think all three of them might be working together?"

"Anything's possible. Temptation comes in many disguises. Whoever strayed might not even consider it wrongdoing; convincing the others to join in would be all the easier with that belief. That's how Lucifer usually succeeds."

"So, what should I do next?"

He began to fade, moving away from her as he did. "There's no need to change anything, Sophia. See if your perceptions continue. The absence of angels will point us in one direction; the obvious presence of evil, another. If there seem to be delays or lack of communication, we have yet another indication. Hector will show us more too. Monitor his progress carefully, and compare your observations with those of the Selected Servants and Ruth."

"So be it," she said, but Gabriel had vanished before the words were out of her mouth. An instant later, she was at the back of the Guidance Room, watching the Selected Servants and Ruth in the midst of what appeared to be an argument.

"Greetings!" she said, stepping forward.

They stopped bickering and turned to face her when she asked for an update on the candidates. Each looked uneasily at each other, reluctant to begin. Sophia wondered what besides guilt would make them so reticent.

"Ruth, why don't you start?" she finally asked. "Pick whomever you want to talk about first."

"Okay. I'll start with the most successful one. Praise be, it's JoJo."

What unfolded was a story that would be called a miracle on earth. Prompted by Sophia's appearance, JoJo began to listen to Pastor Ephraim and those around him who encouraged and supported a change of attitude. Once he repented, he became so full of passion for his faith, he founded a small prison ministry called "Condemned No More."

These activities attracted the notice and eventual praise of the guards, who informed the warden. JoJo was given limited computer privileges to write a newsletter about his conversion, which Tamika handed out to the church congregation. One of the members thought it was so valuable that he offered to distribute it more widely, and a regional mailing list of recipients quickly escalated into a nationwide audience. A literary agent had even made tentative inquiries about JoJo's interest in writing a memoir.

As if that wasn't enough, Maria, the law clerk who had taken an interest in his case, filed an appeal. Mentored by the senior partner who had known Ruth, she was crafting a motion to dismiss the homicide charges because of the tainted drugs JoJo had taken the night he murdered Ruth.

"And just look at the angels around him," Ruth ended proudly, gesturing toward a scene of JoJo in his jail cell with a Bible opened across his knees.

There was no mistaking the happiness in her voice, but Sophia didn't see a single angel. She decided not to comment, sitting silently in her recliner and waiting to hear more.

Faras gave Sophia an apologetic look. "I might as well go to Gustaf, who is also in the news, but for a very bad reason. He and a small group of secret police 'arrested' Blake Armstrong, an American journalist whom they believed was spying for liberation forces. What they didn't know was that Blake's father is a powerful businessman in America, and the real reason for the visit was to see if there was some way to help the children trapped in a particularly violent area near the Asian border. Of course, Gustaf and the others deny they have Blake, but an international incident has broken out over the situation."

Sophia studied the Earth Viewer, which showed Blake Armstrong on his knees begging for mercy and praying to the Almighty Divine for help. His thin brown hair hung in ragged ribbons over his bruised face, while the shirt and pants he wore were not only dirty and torn but splotched with blood in spots. Despite the young man's pleas, Gustaf and the others continued to take turns torturing Blake. The looks on their faces were so similar to the snarling expressions of the Nephilim, she couldn't help making a noise of disgust at their behavior.

"Where are the angels?" she asked Miriam, wishing Hector was there to confirm or discredit what she thought she saw. Ruth and the Selected Servants looked at each other.

"Sophia, I don't know why you don't see them," Faras said quietly. "He's surrounded by them."

"All three of you need to listen to me carefully." Sophia slapped the Earth Viewer off and faced them, her eyes narrowed. "The time has come to be completely honest, and while I know we *think* there are no secrets between us, you saw how I strayed from complete submission and wouldn't admit it to you. If there's anything unusual you've noticed, or if you've felt the slightest temptation from Lucifer, please say so now. It could even be something so subtle that you might not readily recognize it, as it was for me. I heard a Voice that spoke so clearly it could have been one of yours, but I didn't associate it with Lucifer until it was too late."

"What makes you so sure you aren't still under the influence of Lucifer? You're the one who isn't seeing my angels," Miriam said. Faras and Ruth exchanged a look of agreement. "It sounds like you're accusing one of us of wrongdoing, but Sophia, maybe we aren't like you. Maybe the Almighty Divine doesn't see a need to tempt us, for some reason."

"Miriam, temptation is the work of Lucifer—if you don't recognize that, you are already under attack," Sophia said, keeping her voice level.

Miriam stared at her defiantly but Sophia took a step closer to the Selected Servant, returning her look without flinching. Suddenly, Miriam collapsed onto a recliner, covering her face with her hands.

"Of course, you're right. The Testings of Devotion aren't going well. Maybe I've done something wrong. I've tried my hardest, but we can't deny that Anthony's death was a terrible tragedy, and a mistake."

A look of surprise united Faras, Ruth, and Sophia. Tentatively, he leaned over to put his hand on her shoulder.

"Miriam, I don't think Sophia is suggesting any of us have deliberately done something wrong."

"But you have to admit we're failing horribly, Faras. We all know it," Miriam said, raking her fingers through her hair, then jumping back up and pacing around the room with great drama. "What must I do? What can we all do?"

Sophia watched the theatrics, wondering if Miriam was a good actress or truly distressed. She looked at the others.

"Faras and Ruth, is there any chance you've been mistaken in your actions?"

She studied their responses, feeling even smaller than usual. What if all three of them were conspiring? Unless Gabriel came to help, they could easily overpower her.

"Not me," said Faras. Ruth echoed his words.

Sophia waited, expecting Miriam to say the same, which she did. What would it take to get to the truth?

With a sigh, she flipped the Earth Viewer back on. "If no one has anything to confess or share, we should go on. Faras, let's get back to Gustaf. What can turn this situation around?"

Amazingly, Hector appeared on the screen before any ideas could be shared. Michael and Gabriel must have decided to keep him on earth for this very reason, because he immediately comforted Blake, who was still held captive, casting him into a deep sleep that helped him forget, momentarily, what was happening. Sophia waited for one of the others to comment on Hector's presence, or express surprise that he was on earth, but no one did.

"Karl and some of the other men in Gustaf's group are starting to take issue with the way prisoners like Blake are being treated—the same one who urged restraint before. He is going to try to persuade the others to release him when he wakes up, so that's something," Faras said.

"But that doesn't help with the Testings of Devotion," Sophia said.

"Maybe...somehow...I don't know. Ruth and I need to confer further. I'm just so tired right now I can't put the parts together in a way that makes sense. I have to admit, Sophia, I agree with Miriam. The Testings of Devotion are failing, but I don't know why. Please forgive me."

His normally beautiful face was etched with lines of fatigue even deeper than those she observed before, and his shoulders slumped as if carrying a heavy burden. She wondered if he too was being dramatic in an effort to deflect her concerns; it would be easy to mask dishonesty with fatigue.

"The others?" she asked quietly.

Miriam admitted that Kim Lee was not thriving. Before her new friends and faith could help pave the way to a different and perhaps better life, she sank into a deep depression and was on the verge of suicide. Although Ruth, again, was the one to comment on how many angels surrounded the young woman, Sophia prayed that Hector might be sent there next because she didn't see any. How quickly her friend's mission had become more complex than a checkup on one candidate!

The only good news concerned Samuel Olsen. Miriam seemed as pleased with his progress as Ruth had been with JoJo's.

"Now, this was a good choice. Samuel rallied after the fire. He found another building in which to continue his meetings, and every night he's drawing thousands of people from the city into his church, including prostitutes who work nearby. We've kept him surrounded by angels from the beginning, and it's worked. See for yourself, Sophia. He's very charismatic."

At least one of Miriam's claims was true. The auditorium where Samuel was speaking had no empty seats, despite the late hour. His sermon was winding down after a dynamic lesson that was equal parts exhortation, education, and humor. People surged forward to have Samuel lay hands on them in blessing, but again, not one angel was visible to Sophia.

Samuel's strength seems to be growing, so at least we haven't failed completely, Sophia thought, but the way Miriam was staring at his picture on the Earth Viewer made her uncomfortable. It was much the same way as Ruth looked at JoJo. Had the Selected Servant developed a special attachment for the pastor, or was she basking in the achievements of a candidate considered her choice?

Just as Sophia concluded she needed to think carefully about all she had learned, Gabriel signaled that it was time to bring Hector back to the First Level so he could report on his observations. She thanked the Selected

Servants and Ruth, led them in a brief prayer song, and then sent them to refresh in their chambers. No sooner had all three gone through the exit than Faras returned, alone.

"Sophia, there's something I must speak to you about. Privately."

He looked so grim, she understood in an instant that he wanted to talk about the Testings of Devotion. Sealing them into the room, she allowed the comforting blue mist to waft up around them and waited.

Perched on the edge of a recliner, he avoided looking her in the eyes, choosing his words carefully. "You—what you said—well, you're right. There is something wrong with the Testings of Devotion, or at least it seems that way to me."

"What is it, Faras? Please tell me everything. You won't be blamed."

His head jerked up. "I haven't done anything wrong! It's Ruth and Miriam I'm concerned about. Every time I try to intervene with any of the candidates, it's as if there's a barricade preventing me from getting through to them. No matter what I do, I can't overcome it. I think that explains my fatigue. I'm exerting twice as much effort as before and getting no results. All I can think about is refreshing."

She watched his every move, wanting to believe him, but he seemed so reluctant to look at her directly that it was hard to know if he spoke the truth.

"Why didn't you speak up when I confronted you all? Ruth and Miriam should be part of this conversation."

"I think not." He looked over his shoulder, even though there was no way for anyone to enter the room. "The two of them have secrets, Sophia, I'm just not sure what they are. Whenever I come close, they change the subject or pretend nothing happened."

"Have you heard them say anything that suggests they aren't being completely subservient in regard to the Testings of Devotion?"

"No," he admitted, glancing at the Earth Viewer, which was blank. "It's more subtle than that." His brown eyes shifted around the room, bewildered. "I wish I could offer you something tangible as proof, but all I have is my intuition. Maybe I shouldn't have come to you without solid evidence."

Before she could stop him, he darted to the doors and punched in the security code, leaving with surprising speed for one who appeared so weary.

Oh, Faras, Sophia thought, watching him go. *You should have come to me long ago, with or without proof.*

28

Sophia thought about Faras's confession on the way to the Portal, but as soon as she arrived, she shifted her full attention to Hector, who was sprawled on the ground before her, moaning and clutching at handfuls of the velvety grass. Luckily, the Portal had been moved to an area where no other angels would be able to see their director so broken and disheveled.

Before he could say a word, she swept him up in her arms and promised they would talk later. Holding him up, she escorted him to a nearby tree and brushed the bits of grass and dirt from his hair. There was a stream nearby; she dipped the edge of her robe in the chilled water and bathed his burned face, then let him rest while she sang a long prayer song.

Lost in a comforting melody that came naturally to her lips, Sophia couldn't help wishing Gabriel would magically appear and sweep her and Hector off to the safety of the Second Level. How selfish and yet how fearful she felt as the evidence of Lucifer's destruction encroached on the First Level. It had been one thing to watch mortals suffer on earth and try to help, but this was a new challenge—and one she hadn't really been prepared for, in her opinion.

"Thank you," Hector said, sitting up and sighing. "That was just what I needed, in comparison with earth, which was horrible. I don't know what I'll do if the Almighty Divine ever tries to send me back."

"Think of all the angels who do nothing but that. I wonder if we appreciate what a sacrifice they make," Sophia murmured, stretching out next to him and allowing the grass to tickle her bare feet.

"So? What more have you learned?" He ran his fingers through his curly hair and then tentatively touched the wounded spots on his face, which were already healing. "Was it worth it?"

She raised her shoulders noncommittally. "There is some good news. I could see you, Hector, so it's likely the absence of angels I told you about before isn't coming from the heavenly host."

"But then it must be one of the Selected Servants or Ruth." His belly lifted and fell in a vigorous sigh. "This is too much. Look how strong Lucifer is, Sophia. Even you must feel a little afraid."

"You know what scares me? Until recently, I thought he would repent and come back. I can't imagine what keeps him on earth. He has to realize what a horrible fate he's doomed himself to."

"As long as he has mortals under his influence and an army of his own, he'll stay," Hector said. "And like you, I believe mortals are basically good and have a longing to connect with the Almighty Divine, even if they don't recognize it as such. This might be a very long battle."

"What is your assessment of the state of earth and this new candidate? I couldn't bear to watch you in that church with Samuel, but of course I had to. It seemed so odd that there was no one to help until Michael arrived at the last moment."

Hector grew distant. "Perhaps it was planned that way to draw Lucifer out... Anyway, it was by far the worst thing I've experienced as an angel. Until now, there've been such clear boundaries. Earth belonged to Lucifer, and heaven to the Almighty Divine."

"At least we can always count on Michael. He was amazing."

Hector nodded in agreement, leaning closer to her. "While I was trapped in that inferno, I did learn something that may be of value. Some of Lucifer's demons have grown very strong from absorbing the spirits of mortals who succumb to them. Their power is almost as great as Lucifer's. They've sorted themselves into a whole battalion of dark angels and archangels."

Sophia's blue eyes widened. "That's much as Gabriel suspected, but we didn't know they could absorb the spirits of mortals."

"If you look closely, you can see the features of the ones they have overtaken. I wasn't quite close enough, but I thought I saw Anthony's eyes in the face of one demon." Sophia inhaled with a shocked sound, but Hector silenced her by holding up a hand. "I'm not finished. It was hard to tell, given my own circumstances, but there seems to be two factions among the demons who invaded the church that night. One group wanted to kill Samuel and unite their forces against Michael, while the others believe there's a need to wait—for what, I don't know."

"Do you mean to tell me the created angels who originally followed Lucifer to earth are opposing the Nephilim and others who join their dark forces?"

He nodded. "Unfortunately, mortals are caught in the middle. Both sides want them."

She thought for a moment, wishing the news was more encouraging, then patted Hector's arm and switched the subject.

"You've done very well. One last question: is there any chance Lucifer or his demons could pass through the Portal?"

"You mean, could they come through unobserved like we go down to earth?" he asked. "I'd be very surprised if they could get by the Guardian Angels. I had a hard time getting back in until Michael showed up to escort me, and the procedures for reentry of earth angels is equally complicated. Still, I can't say it's impossible." Hector's eyes fluttered shut and he took a deep breath of the air that was fragranced by the flowering branches that sloped overhead.

"So, we have some answers, but not all the ones we need," Sophia said, rising to her feet and mulling over the new information Hector had given her. Dissention among Lucifer's followers could be their trump card, and one she hadn't anticipated. What about Gabriel? Had he known all of this before sending Hector to earth?

Hector grunted, eased himself to his feet, and shook his robe free of debris. "I sense that if we don't do something dramatic soon, Sophia, it might be too late, and the Almighty Divine really will have to close the Portal and just forget about whomever is left on earth."

"Still thinking about that old story, Hector? I'm not, and anyway, the Almighty Divine is the only one to make that decision. Please, before we return to our duties, tell me what you found out about the Testings."

"I don't know what you saw from your side, but I was greatly tempted the instant I hit earth. First there was a beautiful angel who offered to rescue me from my suffering and tried to convince me a loving Almighty Divine would not subject me to such torment as the consuming fire. I heard Lucifer's voice the entire time I was trapped, just as you suggested I might. Although I wasn't in mortal form, I could feel everything, Sophia. It was like being burnt at the stake, except I wasn't.

The torture just went on and on until Michael appeared."

She shuddered, brushing the hair back from his forehead to examine his face. His angelic form seemed restored, but the memories would probably take a long time to erase. "Did other angels come to help you?"

"No. That's what made it so easy for Lucifer and his followers to attack. Had it not been for Michael, I don't know what would have happened to me, or Samuel."

"And afterward, when the human helpers arrived?"

"No angels then, either. Michael and I were the only ones, and then he got sucked up into the clouds and I don't know what happened after that. I heard your voice calling to me, so I went to try to help that poor boy who was trapped by Gustaf and his crew."

"When you arrived there, what did you see?"

"Same thing—no angels. I was able to comfort him a bit, but that's all. Not that it matters, but if it were up to me, I'd forget about Gustaf right now. He must be getting his ideas straight from Lucifer. That poor kid…he wasn't much more than a boy really, and he had no preparation for what happened. The only time he ever played spy was as a grade schooler, I reckon."

Sophia pressed on. "What of the prayer angels and earth angels? Can you check with them to see if they received direction to assist in either situation?"

"Now?" His eyebrows raised in disbelief, but when she nodded, he scrambled to his feet. "I'll be back as soon as possible."

Sophia realized how rarely she was alone after he left, and at first felt uneasy. Then she remembered her enjoyment of long stretches of prayer, and sank into the seat Hector had vacated, reverting to her former job of praising and petitioning the Almighty Divine.

"I thank you for giving me the honor of protecting all your beloved angels from these trials," she whispered, straightening out her robe and brushing back a strand of hair the breeze had blown into her face. A butterfly whose wings were a mosaic of colors flitted in front of her and rested briefly on her leg, which made her laugh in delight. Even in the midst of great difficulties, the Almighty Divine sent bits of beauty. The angels understood this well; mortals were often so consumed by suffering, they missed the uplifting signs around them.

She continued to pray until Hector returned and dropped back in place beside her.

"I've spoken to all the captains of the heavenly host. None of them even knew what I was talking about. It was hard not to arouse suspicion, but when I asked what directions they had been receiving from Ruth and Faras and Miriam in my absence, they told me about every mission but the Testings of Devotion. No one heard anything about that."

A heavy silence passed before he concluded: "There is definitely a problem. As much as I resisted, I now see how wise it was to send me to earth."

She dropped her head briefly onto her hands, but then took a deep breath and stood up. "May the Almighty Divine be with us in a special way now, Hector. We know someone isn't doing their job, or maybe someone has done too good a job of deviating away from the plan delivered to us." She checked his appearance, relieved to see he looked restored to his usual energetic and confident persona. Hugging him briefly, she bade him farewell. "I feel fortunate to have you on my side, but remember, only you, Gabriel, Michael, and I know the truth of these many matters concerning both the heavenly host and mortals. We must be cautious."

She left, sorting through what Hector had shared, as well as her conversation with Faras, but feeling strangely calm as she headed for the Guidance Room. Continuing to pray for discernment, she was randomly flipping through scenes of the candidates on the Earth Viewer when the sound of angry voices in the distance distracted her.

The Selected Servants burst into the room. Miriam and Faras were holding Ruth by either arm, but the mortal continued to struggle as they dragged her forward.

"It was her!" Miriam said.

Faras added: "We've just found out Ruth is the one who's been interfering with the Testings of Devotion!"

"No, it's their fault! Faras didn't stop the bad influences when I asked him to, and Miriam didn't listen when I said we needed more angels. They don't believe I know what I'm doing because I'm new!"

"Stop, each of you, and let go of her. Tell me what you're talking about," Sophia directed. "Miriam, you go first."

"She's been changing things all along, intervening on her own." Miriam jabbed her finger at Ruth. "The Testings of Devotion aren't working because all she cares about is her precious JoJo. She's lied to us, pretending to be submissive to the plan we came up with, while secretly changing everything. First, she diverted extra angels to help him; then she introduced the idea of altering the drug charges, and now this!"

"I haven't done anything wrong! You watched every single thing," Ruth argued, twisting her arms free and moving away from Miriam and Faras.

Sophia made another gesture for them to calm down and began a prayer song, knowing it would be impossible for the others not to join in. As they sang, the beautiful melody slowly eased the tension in the room and smoothed away their overt anger.

"Now," Sophia said when they finished, "let's start over, and please, hear each other out. Don't accuse without some kind of evidence."

"She's been interfering with the Testings of Devotion from the beginning." In an instant, Miriam's hostility flared as she pointed one finger at Ruth. "Didn't I say all along that it was a bad idea to have a mortal here, working so closely with us? I was right!"

"Miriam, it would be more helpful to share what you know, not what you feel," Sophia said.

"After what you said to us, I started to think about all the things that had gone wrong with the Testings of Devotion, and knew it had to be something coming from one of us, so I reviewed every step of the way since we started the plan. I found out why your descent was so difficult. The three of us had agreed on the specifics of JoJo's testing, but Ruth manipulated that drug charge and the supposed drug dealer who got arrested while you were on earth. None of those things were part of it. JoJo needed to confront what he had done and then take responsibility for the consequences. That was to be his way to repentance."

Miriam looked at Faras, who nodded in agreement. Ruth's initial defiance ebbed away until she dropped her head ever so slightly. Miriam continued.

"There's more. Now the charges have been changed further because the drugs JoJo took were laced with PCP, so his attorney can argue he wasn't responsible for his actions. That wasn't enough, though. Ruth altered the autopsy reports to make it look like she died of a stroke, not trauma! That means JoJo will be out of jail in months instead of years, and the whole Testing process is irrelevant! She's probably done more that I didn't pick up on—maybe Tamika won the lottery, for all we know."

"Ruth?" Sophia said. "Is what Miriam said true?"

Ruth didn't speak, her head bowed so low the features of her face were hidden. When Sophia looked questioningly at Faras, he wrinkled his forehead and stared fixedly at his feet.

"Why would the Almighty Divine allow such a thing?" Miriam demanded.

"Mortals should stay in the Community of Resting Mortals. We don't need them," Faras echoed. "Didn't He consider how hard a mission like this would be for her?"

"Stop," Sophia said, "or you will be guilty of rebellion too. We can't question the Almighty Divine—serving Him is our job, whether we agree with what we're asked to do or not. Now, unless the two of you have more to add, I'd like to be alone with Ruth. I suggest you go see Hector and find out what you can do to salvage what's left of the Testings."

"That won't be easy—she's diverted all the efforts to JoJo. No wonder I was exhausted—each time I tried to intervene in the other situations, I felt like I couldn't get past some big invisible barrier—turns out it was her. That's what I was trying to tell you," Faras said over his shoulder, as he and Miriam walked away. The hum of their commentary could still be heard as they went down the hallway.

"Ruth, is this all true?" Sophia asked when the sound of their voices had faded. "You should have been able to let go of your feelings for JoJo by now."

"Well, maybe you don't know as much as you think you do, Miss High and Mighty. You told me all those things, but how do I know they're true? Maybe angels don't feel attachments for each other or people on earth, but that didn't happen to me. The longer I've been here, the more grief I've felt over JoJo. He's a good boy, and I know what he did was a mistake—but just a bad mistake. The Almighty Divine spoke to me himself and told me to do everything I could to help JoJo, even though you wouldn't approve."

"Ruth, that's not the way things happen on the First Level—"

"You mean that's not the way *you* want things to happen. I bet you've never even talked directly to the Almighty Divine, have you?"

"No, but none of us have on this level. Gabriel is our intermediary. Ruth, if you think the Almighty Divine was speaking to you about JoJo, you were deceived."

"I wasn't! You're the one who's being deceived, you and Miriam and Faras. None of you have as much integrity as Pastor Ephraim—you're always fussing and squabbling with each other, even though you tell me this is the place of eternal peace. The Almighty Divine has a special destiny for JoJo, and I know it, even if you don't!"

Stunned by the depth of Ruth's conviction, Sophia couldn't easily explain away her accusations. She was right about the tensions between the three of them, but those had all arisen since Ruth arrived on the First Level.

"You see," the Voice spoke. "That's how easy it is for me, because I am the true power. My way is the true way, Sophia. If it wasn't, how could I convince one 'selected' by the Almighty Divine so easily?"

29

Sophia took Ruth by the shoulders and waited until the woman turned her head and reluctantly looked down into her eyes.

"Ruth, I know that's what it seems like, but you're wrong. The Voice you've been listening to is so clever, it can confuse even the most devout among us. Believe me, I speak from experience."

Ruth looked over Sophia's head. "Miriam knows I'm right. She always says you're different from the rest of us."

"Even Miriam knows Lucifer found your vulnerability and used it to tempt you. You've taken control of situations that aren't yours to manage, and doubted the Almighty Divine's ability to take care of mortals."

Sophia remained standing in front of Ruth, refusing to budge even though there was no eye contact between them. It was difficult to continue avoiding Sophia's stern gaze, and Ruth ended up glancing back, only slightly abashed. The woman's expression then changed from stubbornness to confusion, and finally, shame. When that happened, her face crumpled with dismay and she fell to her knees in front of Sophia, sobbing.

"What have I done? Please forgive me, Sophia. I've been so misled. It seemed absolutely real and right, but everything you've just said is true. I was ready to surrender all those earthly attachments until that Voice came along and started whispering in my ear all the time. It never stopped! I thought it was really the Almighty Divine, wanting to reward me for all the hard work I did when I was mortal," she cried. "Is there any way to fix all the damage I've done?"

Sophia knelt down so that they were on eye level. "I'm not the one you should beg to forgive you, Ruth, and I don't know what the consequences of your actions will be, but I do feel sorry that you're suffering so." She leaned forward and gave Ruth a half hug, both stunned by the betrayal and saddened by the vulnerability of mortals. The heavenly host had been horrified by what happened to the Savior Son and those who followed him, but for an instant she understood how very different angels and mortals were.

Rising to her feet, she let her fingers linger on Ruth's shoulder. "Perhaps it will help if you spend time in a special prayer song for forgiveness while I meet with Gabriel."

"I will, I will!"

Ruth's wavering voice faded away as Sophia was drawn up to the Refreshing Room. What a difference there was between the calm blue stillness and the turmoil she had left behind in the Guidance Room. Hopefully, Miriam and Faras would take pity on Ruth and at least pray along with her.

When Gabriel let his hand rest on the top of her head for a moment, she felt certain a resolution to their concerns was in sight. Now that they knew who was conspiring against them, the Testings of Devotion could get back on course and proceed as planned.

"Gabriel, how wise you are. I guess our worries about Ruth were the more legitimate ones. Once she confessed, it seemed so obvious."

"The Almighty Divine is pleased that you deferred judgment of her."

Previously, she would have seized on the comment as one more compliment suggesting she was on her way to the Second Level of heaven, but instead she was baffled. "What do you mean? If I had been more astute, I could have prevented Ruth from doing further damage."

Gabriel laughed. "What makes you think she has done damage, dearest Sophia? You are gifted with devotion, but now we must work on your trust. Nothing that's happened is outside the will of the Almighty Divine, believe me."

She was speechless. "You mean it doesn't bother you that Ruth listened to Lucifer and did his bidding? That she ruined the Testings of Devotion?"

Gabriel frowned. "It bothers me tremendously that she gave in to temptation, and that Lucifer found a way to keep her bound to her mortal life. But she hasn't ruined the Testings—at least, not according to higher standards than yours. Sophia, you only see one plan and one outcome. The work of the Almighty Divine is more complex than that. Even I can't fully appreciate it—but I know who is always in control."

"So, what am I to do to save the Testings?"

"You are doing exactly as you should. Remember, Lucifer's powers are limited and his plans will always fail in the end. While he's been busy trying to control his own ranks and thwart our plans, other successes have bypassed him."

A tendril of blue mist curled up from the floor to stroke Sophia's cheek, and in that moment, she understood what Gabriel meant. Stunned, she began ticking off the cases on her petite fingers: "Pastor Ephraim and Tamika...the missionary whose wife befriended Kim...Gustaf's friend Karl, who had softened his convictions, if only briefly . . ."

In each candidate's life, there had been others who were touched by the impact of the Testings of Devotion. Even the wife of Anthony Davis had recovered and started her own organization to help families confronting challenges like hers. The support of her parents and other political connections had enabled her to build a tremendous following and help many who would have otherwise suffered even more.

"For now, Miriam and Faras shouldn't be told about this. Let them figure it out on their own, since the Testings of Devotion aren't complete."

"You mean Ruth isn't the only problem?"

"She has started the process of revelation. Continue to be vigilant Sophia, and do as your spirit leads you."

What Sophia felt in her spirit was a surge of dread. How could she confront anything more challenging than what she had already faced when she thought Hector and Gabriel were the only two angels she trusted?

"Gabriel, I don't doubt the Almighty Divine, but I do doubt myself. How can I be strong enough to deal with more of this? I have no idea what to say to Ruth when I return. If more threats lie ahead, I'm afraid I won't uncover them in time."

He touched her shoulder lightly and his smile told her she already knew what he was about to say. "You have been called to do this, Sophia. Have faith, and follow as you are led."

"At least tell me what to do with Ruth—I can't judge her, and yet surely the Almighty Divine will decide on some consequence? She'll be so vulnerable if she's sent back to earth, and even the Community of Resting Mortals might turn on her if they discover what she's done."

"For now, Ruth needs a protector. She should stay with you at all times and do your every bidding. She no longer has the power to intervene in JoJo's or any other mortal's life. You are to take her place as the director of the Testings of Devotion, and I guarantee we shall soon discover other betrayals."

Before Sophia could question further, he was gone. Not knowing what else to do, she allowed herself to sink back down to the Guidance Room, where Ruth was still kneeling on the floor in the exact spot she had been before Sophia left to meet with Gabriel.

"Am I being sent back?" she asked fearfully, looking up when she realized Sophia had returned.

"No, but as you probably can tell, you've lost your ability to see anything on earth, much less intervene." Sophia pointed to the blank screen of the Earth Viewer. "Until more is decided, you are to remain with me at all times."

"Doing nothing?"

"Doing exactly what I tell you to do." Deliberately keeping her voice and behavior neutral, Sophia nodded toward a recliner and indicated that Ruth should sit. "Stay by my side at all times. I'm taking over the Testings, so when Faras and Miriam come back, we'll see what has happened."

Almost as if they sensed that Sophia was back, the Selected Servants returned, barely glancing at Ruth when they passed the recliner where she was curled up with her arms around her legs and her head resting on her knees.

"What's the decision? Will she be sent away?" Faras asked, jerking his head in Ruth's direction. He sounded eager to have a harsh punishment dealt out, and why not? He believed Ruth had thwarted all his efforts in the Testings of Devotion.

"The decision is that I'll be replacing Ruth for the time being. She's to remain at my side, but she won't participate in our efforts."

"That's it?" He looked disappointed. "She ruins everything, and her only consequence is to lose her power?"

Sophia laid one finger across his lips, speaking to Miriam as well. "I suggest both of you let go of your negative feelings about Ruth and focus on working with me. I asked you to review each of the candidates and have an update ready for me. Are you ready?"

Abashed, they shook their heads no. They must have spent the time since they were last together complaining about the preferential treatment they felt Ruth received. Maybe Faras had even taken the opportunity to refresh, but if he had, it must not have helped, since his expression was still tired and frustrated.

"Okay, then we'll do it together, and Ruth will be with us to observe, but that's all. Any objections?"

The two seemed to sense there was nothing to be gained by challenging Sophia, so they turned toward the Earth Viewer, which sprang to life at her signal. On the screen, they saw a young woman in a wheelchair, surrounded by important-looking men in suits and ties.

"I know our efforts with Anthony Davis failed, but I'd like you to see what's happened to his family, anyway," she said. "That's Katie, his wife, and Kyle, the son who survived the automobile accident they were both in. He's almost a teenager now."

Miriam's eyes widened as Sophia explained: "Katie just spoke to a group of doctors about the need for better care of families like hers. They're going to give her money to get an organization started, and Kyle is going to a local church, where he's part of a youth group planning a mission trip in the near future. It seems his faith has grown tremendously because of all he has gone through."

"I think they need extra angels to keep them on course, don't you?" Faras piped in, adding dozens of other angels to the ones already guarding the boy and his mother. "And I'll make sure to protect him from bad influences and prevent the shadows of depression from overwhelming his mother."

"Now Gustaf." Sophia rested her chin in one hand. "I think Karl might be the answer there. Look."

They all watched the Earth Viewer switch screens. Karl and Gusfaf were having coffee in a small café frequented by the secret police. They were sitting a distance from the others, deep in conversation.

"I'm all for the motherland." Karl took a sip of his coffee and grimaced. "Good God, where do they get this stuff? It's like cat piss. Anyway, as I was saying, I'm all for the motherland, but lately things have gotten a bit...extreme, wouldn't you say? The journalist who fled to the United

Northern States and was killed with mercury, the prisons being built in the north pole, torturing women, and now this journalist who was kidnapped—just an innocent boy, as it turns out."

Gustaf swilled the last dregs of his coffee before tossing them back into his mouth like a shot of liquor. "Hush, Karl! That kind of talk will have you arrested next. I don't want to be the one to come to your apartment tonight with a warrant."

"Ah, so you still have some conscience. That's reassuring." Karl caught sight of a beautiful young woman whose entrance into the café temporarily caused the buzz of conversation to miss a beat. Searching among those at the tables, she sighted Karl and descended on him, unwinding her scarf as she did so, but not bothering to unbutton her coat.

"Karl, have you seen my younger brother Torval? He's been missing for some days now."

"Volya, calm yourself. Have a seat." Karl pulled out a chair for her but she perched on the end as if ready to take flight again.

"I'm very worried." A curl of dark hair had escaped from under her hat, and two spots of crimson burned high on her cheeks. What could be unshed tears sparkled in her brown eyes.

"No, I haven't seen him, but he'll show up. Young men have their ways." He laughed and elbowed Gustaf. "Do you know my friend?"

Volya wrapped and unwrapped her scarf around her fingers, as if ready to look for others who might help her find Torval, but Gustaf summoned for a cup of warm tea. That made her turn and study him for a second, and then stomp one foot on the floor.

"I *do* know you! Gustaf Chernoff. We were in lower school together." She winked at Karl and gave a silvery laugh. "Gustaf had a special wooden sword that his father carved for him. He brought it to class every day but wouldn't let anyone touch it, including the teachers. He told us he was going to be a great warrior when he grew up, but I don't think that thing would have helped very much."

Gustaf's cheeks flushed as the waitress slid a mug of tea across the table along with a glass of vodka for him and Karl. "Your memory is very good. My father's patron saint was Saint George the Warrior, but I stopped believing in any of that long ago." His eyes rested on Volya a bit longer than they might in a casual conversation, and his grin was more genuine than any of the ones he had given Karl that morning. Volya smiled briefly, but then turned back to Karl, ignoring her tea.

"Do you think you can help me find Torval?" With a furtive look at the customers seated on either side of them, she leaned closer and spoke in a low voice. "I know I can trust you both, but please be discreet. We've been holding home church services at our house, and I'm afraid Torval has somehow gotten in trouble for it."

"Let me guess. Gustaf will fall in love with Volya, and he and Karl will become men of faith." Miriam's lips were pursed and her arms were crossed high on her chest as she watched the screen. "Very tidy."

"You're right, especially when they discover Torval has been secretly murdered on the basis of trumped up antigovernment charges brought by Gustaf's own co-workers," Sophia added, then noticed that Ruth hadn't joined them. "Ruth, please join us."

Reluctantly, Ruth shuffled over. She hung behind Sophia and stared at the floor to avoid Miriam and Faras's hostile looks.

"I never would have thought of that," Miriam said, turning back to the screen. "Sophia, do you know something we don't?"

With a carefully neutral expression, Sophia looked at her. "What do you mean?"

"I thought the Testings of Devotion were about the candidates, not the people around them," Miriam said, eyes narrowed.

"If we have to take care of them too, it'll mean a lot more work," Faras added. "Of course, if things had gone right the first time, we wouldn't even be having this conversation." Both he and Miriam shot Ruth a pointed look, but she refused to lift her head.

"I'm sorry, really sorry. It's all my fault," she whispered in a chant.

"She's right about that," Faras grumbled, but it was Miriam who nudged Ruth away from the Earth Viewer, forcing the mortal to stand behind them.

"Let's go on," Sophia said.

"Sophia, I can't believe you! How are you coming up with all this extra stuff? If the focus of these Testings of Devotion has changed, Faras and I should know too."

"The Testings haven't changed," Sophia said.

"Yes they have," Miriam snapped. "We were supposed to agree on a plan and work together, but now you're taking over and shifting everything around. That's easy for you, but Faras and I will have to start focusing on the other people around the candidates now too."

"That will make a lot more work for all of us," Faras added.

"What makes you think this wasn't part of the Almighty Divine's plan all along? We weren't given full knowledge of the Testings of Devotion, which is fortunate, since Lucifer has found a way to penetrate our circle. I have to assume Ruth shared every strategy we used, but in His infinite wisdom, the Almighty Divine didn't reveal everything to us," Sophia said. "And we've yet to complete the Testings."

She gave Faras and Miriam a long searching look, pretending not to notice as they exchanged glances when she started to turn away. Neither of them protested as she moved on to Kim Lee, who was living in America with her missionary guardians, Janet and Lee Davis. She was working as a museum docent during the day, but had helped Janet and Lee seed a small Asian-American Christian church that had already outgrown the elementary school cafeteria where they met for Sunday services."

"You won't believe what's happened, Kim!" Janet said one night as the two of them prepared dinner. "Lee has been giving this a lot of thought and finally decided to go into full-time missionary work."

Kim gave her a genuine smile and long hug. "That is wonderful, Janet. I only wish God will reveal my life purpose to me. I like this job, but I can't see how I make any great contribution to society. And look." Kim knelt to pick up mail that had been shoved through the slot in the door. "Probably more rejections for my book."

Now Miriam's hands rested on her hips and her eyes were rolled upward. "Let's see if I can guess this one. Kin will write a best seller, maybe even land a movie deal, and that will launch a glorious career. At this rate, I can't wait to hear what you have planned for JoJo."

Sophia forged ahead. "That sounds like criticism, Miriam."

"Oh no, far be it from me to find fault," she said sweetly. "Are we just about done here? This is a lot to absorb." Faras seemed about to agree with her, but then began polishing the buttons on the podium with the sleeve of his robe, as if that was far more important than anything Sophia had to say.

"Just in case either of you are questioning the Almighty Divine's wisdom at this point, let me advise you to avoid the same mistakes Ruth and I made," Sophia said. "I admit I was a bit overcome by all this too, but it's not our job to question or ask for explanations."

She waited for one or both of them to disagree, but Faras merely closed his eyes and mouthed what might have been a prayer. Miriam tossed her hair back impatiently and sighed so everyone could hear her.

"We might as well go on. I can't wait to see what's in store for JoJo," she said.

30

Ruth continued to stand silently, less distraught, but still unwilling to look at the others directly. Sophia wondered if she was longing to return to the Community of Resting Mortals where she could try to forget about what had happened during her time on the First Level.

"As you know, things are progressing with JoJo," Sophia said. "It looks like he'll be released from prison earlier than we thought, but Gabriel assures me this is genuinely part of the Almighty Divine's plan. Another thing we didn't predict is that Tamika would change so much too. She's begun helping Pastor Ephraim with prayer services and enrolled in a Bible school where she can take classes at night. She's quite a dynamic speaker, as it turns out."

All four of them watched a new version of Tamika appear on the screen, vibrant and full of confidence. She held a microphone, and was swaying in time as she sang a song of praise to an audience packed to over-flowing in Pastor Ephraim's church. Her children, better clothed and full of excitement, were sitting with Anita, clapping along with the rest of the crowd and grinning at their mom.

"Unbelievable," Miriam said, staring at Tamika. "Just a few small changes and she really blossomed...of course, who knows what might happen next?"

"Exactly. She'll need the protection and encouragement of the angels, as well as release from the bondage of her relationships with abusive men. Both of you must be especially vigilant," Sophia said to Miriam and Faras.

"Was this the plan all along: to make those around the candidates flourish, while we were thinking the focus was on Kim and JoJo and Gustaf?" Faras asked.

"I don't know, but you can see the results are exceedingly good," Sophia said. "Once more, we witness how wise our beloved Almighty Divine is."

"I don't understand why we weren't trusted with this plan? We could have helped even more. I feel as if I've been of no use." Miriam tapped her foot against the floor restlessly and drummed her fingers against her thighs. Sophia patted her arm. "I understand. I felt much the same when I learned the full scope of the Testings, but it isn't our place to know everything. Don't take it as a sign that you weren't trusted." Instead of relaxing, Miriam tossed back her hair and bit her lower lip so hard the tips of her teeth showed; her foot continued its noisy cadence against the floor.

Suddenly, she stepped up to the Earth Viewer and switched to Samuel's picture. "What about him? Who else is benefiting from his misfortune?"

"Samuel's still a mystery to me," Sophia said, examining his image.

Now that Anthony's wife had emerged so strongly as a leader, Samuel was really more of an understudy candidate, but there was something about him Sophia still couldn't reconcile. Perhaps it was his lifestyle, which seemed more earthy than appropriate for a spiritual leader, or maybe there was the nagging feeling he too was hiding a secret. She didn't want to think that she hadn't bonded with Samuel because he was the candidate that Miriam had selected.

She moved to stand next to Miriam at the screen, feeling sure she was on to something. No one would guess that Samuel ever experienced a hardship. He wore an expensive suit, perfectly cut to accent the lines of his trim body, and his facial expression was relaxed and confident. Even his walk suggested self-assurance, but there was no doubt he was using his talents to serve the Almighty Divine. He was teaching a Bible class, treading up and down the aisles of the large classroom to make sure everyone was following his lecture. Now and then he would pause to rest a hand on a student's shoulder and point out a passage, or even kneel down to be on eye level and answer a question point by point. At times, his followers almost seemed to cling to him with cultlike devotion.

"He could be an angel," Faras said with admiration. "What other man could lose everything he worked for in a fire, be accused of terrible wrong-doing, and yet look so completely innocent and assured? Imagine having your closest supporters turn against you and yet continuing to stand so strong you attract a crowd wherever you go. They must sense how great his faith is."

Sophia looked sideways to see if he was being skeptical, but his eyes were shining and a smile of admiration turned his mouth upward as he stared at the screen. Ruth was the one who looked unconvinced, but that could be because the only positive thoughts she had were reserved for JoJo.

"Either that or someone did an excellent job of shielding him from further harm and encouraging him with the support of angels," Miriam said proudly. She turned to Sophia. "At least we can say we've succeeded with the Testings in relation to him. The people who left his first church because they suspected him of foul play were quickly replaced by twice as many others. His new congregation has raised enough money to build a church twice the size of the one that burned down."

"No." It was the first word Ruth had spoken since her abject confession. She was watching Samuel dismiss the men and women from his class, smiling at each one and giving them a handshake or hug. She shook her head back and forth. "It's all too easy."

"Too easy? He was nearly burnt to death and lost everything, but of course when you don't start out as a criminal, it's a lot easier to bounce back from difficulty." Miriam looked Ruth over from head to toe and gave a sniff of disdain.

Sophia watched the two women carefully, ready to intervene if needed, should the exchange escalate into an argument. There was nothing on the Earth Viewer that should cause concern: no excess angels bearing blessings or other signs that Samuel's Testing was being altered in any way, but Sophia couldn't help feeling that Ruth was right. Something seemed too perfect.

"That was intense," Faras sighed, turning off the Earth Viewer before they could discuss Samuel further. "But I hope the Almighty Divine is pleased with what we've managed to do. And now—"

"Let me guess. You want to refresh." Sophia couldn't help laughing at his predictability, but this time his request was reasonable. They had just worked hard, and a period of renewal would give them a new beginning of sorts. "Actually, I agree with you, Faras. The Testings of Devotion seem to be in better shape than I thought possible before we went through this latest review. Good things can come from unfortunate mistakes."

"Well, I'm more than a little put off by all this deception," Miriam said.

"We all get advised about being honest and straightforward with each other, but the Almighty Divine doesn't seem to feel the same consideration toward us."

Faras nudged her gently. "Watch yourself, Miriam. Sometimes too much knowledge can be a bad thing."

"I just think we deserve an explanation for being duped," she said, turning to Sophia. "Am I excused now?"

Sophia nodded, and Miriam flounced out of the Guidance Room, her dark hair swinging across her shoulders with each step. Faras and Sophia watched until she had gone out the doors, then he asked what was going to happen in response to Miriam's behavior.

"She has vulnerabilities like all of us, but she does her job well. Hopefully, the success she's had with Samuel will settle her down. Please, go and refresh for as long as you need." Without further comment, Sophia dismissed him and motioned for Ruth to follow her. "Gabriel wants us to share these latest developments about the Testings of Devotion with Hector."

"Do I have to go?"

"Ruth, at first I was angry with you for your interference with the Testings of Devotion, but then I realized we've all been treating you as if you were one of us, when you're not. You're mortal, and that makes a huge difference. This is an experiment that has led to many revelations."

"If I had it to do over, I wouldn't have pushed so hard to be the test run," Ruth grumbled. When they arrived at Hector's, she sat silently at Sophia's feet while the two angels discussed the Testings of Devotion. Although Sophia didn't reveal everything she knew, she reassured Hector they were seeing progress and could be pleased with the outcome of the Testings of Devotion to this point.

Hector looked down at Ruth, then leaned over and took her hand. "Stand up, sister, please. You are a valuable part of this team." She obeyed, but continued to cower behind Sophia, still dejected.

"Gabriel wants you to continue paying attention to anything unusual, Hector. You know sometimes one event becomes connected with another in a way we can't quite foresee," Sophia said. "You haven't sensed anything out of the ordinary since you returned from earth, have you? And we sorted out the issues around JoJo's Testing."

Hector hesitated, glancing beyond her at Ruth. "This *all* seems out of the ordinary, but as you've explained, even when things don't go according to our plans, they are still under the direction of the Almighty Divine."

His point stopped Sophia short. Had Ruth really done anything wrong by intervening in a way that caused those around JoJo to be impacted by his Testing too? Miriam and Faras didn't know about the other details she had discovered: the senior law partner who attended Pastor Ephraim's church unexpectedly won a large medical malpractice case, resulting in a fee so unbelievable he felt compelled to donate a tenth of it for a fund in honor of Ruth. That money had been enough to pay for Tamika's tuition to Bible school and JoJo's legal fees. What, if any, role had Ruth played in those outcomes?

Hector was staring at her, waiting for a response. "You're right, Hector— that's why none of us can judge others. Only the Almighty Divine knows the ultimate plan for His universe." She moved so Ruth could stand between them. "Ruth, can you tell us how this all happened so Hector and I can at least make sure we don't have any other problems?"

Ruth swallowed hard and then spoke haltingly: "I knew I could do it. It was the Voice. He told me to just use the Earth Viewer like Miriam and Faras do. I overrode their instructions. At first I just pulled one angel away from another place and sent him to JoJo, and no one knew. That made me think I was on the right track, because none of you caught on or seemed to care, so I kept going." Her head dropped again. "How could I have been so misguided, thinking it was the Almighty Divine talking to me? I've ruined everything!"

Hector's eyes met Sophia's, concerned. He turned to his Angel Viewer, and flipped through several screens while the other two watched. After some time he turned back to them.

"Ruth's right. Looking back, I see how it happened. She diverted them after I had given them their orders, just as any Select Servant can."

Still, Sophia thought, *why did Miriam and Faras see angels on the screen when I didn't? Surely Ruth didn't engineer that.*

Hector seemed about to speculate further, but then turned the Angel Viewer off and shrugged his shoulders in resignation. Sophia remembered

Gabriel's warning that there was more to come. Would it be from Ruth or one of the others? Even Hector had to be a suspect, if that was the case.

She hugged Hector and left with Ruth trailing behind her. The entire way back, the woman chanted requests for forgiveness, insisting she wasn't worthy to walk at Sophia's side or even be allowed to remain on the First Level of heaven.

"What's going to happen to me?" she asked Sophia as they mounted the steps in front of Operations Central. "Will I be sent to hell now?"

"I don't know," Sophia answered sadly. How much she longed to refresh with Gabriel and receive further directions, but in the absence of a summons, she would have to muster on singlehandedly. At least she could rest in the Guidance Room, so when they arrived, she settled Ruth in a recliner and took the one closest to it for herself. Part of her wanted to stay vigilant and protect Ruth, but then the telltale relaxation crept over her, and she closed her eyes lightly at first, but soon without effort.

Usually, no one would interrupt an angel during refreshing, but just as Sophia drifted into a state of complete oblivion, someone shook her shoulder. Startled, she opened her eyes and saw Ruth holding one finger across her lips in a gesture indicating silence.

Taking Sophia's hand, she pulled her to her feet and led her toward the Earth Viewer, where Miriam stood, hands embracing either side of the podium. Her expression was rapt as she stared at an image of Samuel Olsen reaching longingly toward her from the screen.

"Don't worry about what they've done, my darling. Our plan is still in place. Not much longer," Miriam crooned. "Then, beloved, as Lucifer has promised, we shall be together forever."

31

The sight of Miriam so fixated on Samuel that she was oblivious to their approach shocked Sophia. She had never heard any angel speak with the kind of naked desire so clear in Miriam's voice. Was this what had happened to the Watchers, who gladly flew from the First Level of heaven to mate with mortals?

A flash of understanding revealed how Lucifer had been able to penetrate the First Level of heaven: lust. Miriam wanted this mortal man so desperately, she had helped Lucifer gain access to Ruth and Operations Central. She had blinded Faras's and Ruth's vision to the absence of angels and thwarted Hector's efforts to help, but she still hadn't succeeded completely.

Sophia leaned close to Ruth so Miriam wouldn't hear. "How long have you known about this?"

"Just now, Sophia, I swear! I heard her speaking when I was about to settle into refreshing."

Sophia believed her. She swept forward and slapped her hand across the podium so the picture of Samuel disappeared. "Miriam, stop this right now while you still have a chance to redeem yourself."

Miriam gave her a vicious shove backward and punched the Earth Viewer on, her features no longer lovely. "What a stupid idea. This can't be stopped, even if I wanted to, you silly thing! Our plan has been in place since before you became Senior Servant, and you've helped us quite nicely, thank you."

Sophia had nearly fallen on the floor when Miriam pushed her; now she looked from Ruth to Miriam and back again. She was shorter than both of them, which made her feel even more overwhelmed by their duplicity. If they joined forces against her physically, she wouldn't stand a chance.

"Ruth, what's going on here?" She tried to make her voice bolder than she felt.

Ruth took a step back, distancing herself from Miriam and Sophia. "I told you, Sophia, I don't know. I already confessed all my transgressions to you. Miriam must have thought I was asleep, because she came in and started sweet-talking to Mr. Sam there."

"That's right." Miriam tossed her hair over her shoulders and smiled at the image of Samuel again. "Our little mortal has done everything we needed her to, hasn't she, darling? She's created such a distraction with her little JoJo that you've all been too busy to notice what's really going on." She looked at Sophia briefly and smirked. "You wouldn't have had any idea if it wasn't for the missing angels on the Earth Viewer. I'm still not sure why you weren't blinded like the others, but it doesn't matter now."

Sophia couldn't contain her sarcasm. "Could it be the power of the Almighty Divine is stronger than yours?"

"I know you want to think that," Miriam cooed. "But I've been a Selected Servant for a long time, and it's clear to me whose power is greater. It's obvious the Almighty Divine doesn't really care about you or any of the angels, just as it's obvious mortals don't really want to be rescued from the temptations of earth. My lord, Lucifer, is the one who wants to restore heaven—and earth—to their rightful ruler: him. We have no need of intruders like that one." She jerked her head back toward Ruth.

Sophia said, "Lucifer will tell any lie he thinks will be believed."

Miriam's eyes, once a beautiful purple, were now flinty. "Really? Well if the Almighty Divine made mortals just as He made us, why don't they all believe in Him? Every angel knows the Almighty Divine exists—even if some of us have come to realize Lucifer is the better leader."

"That's right, my love," Samuel said from the screen, his mouth resting in a wry half smile.

"No, mortals do believe for the most part. They are—"

"Good?" Miriam interrupted Sophia. "Come on. Why did you and Gabriel have to come up with these Testings of Devotion, then? And then have them fail so quickly and completely?"

Sophia lifted up her chin and took a step closer to Miriam. "They didn't fail, Miriam. You just didn't understand their true purpose. It was never just about the candidates."

She edged her way between Miriam and the podium, giving Samuel a look of pure disgust before she switched the Earth Viewer to another scene. "Get out."

She pointed toward the doorway and busied herself checking on the other candidates as Miriam stood next to her, momentarily speechless. Without looking away from the screen, Sophia waved her hand in dismissal.

"Still here? Go on, join your beloved Samuel and live as a mortal, because you know that's what will happen. You can only stay on earth so long before you're trapped in a mortal body, Miriam. Even if Lucifer lets you keep some of your powers, it won't be pleasant." She paused and tipped her head. "Then again, maybe you can have some Nephilim children and spread evil, instead of love."

With a roar, Miriam lunged at Sophia and seized the neck of her robe, twisting it so tightly that she was forced around to face the larger woman.

"Didn't you recognize Samuel? He's Isaac, our former Senior Servant. He and Lucifer have been collaborating to take over the First Level of heaven since the beginning of time, but that fool Gabriel somehow kept getting in the way. Like you, he's misguided, but devoted."

Sophia felt a tingle of fear begin to creep through her spirit. How much did Gabriel know, and why had he kept so much hidden about Isaac?

Miriam threw back her head and laughed, the nails of her fingers digging into Sophia's shoulders. "Our power will overwhelm the heavenly host *and* the Almighty Divine—then Isaac and I will rule over earth, and Lucifer will reign supreme on the First Level of heaven. You're finished, Sophia."

From the screen, Samuel/Isaac, who had reappeared, joined in. "Poor Sophia. Maybe Lucifer will take pity on you and find something you can do to serve him. He always has seemed rather partial to you."

Sophia squinted up at Miriam. "You and Isaac may have given in to Lucifer's influence, but I never will. The only way he'll get back into the First Level of heaven is to repent for all he's done, and beg the Almighty Divine for forgiveness."

"Do you really believe that?" Miriam gave her shoulders a half shrug. "Right now, Michael and Gabriel are both in the midst of a battle with Lucifer—but this time all the demons are united to help overwhelm them. See for yourself."

The screen faded to a scene of the two archangels, surrounded by legions of evil warriors. Michael's sword was in constant motion, but for each monster he struck down, two more leaped forward to attack. Gabriel was pinned in place by hundreds of others. At Lucifer's side, Azazel shouted encouragement and roared with laughter as troop after troop of Nephilim approached, snarling with hatred.

"After he's defeated the archangels, Azazel will destroy the mortals and Lucifer will come here." Miriam smiled slyly at Sophia. "Guess who will be waiting to let him in the Portal? Yours truly! Once he's safely in, I'll be on my way to earth and to my beloved Samuel, as he prefers to be known. The devoted Isaac you remember is dead, now."

Sophia tried to wrest herself free, but Miriam easily held her captive. Despite her fear, she lifted her face to Miriam's defiantly.

"Lucifer might be on your side right now, but once he gets what he wants, you and Samuel will find yourselves under his complete control. He'll never allow you to rule over earth." Sophia snickered, and a brief look of indecision flickered across Miriam's face. "Anyway, even if Lucifer does get into the First Level of heaven, do you really think he could convince every angel here to do the exact opposite of what they've been doing for eternity?"

The words sounded braver than Sophia felt, but something within Miriam seemed to hesitate. Raising one foot, Sophia pushed against Miriam's midsection with all her might, and was able to free herself, falling backward. She scrambled to her feet, knowing that she needed to get back to the Podium, but keeping as much distance between her and Miriam as she could. Ruth stayed fixed in her place, an equal distance away from both of them, cowering on the floor and visibly trembling.

"No. It worked with Ruth, and it will work with all the others," Miriam said, turning back to the Earth Viewer and watching as Michael and Gabriel continued to do battle. Was it Sophia's imagination, or did they seem to be weakening? "She may be a mortal, but she was our test case, and it worked beautifully. Even now, she hasn't truly repented; all we have to do is offer her the chance to regain her power and save JoJo and she'll join us. Don't count on Faras to help, either. He's still back in his chamber refreshing, too 'tired,' thanks to our intervention. You have two choices, Sophia: join us, or cease to be."

She glared at Sophia, but then, as if hearing a call from far away, grew perfectly still. Her body stiffened and her long arms lifted upward as her head fell back. A strange guttural speech came from her mouth and her appearance began to change.

First, her hair grew fuller and wilder, like a mane of jet black fur tumbling down her back. Next her eyes narrowed and receded into the curves of her face, glittering and hooded. The rest of her features hardened as her skin turned slick and darkened to the color of ash.

Sensing danger, Sophia began singing a prayer song and reached out to protect Ruth, who was crouched on her same spot on the floor, whimpering.

"Come stand behind me, Ruth," she said between notes, easing further away from Miriam. "You'll be safe."

"You see how little power they have!" Miriam screamed, stabbing a clawlike finger toward the screen of the Earth Viewer. Michael was pinned down by a hoard of demons, while Gabriel, nearly transparent, was struggling against Lucifer.

"It's an illusion," Sophia cried, "don't believe it, Ruth!" She held out her arms imploringly. "The Almighty Divine loves you. He wants to be your defender."

"Never!" Miriam screeched, facing Sophia and pointing with her hands like weapons. "In the name of Lucifer, Prince of Light and Lord of the Earth, I cast you out of the First Level of heaven forever!"

A dazzling electric cloud crackled around Miriam, then condensed at the ends of her fingers like a dangerous ball of static. With a shriek, Miriam arced back and hurled the globe at Sophia.

"No!" Ruth leapt up and plunged between the two of them, absorbing the impact of the strange force.

In an instant, she vanished, as did Miriam. Sophia sang louder and louder, stretching her arms upward and raising her eyes in the hope she could somehow save both women from the curse that had just overpowered them. On the Earth Viewer, she saw Miriam, screaming in pain as she hurtled through the Portal and out of the First Level of heaven, but there was no sign of Ruth.

"Sophia? What is it?" Faras rushed in the room, as vital as he had been before the Testings of Devotion began. "I was in the middle of refreshing when I felt pulled up and sent here to help you." He looked around quickly. "Where's Miriam, and Ruth?"

Sophia leaned against Faras gratefully as he guided her to a recliner. On the Earth Viewer, she saw a sudden change in the standoff between the archangels and Lucifer as Hector and a battalion of the heavenly host swarmed onto the scene. Charging forward, the angels took on the demons with a new energy, destroying so many so quickly that Lucifer was forced to retreat, howling in fury.

"Ruth and Miriam are gone, Faras," Sophia said dully.

He examined her closely, as if unable to understand. "What do you mean, 'gone'? Angels don't just vanish. What happened?"

Something occurred to him, and he went over to the Earth Viewer, which was lit up with thousands of points of light, each flashing red. "I've never seen earth like this. Lucifer must be furious with someone up here." He turned back to Sophia. "You?"

"No," she said. "It's never us, really, is it? It's the Almighty Divine, who always defeats him. Come, sit down, and let me tell you everything."

32

After she finished updating him, Sophia dispensed Faras to greet Hector and the other returning warriors at the Portals, gratefully collapsing on a recliner as soon as he left the Guidance Room. She shut her eyes, but the room seemed to echo with the sound of Miriam's tormented cries as she was cast out through the Portal and hurled toward earth. The uncertainty of Ruth's whereabouts might be even worse, though. How courageous the mortal had been in the end!

When Gabriel appeared, she nearly wept with joy. He gathered her up and they drifted to his Refreshing Room. Although his face was lined with fatigue, his arms held her firmly until he carefully deposited her in one of the fleeced blue recliners and sank down in the one next to her. The blue vapor—more soothing and sweet than ever before—drifted up to bathe them with a gentle caress.

"How could such things happen?" she murmured after a prolonged period of silence. Part of her wished to put the ugly memories behind her and try to forget them, but another more demanding part needed an explanation so the experience would not be repeated. "I don't know what I did wrong. How could Miriam deceive all of us so completely? Or was there a chance she could have been saved before the very end?"

Gabriel turned toward her and leaned on one elbow, his cheek resting against the palm of his hand. For a moment he studied her as if they were meeting for the first time. "Just as you've discovered how different mortals are from angels, I continue to discover how different you are from me." Flopping onto his back, he clasped his hands together behind his head, staring up into the clouds of turquoise mist that still hovered over them. "You've never given up on the idea of Lucifer repenting and coming back to heaven or the opportunity for any angel or mortal to be forgiven." She made a sound of disagreement, but he closed his eyes and shook his head slightly. "It's all right, Sophia. In a way I suppose your naïveté is even a good thing—it keeps me from becoming too jaded, and it's your version of Ruth's love for her family—but Miriam made a choice, just like any of us can. She listened to Lucifer, just as Isaac did. We knew he had gone through the Portal to earth, but even I had no idea where he was or what he and Lucifer were up to. Now he's trapped there as Samuel."

Gabriel waved at one wall and it became transparent so they could look down on earth. Miriam, in mortal form, was with Samuel. Although she no longer looked like the feral creature who had tried to destroy Sophia, the striking features that made her beautiful in heaven were hardened and coarse. Her eyes were slits of anger, and her mouth was twisted in a grimace of rage; her flawless body was gaunt and knobby, and her black hair was short and frizzed.

"It hurts! It hurts so much!" she screamed, clinging to Samuel. "You told me I would rule the earth as your queen, but I'm too hideous to leave this room. I can't even move without pain."

"My love, Lucifer will change all that. It was the same for me, and look at how handsome I am now. You must believe that we will still succeed and have our revenge." Samuel patted her head, then closed his eyes, lifted his arms, and began to chant a summons to Lucifer.

Sophia shuddered. Miriam was an angel—or had been. It was terrible to see her stripped of all her heavenly attributes and equally distressing to realize she wasn't crying because she regretted her actions.

"What of Ruth, Gabriel? Please tell me she hasn't been sent back to earth. In the end, she did the right thing. Her sacrifice saved the First Level of heaven, even though she had no way of knowing what would happen when she protected me."

"Ruth is back in the Community of Resting Mortals for now, and I suspect that's where she'll stay, although I agree that she acted admirably, especially for a mortal. Isn't that your mantra: all mortals have the capacity for incredible goodness?" he said, teasing.

She swatted his arm playfully, then sobered again. "How about Miriam and Samuel? Do you know what will happen to them?"

"I suspect Lucifer will find a way to use the two of them against mortals, and their spirits will gradually become completely consumed with evil. When mortals speak of hell, they cannot know that some are already living in a form of it, but Miriam and Samuel will discover for themselves.

Angels are meant to exist in heaven: when they leave, it's only a matter of time before they suffer the torment of being separated from the Almighty Divine."

Sophia turned away from the screen, flinching. "So, someone will replace her and Ruth here on the First Level? I can't imagine that Faras and I can handle all the chaos that's likely to occur in the near future, and the rest of the heavenly host is bound to be disturbed by what's happened."

"The heavenly host already knows. Hector recognized the danger at exactly the right time and made sure the Portal was secured before he came to help us. He brought his strongest angels with him, and they're the ones who turned the tide of our battle. We didn't lose a single spirit, while many of Lucifer's followers were destroyed."

She sighed. "Faras and I must be even more diligent with the Testings of Devotion. We'll do whatever it takes," she promised. "Developing those candidates seems especially important, now."

Gabriel sat down on the floor so they were on eye level. His blue eyes were playful as he tilted his head. "You're right about the Testings of Devotion. They will be even more vital to our efforts in the future. However, I have an invitation for you. It will involve a different kind of diligence. Come."

Taking her hand, he raised her up from the Refreshing Room and beyond the Separation Zone. As they floated through the clear crystal canopy of the sky, rays of every color created caressed her, and the sweet song of praise angels whispered in her ears.

When they emerged above the Separation Zone, she found herself standing before a pair of enormous filigreed golden doors, set with every type of precious jewel imaginable and sparkling with light. On either side, oddly serene sets of cherubim stood guard, staring straight ahead and standing perfectly still, their wings folded around their bodies. Each one had three faces: an angelic one that looked forward, and, on either side, one of a lion and one of an eagle. Their energy was so consumed by singing a continuous song of adoration for the Almighty Divine that they seemed unaware of Sophia and Gabriel, yet she had little doubt that if intruders arrived they would instantly be driven away by the potentially fierce creatures.

Tentatively, she touched the door, and the tips of her fingers felt a pleasant tingle. She turned back to Gabriel, her mouth caught open in delight but unable to speak. He nodded at her unasked question and lifted one hand to push the doors open. Briefly blinded by the light that poured forth from within, she stretched her arms out to feel her way.

"Sophia."

It was the same voice that had spoken her name with complete love on a previous occasion in Gabriel's Refreshing Room. This voice knew everything about her but delighted in her existence regardless of transgressions or mistakes. She moved forward, still unable to see beyond the brightness before her, but filled with delight at her arrival in the Second Level of heaven. It was not the dwelling place of the Almighty Divine, but it was one level closer to Him.

At her side, Gabriel took her arm and pivoted her slightly so she could see row upon row of the Holies who made up the Council of Elect, formed to serve the Almighty Divine in decision making and oversight of both angels and mortals. They were all smiling and nodding at her in greeting.

"So this is it, Sophia, the Second Level of heaven you have so longed for."

She knelt down, and lifted her hands toward the light. "Thank you, beloved Almighty Divine. You know how I have craved this moment, and although I know you are still further removed, I am so blessed to be even somewhat closer to you."

"Yes sweet child, your wish has been granted, and if you wish, you may remain here, serving Me in a different capacity of your own choosing," the voice of her Creator said.

Sophia's head jerked up toward Gabriel.

"Surely it can't be true?" She laughed. "But why shouldn't it be, of course? There are always choices, aren't there?"

He indicated that she should come with him before the Council of the Elect. She scanned their faces, amazed to see the familiar countenances of the many devout beings she had watched throughout history. Her eyes locked on Enoch and she smiled, remembering their long-ago encounter.

He was the one who spoke, after looking right and left at his peers to make sure they were in agreement. "Sophia, because I have lived on Earth, my spirit is always in sympathy for mortals. Some of us look up to serve, while I have happened to keep my gaze downward. The events set in motion by the Testings of Devotion are going to cause mayhem on many levels. I would implore you to remain on the First Level of heaven for a while longer, guiding the heavenly host as only you can at this particular moment in time. However, this is only a request. As the Almighty Divine and our dear Gabriel have indicated, you make the final choice: you may stay here and lend your talents to all of us, or return to the First Level of heaven."

Gabriel added: "Your desire to be here has been granted, Sophia, but your motivations for longing to stay might be different now. Surely you realize you are strong enough to resist and even defeat Lucifer without being removed from the First Level of heaven, and your wish to be closer to the Almighty Divine has already been fulfilled."

Her eyes widened. "You knew all along why I wanted to come here. But now that I'm here, it's so wonderful! Surely I would be so content that I could help mortals even more from the Second Level of heaven than I could from the First. And all of you could provide such wise advice…"

Gabriel was silent, and when she looked back to Enoch, he was too. Scanning the Holies on either side of him, she waited for someone to answer her, but when no one did, she realized she would have to come to a decision on her own.

"If I stay here, can I go back later?" she asked hopefully.

Enoch bent forward, but not in time to hide a smile. "Sophia, you are a wonder. We all enjoy you very much, and as we've looked down on the First Level of heaven from time to time, we couldn't help admiring your very being. The Almighty Divine may have created you as a tiny angel, but you certainly are an insightful one."

Gabriel patted her shoulder. "Sophia, I go between the First and Second Levels all the time, so that arrangement is not impossible, but I'm an archangel. I think you are being asked to choose where you will remain from this time forward."

"Does that mean if I go back to the First Level I will be there forever too?"

"He doesn't know the answer to that question, Sophia. Only the

Almighty Divine does," Enoch interjected.

Perplexed, Sophia sank back down to her knees and looked up at Gabriel, unsure of whom to address.

"May I pray?" she asked.

"Of course," he and Enoch answered at the same time.

Folding her hands before her, she bowed her head. Her spirit traveled away from the Second Level of heaven, first hovering over earth from a great distance and hearing the cries of many mortal voices lifted up in grief. There seemed so many problems she and the other angels could help with, and the Testings of Devotion held such promise!

Then she soared to the First Level of heaven and saw Hector and Faras in the Guidance Room, studying the Earth Viewer. Drawing closer, she heard them speak.

"Better you than me," Faras said, shaking his head at the screen, which depicted the outburst of war between two countries on earth. "I can barely stand to watch mortals fight each other, let alone be in direct battle with Lucifer and his tribe."

Hector squeezed Faras's arm. "But it was incredible, Faras. Joining our power with Michael and Gabriel was like nothing I ever experienced before. Not that I didn't always believe we would defeat Lucifer once and for all, but now I know it to be true!"

"The sooner the better," Faras said with a sigh, then after a silence, he glanced sideways at Hector. "So that's it, then? You've agreed to become Senior Servant, and we'll have to find at least one more Selected Servant?"

"That's the plan for now, until I'm told otherwise."

"And Sophia's on the Second Level of heaven, where she's always wanted to be." Faras sighed. "I thought she was comfortable here, just like you and me. It's rewarding to be among others like us."

His eyes met Hector's, and something about the angel's expression made him wrinkle his forehead. After a moment, he spoke again.

"It isn't decided for sure yet, is it?"

Hector laughed and clapped one hand on Faras's back. "You understand very well, Faras. No, it's not absolute. I suppose Sophia has to search her spirit to truly know what the Almighty Divine desires for her, but for now, you and I have to help those mortal candidates make earth a better place. I think I'll go check with the new director and make sure he's ready to send some earth angels down to help the injured soldiers. You'll be okay by yourself for a bit?"

"Absolutely."

Once alone, Faras touched the panel set into the podium and focused on the Portal, waiting until he saw a flock of earth angels arrive there with Hector at the lead. Slowly, the Portal opened so they could descend, each of them accepting Hector's blessing as they left with great jubilation.

Rubbing his chin, Faras glanced over at the recliners, then flipped the Earth Viewer off and shut his eyes and whispered, "Sophia, if you can hear me, know that I'm pleased for you, but also know that it just isn't the same without you here."

He lifted his head up and opened his eyes, almost as if he knew Sophia was watching him. From her spot back on the Second Level of heaven, Sophia gazed down thoughtfully and then suddenly jumped to her feet, eyes wide.

She turned to Gabriel. "The Almighty Divine didn't *ask* me to come to the Second Level or *tell* me to do it—he offered. He knows I wanted to leave the First Level because I was afraid of Lucifer and didn't trust myself."

"And because you wanted to be closer to Him," Gabriel added.

"Oh yes, of course, and because I wanted to be closer to Him," she echoed.

Gabriel's eyebrows lifted. "And now?"

"Now I know I can."

"And?"

She linked her hand through Gabriel's arm and turned away from the Holies after bowing respectfully. "Having survived my own Testing of Devotion, I confess I'm pretty curious to see how the mortal candidates handle theirs. It seems I've gotten attached to them, which must be what Ruth was trying to tell me about parenting."

As she and Gabriel walked toward the gates, a song of rejoicing surrounded them like a gentle breeze, carrying them effortlessly forward. When they reached the golden passageway, the voice of the Almighty Divine sounded above the chorus of saintly music.

"Yes, Sophia, my precious one, you have discovered just how much it is possible to care for those placed under your care. Go now with my blessings, and find new joy in the gifts you have to offer to all those on the First Level, and know that I am always close by."

When Sophia and Gabriel arrived back at the entrance, the light surrounding her was bright again, glinting off the jewels of the gate in multicolored sparkles of light and making the gold posts glow. The cherubs maintained their odd vigil, and in the background she could hear the Council of the Elect calling out blessings and encouragement. When the gates swung open, Sophia almost changed her mind and ran back inside to the place of her dreams, but then she remembered reality: the sweet smell of flowers on the First Level, Hector's bubbly laugh, the soothing songs of the praise angels, and so many other comforts she loved.

He gave her a half bow in farewell and promised they would talk again soon, then she began to drift away from him. He was swinging the gates shut behind her when a thought occurred to her and she hesitated, a puzzled look on her face.

"Gabriel, you haven't told me what *your* Testing of Devotion was about," she said.

"You've just completed it," he answered, with a twinkle in his eyes that matched the sapphires in the gate. "I helped develop the best Senior Servant the First Level will ever have."

She laughed, sure he was both teasing and serious, but couldn't help flying back to give his cheek a farewell kiss one more time. "You're the best archangel ever—but don't tell Michael I said so," she whispered in his ear.

Then, as the Separation Zone opened and the sound of the heavenly host chorus swelled up to greet her, she looked toward the First Level with joy in her eyes and contentment in her heart. Gliding on the wings she used so rarely, she coasted happily back to her home.